Muhammad Abdelnabi, born in 1977, is the author of two novels and four short-story collections. His *The Ghost of Anton Chekov* won first prize in the Emerging Writers category of the Sawiris Cultural Award for short-story collections in 2011. *In the Spider's Room* was shortlisted for the 2017 International Prize for Arabic Fiction and was joint winner of the 2017 Sawiris Cultural Award for novels in the Emerging Writers category. He lives near Banha in Egypt.

Jonathan Wright is the translator of the winning novel in the Independent Foreign Fiction Prize and twice winner of the Saif Ghobash Banipal Prize for Arabic Literary Translation, and was formerly the Reuters bureau chief in Cairo. He has translated Alaa Al Aswany, Youssef Ziedan, and Hassan Blassim. He lives in London, UK.

In the Spider's Room

Muhammad Abdelnabi

Translated by
Jonathan Wright

hoopoe
AN IMPRINT OF AUC PRESS

First published in 2018 by
Hoopoe
113 Sharia Kasr el Aini, Cairo, Egypt
420 Fifth Avenue, New York, 10018
www.hoopoefiction.com

Hoopoe is an imprint of the American University in Cairo Press
www.aucpress.com

Exclusive distribution outside Egypt and North America by I.B.Tauris & Co Ltd., 6
Salem Road, London, W4 2BU

Dar el Kutub No. 26459/17
ISBN 978 977 416 875 8

Dar el Kutub Cataloging-in-Publication Data

Abdelnabi, Muhammad
        In the Spider's Room / Muhammad Abdelnabi.— Cairo: The American
    University in Cairo Press, 2018.
        p. cm.
        ISBN 978 977 416 875 8
        1. Egypt—Social Life and Customs—Fiction
        823

1 2 3 4 5   22 21 20 19 18

Designed by Adam el-Sehemy
Printed in the United States of America

To my elder brother and the finest human being,
Ibrahim Abdelnabi

What is love?

A nobleman fell in love with a boy who sold beer, and in pursuit of his love went wandering far from his family. Malicious gossip about him spread far and wide. The nobleman had properties and estates, which he sold to buy beer from the boy. After selling his property he descended into poverty, but his love for the boy increased. Although people constantly provided him with bread as alms, he was always hungry, because he sold all the bread to buy more beer.

Someone once asked him, "You poor, confused man, what is love? Please explain the secret of it to me."

"It is to sell a hundred worlds of goods for the sake of a single glass of beer," he replied. "And if this act does not make a man happy, how could he understand love and pain?"

Farid al-Din al-Attar

1

I CLEARLY REMEMBER HOW THE nightmare began.

Abdel Aziz and I were coming out of his apartment on Qasr al-Aini Street, walking along in an unusually serene state of mind, on our way to have a drink in a place near Falaki Square. Suddenly I had a whimsical desire to hold his hand. Something may have sent a shiver of fear up my spine, and I wanted to cling to him.

It might have been the first time I had held his hand in front of people in the street, and the strange thing was that he didn't move his hand away or discourage me, as I had expected. We held each other's hands and my fear, which had no known cause, evaporated. The next moment rough hands came down on our shoulders. We turned in surprise to make sure it wasn't just a prank by some annoying friends. They asked us for identity papers, still holding on to us as if we might run off if they let go. For a moment I felt guilty: maybe they had appeared out of nowhere to punish us just because I had reached out my hand to my friend and he had held it.

"May I know who you gentlemen are?" asked Abdel Aziz, before taking out his identity card.

He spoke excitedly and with confidence, while I was struggling to hide the fact that I was trembling.

"No need to hurry, my dear. You'll find out everything in good time," replied the one who seemed to be senior.

Then he looked behind him and we noticed there was a police truck not far off. The man called over someone called Hayatim. I recognized Hayatim from a distance—a pale, plump young man with thin eyebrows that looked as if they had been drawn on with a ballpoint pen. Hayatim, a name usually given to girls, was his nickname. I don't know his real name. He was their guide that night.

Hayatim came over, walking confidently between two security men in civilian clothes. "Which one do you mean?" Hassan Fawwaz asked him.

Hayatim pointed toward me without looking at me, as if he were slightly embarrassed. "But I don't know that other guy," he said. "It's the first time I've seen him."

The man in charge looked at me. "Are you *gay*?" he asked, using the English word and speaking rapidly in order to confuse me.

"What does that mean?" I answered in a trembling voice.

"Okay, come along with us, my dear, and we'll tell you what it means."

Then he looked at Abdel Aziz and gave orders to his men: "Bring that one too and we'll see what's up with him."

In less than five minutes we were inside the truck, among more than ten other men. Our gentle world receded into the distance with each passing moment while the nightmare spread its black wings over everything. I clung to my friend's hand in the darkness of the truck.

2

MY NAME IS HANI MAHFOUZ and I was an only child, pampered by everyone as if my mother were the sun and my father the moon.

But the person who pampered me most and loved me most was my grandfather, who was known as Khawaga Mida. When I was six years old I thought I had killed him, after seeing him in a dream. In the dream, he woke me up, kissed me, and touched my hair, and then opened the window, went through it, and rose up until the hem of his striped gallabiya and his bare feet disappeared into the darkness of the street. As soon as I woke up, I went to Mama's bed and told her about the dream, whispering in fear for some reason. She hugged me and told me not to tell anyone else, especially my grandmother Sakina, because "it would bring bad luck on your grandfather, and Grandma would be angry with us and would make a scene."

Only a week or less later Grandfather died, and then I was surprised to find Mama herself revealing our secret and telling them about my dream as if she were proud of me. She declared that I was a spiritual, clairvoyant child with a touch of the divine in me. I didn't understand any of this, but I felt a change in the way they saw me, if only for a short time, before they completely forgot the subject—except for my grandmother Sakina, or Sikkina Hamya ("sharp knife"), as my mother and I called her in secret. She had started to bribe me with candy and money, perhaps in case I dreamed about her death too and made her fly out of the window after Grandfather. This didn't relieve my sense of guilt. I felt I had killed him deliberately; that I had killed the person I loved most out of all of them, the only person whose heart had listened to me when I implored them to postpone sending me off to primary school for another year. He was the only one who loved me, and he had pampered me as if I were the only star in the night that was his life.

My grandfather's real name was Mohamed Mahfouz, and he was called Mida by the Jewish woman who had adopted him when he was in his twenties. She gave him a job in the small dressmaking business she owned on the first floor of an old building in Adli Street in central Cairo. It is said that when he came to her he was a complete oaf who couldn't even thread a needle, and she had taught him the art of tailoring. "And how to be charming as well," Grandmother Sakina would add, fluttering an eyebrow.

I imagine him as a tall, thin young man with a trim figure and sparkling honey-colored eyes, light on his feet, sweet-talking, and, most importantly, with a fine clear voice. In his later years, whenever he secured a short truce with his dry cough and his arthritis, he would sing to me in a voice that was gruff and yet pleasant: "Dawn has broken, the night is gone, and the sparrow has chirped." I sang it back to him, rocking back and forth in dance.

He had moved from Mahalla in the Nile Delta, almost a fugitive from his family, to break into the world of "art," as they called it—the obsession that spared almost no one in my family. He left behind him a poor family with many children. Most of the menfolk were workers in the textile factories and their lives were set out in advance, from birth to death, caught up in thread, cloth, and the cogs of machines, from which they could be disentangled only by death from chronic chest diseases, or by running away, as my grandfather did when he let go of the thread at the right moment. Maybe it was because he was different from his brothers and other relatives, or maybe he felt this difference because of the particular admiration that those around him always showed for him—admiration for his appearance and his fine voice. In the end ambition seethed in his veins and drove him to the capital without money or acquaintances or any clear plan.

They say that on one occasion he waited at length for the actor Naguib al-Rihani outside a theater, and when Rihani appeared my grandfather threw himself at him and begged him to let him join his troupe or just to listen to his voice, if only for a minute. Rihani may have been distracted or upset for some reason, or maybe his troupe was going through a rough patch, and he was sharp with Grandfather.

"Is the morgue short of dead people?" he said. "Off you go, son, God help you."

But when he saw the disappointment on the face of the pale young man as he walked away, he called him back and pressed a large coin into his hand, saying, "Find yourself another line of work, rather than die of hunger."

From a job as an assistant in a coffee shop to selling nuts outside theaters and cinemas, Mohamed Mahfouz lived like a street dog, sleeping anywhere, eating whatever was available, and dreaming of glory on the pavement as he examined the posters. Then a woman who worked in the ticket office decided to help him. She took my grandfather to Mrs. Biba, dressmaker to society ladies of the upper classes, who took him under her wing. Biba gradually taught him everything: how to dress, how to speak and smile at people, and how to deal with her lady customers when he was showing them samples of new fabric. He was a quick learner, and after a few months he cut his first dress pattern by himself.

She gave him the name Mida as a pet form of Mohamed and because it sounded rather like her own name. His Egyptian friends later added the title Khawaga to the name on their own initiative, because it sounded amusing or mildly derogatory. Her customers often thought that Mida was Jewish like the owner because he was the only person she trusted and he looked like he was the only person left from her family, since no one ever saw her with a husband or a child.

I imagine him visiting her in the evening after shutting up the workshop. He would take the elevator up to her apartment in the same building where the workshop took up half of the first floor. He would ring the bell and she would open it herself because the maid had gone. She wouldn't move far back from the door, but would just leave him a small gap to come in so that his body almost brushed against her soft gown. He would find waiting for him everything he might dream of as a young man away from home and pleased with himself—food, a house, a woman who was pleasing to the eye even if she was old enough to be his mother, and like his mother she delighted in his pleasant voice and laughed at his ready jokes. She bought him an oud, and arranged lessons so he could learn to play. Every Friday she looked up from whatever work she was doing and reminded him: "Lesson time, Mida."

He rose in silence with a smile to put on his jacket and fez, pick up the oud, and walk to Emad al-Din Street, where he met his teacher, a blind sheikh, in a coffee shop. The sheikh never ended a lesson without referring to "the lady," saying, "How is Mrs. Biba? Give her my best regards," or asking in jest, "I wonder whether you'll stay on as private oud player to the lady, or do you plan to turn professional, Si Mida?" Mida swallowed his teacher's sarcastic remarks in silence with a smile. That's how I like to imagine him now, shy and smiling and taciturn. In his smile there might be a certain disdain for people and for everything in their world, except for music, good cheer, and his patron.

I assume she didn't give herself to him suddenly. She laid her preparations and was patient. She didn't rush the fruit and pick it green and eat it unripe or too quickly like the hungry and deprived. No, she let him come and go in front of her big dark eyes, slowly losing his Mahalla accent, and warbling English and French words he had picked up from her and the customers. He knew how to dress, how to choose the color and size that showed off his slim figure and well-toned muscles. I imagine that the first physical encounter between the patient old woman and her young fancy man took place long after she adopted him, a year or more. I can see him now, sitting cross-legged on a comfortable sofa in her apartment, playing the oud and singing to her:

Light of spirit, he flashes his eyelashes and eyebrows.

She stands up and goes over to sit next to him, close enough to stroke his curly, shiny black hair with her hand. He keeps his eyes closed and smiles till the end of the song, then turns toward her, happy that the moment has come that he has awaited so long. He sets the oud down nearby, turning it onto its front, and sees that her eyes are tearing up and fluttering. He embraces her tenderly and gently, as if afraid of breaking her fragile bones. At that moment, Mohamed Mahfouz or Khawaga Mida might have grasped the real reason why he ran away from his hometown and family—not from fear of death through some chest disease, not in pursuit of the glories of art and fame, and not in search of adventures or to discover the world. He had come here, to the great city, only to go back to his real home, promised to him long before, in the body of Biba.

On that tender night maybe she said to him: "I don't want you to do anything against your will."

And he answered in a voice that had the swish of silk: "This is what I want, madam."

3

IN THE FRIGHTENING DREAM EVERYTHING looked real. I was touching things and smelling them, and I could see sizes and colors and faces. I suddenly had an urge to tell my dream to someone and, without thinking about the embarrassing content, I found myself looking for my wife Shireen in the apartment. I moved slowly and calmly, like a homeless person who has broken into a stranger's house, though I wasn't embarrassed that I was naked.

She was sitting alone at the kitchen table, busy reaming out zucchini with a corer as bright and sharp as a knife. I started to pour out to her everything I'd seen in the dream: how I had been walking alongside Abdel Aziz, then my sudden fear, and how I held his hand and we were arrested, Hayatim the informer, the police truck and the cell, then the release of Abdel Aziz and how he had left me there alone. She worked the corer more rapidly, and I felt a strange and embarrassing desire throbbing below my waist. I simply reached out, took some of the pulp from the zucchini, and put it in my mouth. It was indescribably delicious, but then I found that my hand had been cut by a careless turn of the corer, and the little cut produced as much blood as you would expect from a bullet hole. But when I looked to Shireen for help all I saw in front of me was Aunt Husniya in the prime of her youth, calmly smoking a cigarette and laughing with abandon, and she soon started to sing the opening line of one of her songs: "Who will guide the stranger to the land of his beloved?" And as she sang, she raised her knee little by little to show her skeleton, bare of skin and flesh. I ran out of the apartment in horror at my dead aunt and her voice, which was a harrowing wail. Or perhaps I was trying to bandage my finger, which had covered the floor of the apartment with so much blood that I nearly slipped in it several times. I soon realized that I was wearing wooden bath clogs and that steam was rising around me and Abdel Aziz was sitting next to me, patting my shoulder and trying to comfort me with friendly words, and when I wanted to show him my finger I couldn't find any cut, and he said he had to go now, and I found the steam around him was consuming him from bottom to top so that he gradually began to fade away in the billows. In the end the features of his face dissolved as he smiled in pity and embarrassment.

The first massive black spider appeared. I don't know where it suddenly sprang from, but it headed toward me, and behind it marched two others, then five, and then I could no longer count the vast army of spiders, and I didn't know where to hide from them, and then I felt the first of them climbing up my naked body. I screamed, but no noise came out, and I woke up to see the terrified faces of my fellow detainees.

4

IN THE HANDS OF HIS patron Grandfather matured with time into a handsome man. His passion for theater and music abated; he played the oud and sang only as a pastime in his spare moments or when he was alone with Biba. Without hesitation he turned down an offer from his teacher to work as an oud player in a reputable group. He must have loved Biba, and he also loved his new trade—in his hands cloth was transformed into objects that almost breathed when they swathed the bodies of women and girls.

He stayed with her as she advanced in age and gradually lost her looks, like a wilting flower. In the end Mida became her nurse and masseur, and it was she who encouraged him to marry Sakina, the girl who did the embroidery, after she noticed that he talked about her and after she heard him arguing repeatedly with the girl. She helped him rent and furnish the apartment in Abdin and then welcomed their only son, my father Ahmad, like a kindly grandmother. My father had confused memories of his visits to the old lady on feast days and his disgust at kisses from her moist lips, which he wiped away immediately. As she approached the age of ninety her health no longer permitted her to leave the apartment and go downstairs to supervise the workshop, which still bore her name though Mida was now in full control.

When public opinion in Egypt turned against the Jews, angry young men threw firebombs at the workshop window.

The damage was slight and the fires were put out as soon as they started. Grandfather suggested she wind up her business and migrate to some other country, as many Jews had done, or that she move in with some of her own people who had stayed. "What do you mean, my people?" she replied bitterly. "You're the only one I have, Mida. I have one niece, who's like a scorpion waiting impatiently for me to die."

To ward off evil, they merely changed the name of the place to Atelier Mida, on her insistence, and at the time Grandfather didn't know he had become the real owner in the official documents, even before they put up the new sign. At least that's what he claimed. A few months later she passed away in her sleep. The night before, he had been sitting with her and singing an old ditty that she loved:

We died for love of you, light of our eyes, and survived.
As if, full moon, we'd really done nothing at all.

He stopped when he felt she had fallen asleep and heard her snoring gently. He looked at her smile, twisted at the side of her mouth, then lightly kissed her smooth, waxy forehead.

After Biba died, everyone was surprised to find she had left the workshop to Grandfather. He was surprised too, or at least he pretended to be, but no one believed him, least of all Biba's niece. The niece sent her lawyer, who put Grandfather through hell before admitting that the contract was valid. Did Mida still feel ill at ease despite his joy? Or is that how I like to portray him, not as my father or grandmother depicted him, in a version that's different from this gentle love story? They had a less romantic version that can be summarized thus: the shrewd and handsome young man tricked the childish old woman and won her over with sweet words and a laugh, then with a wink and one song after another in his fine voice. Then the door opened that led to a garden of pleasures, and in the middle of the garden he came across a well, and the young man had a long and skillful tongue and he started licking and licking until the water in the well trembled and overflowed. The woman who owned the garden gasped, and muttered in a stifled voice, "I'm all yours, Mida. Do with me what you will."

And so she wrote out the contract handing over ownership of the workshop to him, at a time when she was in raptures in another realm. I don't imagine it that way, maybe because I came to know him after time had rounded off his edges and shaken the last feather off the peacock he had been. I also didn't have much confidence in my father's and grandmother's accounts of him because of their constant disagreements with him.

I have distinct memories of him that I didn't borrow from anyone else. He used to take me with him to the workshop, before he raised the white flag of surrender to arthritis and left everything in my father's hands. I was five or six years old at the time, and looked like one of those dolls that they put in shop windows or in commercials for toys or dairy products. My mother worried about me, and she hung a charm in the shape of a blue glass eye around my neck and stuffed an amulet under my clothes that hurt me like a large pebble. But none of this could fend off assault by the evil eye: I fell ill and had fevers, and then she would burn incense, cut out paper dolls, and stick a needle into them as she named possibly malevolent people one after another. In the meantime I was under the covers and the cold sweat felt lovely on my skin, and I imagined all those people hating me for some reason, maybe because I was a boy or because I was pretty. I felt there was something wrong with me that made those around me want me to suffer, to fall ill and die.

The fever would pass every time and I would get up hungry. I would go back to being a shiny china doll, with masses of soft black hair that fell over my forehead and shoulders, and again I would cling to Grandfather when he went out so that he would take me with him, indifferent to my mother's opposition, my grandmother's orders, and their anxiety for my sake. In the workshop I went back to playing with the scraps of colored cloth, looking through fashion magazines, and delighting in the smell and sound of the steam iron. I daydreamed as I played with little mannequins, headless or standing on one leg like a stick, imagining them as bewitched women from the stories my mother told me. Sometimes I imitated Grandfather, holding the tape to take the measurements of beautiful women as far as I could reach up their bodies when I stood on my tiptoes. Some of them would suddenly notice the little angel running between their feet, his head hardly reaching their bare knees. Some of them were well-known stars. Once one of them bent down, picked me up, looked at me with a surprised smile, gave me a hug, smothered me in kisses, and said, "What a pretty boy! And what's your name?"

"Hannoun," I said.

She was the actress Madiha Kamel, in the prime of her youth. Her laugh was slightly husky and her eyes sparkled. I went home that day laden with a small fortune in chocolate and told them I was going to marry Madiha Kamel. When they asked me why, I said because her face was like an apple and she smelled nice.

5

I soon grew used to Grandfather's absence and looked to my father to provide me with an alternative or a substitute. Some days he would forget me and then suddenly notice I was there, as if I were the child from next door who just happened to be in his house, and he would invite me to go with him to the coffee shop or to work. I loved going back to Grandfather's workshop. I loved the tension that ran through the place, with the girls behind their sewing machines or busy finishing off pieces with needle and thread. People never stopped visiting my father, especially when evening fell and the women workers were gone.

The place changed with time. The movie stars in high heels and with bare knees stopped coming, and gradually the business started to attract civil servants and mothers preparing trousseaus for their daughters' weddings. My father also worked with television celebrities and producers of low-budget movies. He had met many of them in his tumultuous youth when he had delusions of a career in show business. He would reach an agreement with one of the production assistants on what was needed, make some preliminary sketches, then give instructions to the seamstresses and leave them to do all the work, freeing himself to manage the business and party at night with his show-business and bohemian friends. I don't think he had inherited Grandfather's flair for cutting cloth, sensitivity for the female form, his artist's wandering gaze, or fine voice. Even so, behind his immersion in the world of show business there maybe lay an enthusiasm inherited from his father or an envy that he harbored toward him.

In his early youth some of his low-life friends in the artistic world convinced him he could become the new screen idol if he were given the right opportunity. He did make some efforts, but his sense of dignity prevented him from accepting any minor roles. In those circles he saw a young woman who pleased him and he thought of marrying her, although she was only a small-time actress. She was my mother, Badriya— or Badridar or Badara, as I sometimes called her—who had been brought up in Old Cairo. She and her elder sister Husniya, or Husna as she was known to her fans, had run away from a troubled background that was not very different from the plots in the movies that drew them to the bright lights. The younger sister was prettier and more congenial. My father saw her in Studio Galal and made overtures to her but she rebuffed him emphatically. "I came here to make a living, not to have romances. Is that clear?" she said.

He went back to his father in a rage the same day and asked him to come with him at once to Studio Galal. Grandfather made fun of him, saying, "Good news? Are they going to sign an exclusive contract with you? And they want your guardian?"

Upset, my father told him he wanted to marry a small-time actress who was acting in a film there. He persuaded Grandfather only after Grandmother Sakina had pestered him for days and nights. In the end he gave in to them, in the hope that the marriage would put his wayward only son on the right track. Father was already over twenty but he had no job or qualifications and spent most of his time chasing women or in bad company.

Badriya and her sister had left their home in Old Cairo a long time ago and moved into a cheap hotel in the city center—two branches cut off a tree, with only an elderly uncle who was already descending into senile dementia. So Grandfather couldn't find anyone he could ask for approval of the marriage, other than the director Fatin Abdel Wahhab. He went to see the director with my father in the place where he was filming his last movie, *City Lights*, and Shadya and Ahmad Mazhar are said to have congratulated the couple on their engagement, or so the family story goes.

My father stipulated that his bride must cut off all relations with acting and the world of show business, and she agreed without hesitation. I think Badriya said to herself, "Better to marry than to live alone," or maybe she had taken a liking to Ahmad, who was dark, adventurous, and amusing. She had always seen acting as just a way to make a living. But she knew that people saw it as suspect, so maybe marriage was an alternative that would protect her reputation. Maybe she hoped her elder sister would also find her own Mr. Right, and she started praying that would happen once she had tasted the benefits of security.

When Aunt Husna visited us in the apartment in Abdin, all my father's family would suddenly disappear on urgent errands or shut themselves into various rooms. No one welcomed her except her embarrassed sister and her beautiful boy. Maybe that was because she wore short skirts and dresses, laughed loudly, smoked like a man, and raised her voice when she joked with me. "If it wasn't for you, sweetie, I would never have set foot in this house," she would say.

The more my mother advised her to be sensible, the more outrageously she behaved, especially after she started singing in third-rate vaudeville theaters. Apparently my father would hear reports of her behavior when he was partying with his friends—the reports were exaggerated for effect, and he would annoy Mother by passing them on. Maybe this was what encouraged him to make advances on Husna one day when she was visiting us and Mother was in the kitchen. My aunt raised her voice and insulted him in front of his wife and his mother. He didn't take that lying down and they swore at each other. She stormed out, leaving the house in turmoil, and came back to visit us only after my father had died.

The flame of love between Ahmad and Badriya died down as fast as it had flared up, and he went back to his old ways, with endless partying and making merry, some of which I witnessed whenever I managed to tag along with him when he went out. Once I saw him arranging sticks of hashish in an elegant wooden box inlaid with mother-of-pearl. He looked at me out of the corner of his eye and said with a wink, "This is what the pashas smoke for pleasure, Hannoun. When you grow up, you'll try it and discover why."

How I longed to grow up and try it and discover why. Another time I saw him going into the bathroom after one of the girls in the workshop, and come out a little later wiping his mouth. I was sure they had been doing what actors did in the movies, and for that reason too I was impatient to grow up and try it. Probably because of the hashish, my father shared the workshop with the owners of other workshops, and it became as public as a market.

I can see myself, aged about ten or so, sitting by the small window with thin metal bars to breathe some fresh air rather than the air in the room, which was thick with whatever the pashas smoked, my head spinning slightly. That window allowed me to play my secret game, because it looked out on a small corridor and in the corner there was a urinal that some of the workshop owners had installed because most of them worked in one or two rooms without a bathroom. I loved to sit in this corner, because there I was invisible to my father and his friends, and also because I could snoop on the men who were urinating. No one would notice the boy slouched indolently behind the window. I would have a peek when I caught sight of a man standing at the urinal and taking his penis out from under his clothes. Furtively I looked at all these hamamas, doves, as they called them, and wondered what lay behind the name. Did they fly like doves?

No one noticed me spying except Ra'fat. Ra'fat worked as a cutter. He was a young man with a thin, straight mustache who parted his thick black hair to the side. I remember that he always wore a red sweatshirt of some shiny material, with a high neck. He must have liked it very much. I never saw him in the kind of dirty or ragged clothes most of the men in the other workshops in the building wore, and the sound of his clear laugh would ring out on the stairs. He was the only one who noticed me snooping. In fact, he liked me looking at his penis but he pretended that he couldn't see me. Over time he began to go a step further and play with his soft white penis until it stiffened and I saw for the first time the miracle that took place. His hamama inflated as though it were going to take off. Would it coo like the doves in the light well at home? On one occasion, he unexpectedly looked at me and caught my eyes feasting on the sight of his penis. I had been discovered. I anxiously expected he would complain to my father, but he never did.

The next time he stood there, as soon as I could control myself and look at him, he gave me a slight smile and made a little nod as if inviting me to carry on playing with him, but I looked away, my heart beating violently. I could feel my heartbeats in my arms and legs and the pictures in the magazine I was holding dissolved into meaningless blotches of color. Then I noticed my father chuckling because someone was making ribald fun of one of his friends, who was stoned and talking incoherently. Father might suddenly notice I was there and ask me to imitate Farid al-Atrash for them. When he did that I put my magazine aside, jumped up off the armchair, and stood among them in the middle of the room, my face and mouth in contortions, reproducing the sighs and laments in Atrash's performances. Then I would sing comically, inspired by Lebleba when she was a child, because I had seen her on television imitating singers:

That's not enough, my love, not enough.
I want you, I want your heart.

Bursts of laughter broke out around me, like the firecrackers people throw on feast days, and sometimes Father would say, both proudly and in jest, "Acting runs in his blood on both sides of the family."

On those occasions Hani turned into something else—the court jester and the center of attention, something for the men to laugh at and gaze at from under drooping eyelids. For ages I loved playing this role and identified with it. From time to time, when I was wrapped up in playing my game with my father's friends, I caught sight of Ra'fat's face behind the little window, standing there, following the free show, and smiling like someone who keeps a secret.

6

THE FURTHER MY WRITING ADVANCES, the bigger this small room grows and the more the walls recede. Eventually they disappear completely. The notebook in front of me is the only place left. I prevaricate. I take memory as far as it can go, to put off the confrontation. I feel as if I'm saying goodbye to my life by shrouding it in lines and words. I haven't gotten close to the open wounds yet. I'm still twisting and turning on paper, in the same way I walk around in the downtown crowds every night, letting my body lose its way.

Two days ago I went out for my evening roam and realized I'd forgotten my dark glasses and had gone out with my face uncovered. I raised my right hand to adjust my glasses on my nose and was surprised to find that they weren't there. I felt as if I'd gone out in the street with nothing on. I had gone only a few paces from the door of the building that includes the hotel on its top three floors. I looked around quickly, just to be safe, and didn't see anything suspicious. Even so I found myself shaking—at least my fingers were clearly trembling. I pretended that everything was normal, on my guard for anyone monitoring me, as though a great big eye, open day and night, were watching my slightest movement, and maybe my thoughts as well. I felt that I wasn't alone and hadn't recovered yet. I looked through the pockets of my coat and pants, though I was sure the glasses were still on the glass surface of the dressing table in the room upstairs. I behaved as if I had forgotten something, just to send the right message to that hidden eye. I turned and went back, almost tripping over my feet. All this happened in less than three minutes, but it was enough for me to know I was still a long way from full recovery.

I still wake up in panic in the middle of the night. I don't know where I am. In one of these suffocating fits I went and looked at the packets and strips of pills in the drawer of the bedside table, tempted to take them all, to put an end to everything and find relief. Holding back my tears, I reached out for them and started to tear off the plastic bubbles over the Xanax tablets, which were a sad, pale pink. My only friend turned up right then—the little black spider I had met in the same room weeks ago when I came out of prison. It started to climb up my fingers casually and affectionately and without fear, as though it were holding back my hand, trying to stop me from taking the pills and whispering to me to calm down and think again. I backed down and watched it walk over my wrist and the palm of my hand, and then I went back to writing, imagining myself as a dumb spider spinning a frail web around himself to protect himself from destruction.

My psychotherapist, Dr. Sameeh, said, "Write, Hani, please. Send me emails regularly, or even text messages on the cell phone. You may have lost your ability to speak but you can still write. Whenever you feel you're suffocating, write. Say on paper what happened, if only for yourself. Purge yourself of everything that made you feel dirty there." When he said "purge yourself," I felt he could see inside me. Maybe he knew that since coming out of prison I've spent a long time under the shower trying to get myself clean. I started thinking seriously about his suggestion. I wrote the first sentence that night on a page in one of the little notebooks I use for communicating with other people: "My name is Hani Mahfouz," I wrote. But I tore it up and threw it away, then took a sleeping pill and was out within minutes.

I sleep. I sleep all the time. I sink into long periods of stupor interrupted only by the need to stay alive. I'm woken by thirst or by the need to urinate, or by nightmares, of course. I hardly remember anything of them other than the shock of how they end. I might have ordinary dreams sometimes. Some of them take me back to prison, back to the most intricate details of the cell and my fellow prisoners, and during those dreams I feel a warm familiarity, like someone who's finally gone back to his home and family. I still haven't come out of the long nightmare, though physically I have distanced myself. The black bird is still perched on my head. I avoid looking other people in the face, in streets and public places, and if any of them stares at me, even for a few seconds, I get flustered and look away, and then I move off quickly, my fingers trembling and my throat dry.

I've confessed to Dr. Sameeh in an email that sometimes I imagine the worst possibilities. I seem to enjoy being frightened and sinking into the dark oozy mud of my fear. When I'm walking around aimlessly, I imagine a heavy hand landing suddenly on me, a living pincer on my neck. I expect it to come down on me at any moment and at every step. I feel it's a small victory when I manage to ignore this threat and steer my thoughts away from it. But within five minutes it comes back to me again and I can sense that unknown person coming up to me, pinning me down and taking my glasses off my face in a single violent gesture. The glasses fall to the ground and other people gather around us in the blink of an eye. Some of them recognize me or he introduces them to me, like a hunter who's happy to have finally found his prey. I see them taking his side, all of them without exception, some of them laughing, and others upset and disgusted when they find out the truth about me. One of them takes part in the public performance with a well-aimed spit right in my face, and another with a firm slap on the back of my neck. Then the others pull at my clothes, which tear easily in their hands and fall off my flesh like paper handkerchiefs. I'm soon naked among them. I try to cover up my genitals but they prevent me. I curl up on the ground while they kick me. The exquisite horror keeps toying with my imagination. Cigarettes are stubbed out on my back and stomach, stiff fingers reach toward my asshole, and I don't even have the energy to scream or cry. I scurry between their legs on all fours like an animal, looking for a gap, but there's no way out.

I don't describe these imaginary scenes to Sameeh in as much detail as I do here. There's also a clear distance between what I write to him by email and what I write for myself here in my notebooks. In one of his messages he said I was trying to overcome my fears by imagining them and magnifying them as much as possible, which is a good start but not a proper solution, and he again encouraged me to write.

When I'm writing, facing the dressing-table mirror yet trying not to look at it, I succeed in forgetting—forgetting not just what has happened to me over the past few months, but also what I have to do now, and tomorrow and the day after tomorrow, and on all the days that I'll have to bear on my shoulders until death brings me relief. I avoid the pressing questions and escape to the happy past, to my grandfather and the workshop and the family house in Abdin and my first relationship. But as soon as I go out roaming every evening, questions circle around my head like birds of prey with horrible screeches. What will I do with my life? Should I emigrate, as some of the people released with me are trying to do? If I wanted to leave the country, how could I go through with the procedures when I'm still completely unable to speak. I'll have to get my voice back first, and to get it back I'll have to have regular therapy, follow Dr. Sameeh's orders, make an appointment to see the speech therapist he recommended, and do countless other things. Thinking of all this, I feel like a dead man walking, a corpse that fights the smell of its own decay every day, and does nothing but this rabid wandering every night.

When my feet tire, I head to the small local bar I recently discovered. It's not one of the places I frequented in my former life, before the nightmare. There I drink one beer after another, and my hand sometimes loosens up enough for me to write in the little notebook I keep with me all the time. The damned questions keep swarming. As soon as a new question is born, within seconds it branches out into other questions, each one hurtling off in a different direction, until I envision a network that branches out to infinity. The new question becomes in turn a hub from which further questions branch out, and so on. It's not like the web that would be spun by my friend the little spider that I check up on every now and then in his place in the drawer. I once addressed him without speaking. "I would have liked to sing to you, but now I can't even speak," I said.

7

SO THE CHICK MANAGED TO break out once he had broken the eggshell with his beak. He stuck out his bare head and his blind eyes, then smashed the egg completely, ruffled his short, scrawny feathers, and teetered along the surface of the earth like a black, ill-intentioned nightmare. He opened his eyes and jabbed his pointed beak in every direction, searching for the taste of flesh and following the smell of blood.

During the hour, which seemed to last an age, between the moment when Abdel Aziz and I were arrested and the moment we were thrown into the cell in Abdin police station, Abdel Aziz managed to bribe the policeman to let him make a quick phone call. He called his family's big-shot lawyer. Some of us managed to do likewise, but others, like me, didn't know anyone they could contact.

The big-shot lawyer sent a young man who worked under him—a joker with a glib tongue who had acquaintances in almost every police station. I didn't see him myself, but that's what I gathered from a policeman who told me later what had happened. He said the young lawyer arrived an hour after we were put in the cell, and they took from all of us our phones, identity cards, money, and everything in our pockets. Suddenly this joker made a scene in the whole police station, which led some of the officers to call Hassan Fawwaz, the head of the vice squad, who only a few hours earlier had supervised the process of rounding us up from various locations. They called him because it was his case and the people in Abdin had nothing to do with it and the whole story was a mystery to them and they didn't know how to respond to this parrot, who kept repeating to them the names of people from the Qadi family, Abdel Aziz's family, who held positions in all the important branches of government. Some of these people often appeared in the media, and with a single word they could advance those who were lucky or reduce the unlucky to the lowest depths. The lawyer deftly managed to slip in some threats, in such a way that an astute listener wouldn't miss them.

Hassan Fawwaz arrived and countered the lawyer's shouting with even louder shouting, along with curses and insults. Despite the rowdy exchanges, Abdel Aziz was summoned and they had a few words with him. Hassan Fawwaz remembered that the informer, Hayatim, hadn't recognized Abdel Aziz and had rounded him up solely on suspicion. He backed down a little, especially when he heard the names of some of his relatives. They didn't argue long, and so far Abdel Aziz hadn't been formally detained. No police report had been written and no grounds for detention had been cited. They didn't need any fuss or headaches over detaining someone from such a family, and their scheme was still in its early stages. Emboldened, Abdel Aziz asked Hassan Fawwaz to set me free too, but Fawwaz refused outright and shouted at the top of his voice that he would cut his arm off if I wasn't a "certified queer," and that if he gave way in every case of special pleading he would have to release all the gays he had spent days rounding up off the streets. The policeman almost died laughing when he told me all this.

Hassan Fawwaz did try to sound reassuring, however, claiming that it was all just a survey he was carrying out on the phenomenon of sexual perversion, which was alien to our society and definitely a recent intrusion from abroad. He wanted to start his survey by finding out roughly how many gays there were in Cairo, and whether they were passive or active or played both roles—just a sociological survey, no more and no less. He wanted to collect statistics and information, and the most important outcome might be to persuade the state to tackle this terrible plague that was spreading among us, so it would only be a matter of hours before we were all back home safe and sound. In my case, these few hours stretched into about seven months, from the heat of May to the cold of November, when some of us were pardoned. And some of us are still serving terms in prison as I write these lines.

Abdel Aziz came back to the holding cell with a policeman to say a few words to me. I moved toward the door with impatient joy, certain that relief was at hand, but as soon as I saw the expression on his face I knew he would go and leave me behind. He took my hands and pressed them between his large hands as he looked into my eyes. All the other detainees watched us attentively and in silence. In a whisper, he promised he wouldn't leave me or abandon me, and he would leave no stone unturned to make sure I escaped from this ordeal as soon as possible. I was happy because at least one of us had saved his skin, in order to help the other and take an interest in his affairs. I suddenly found myself playing the role of the calm, courageous one, and I told him to get in touch with Shireen and make up a lie about how I had had to travel out of Cairo and turn off my cell phone, or that I was with Prince in the hotel to calm my nerves away from home—anything to explain my absence for two or three days. Then I took his pack of Marlboros, though I didn't much care for that brand.

I didn't cry. I was in a state of shock and was focusing on small, practical matters, as if I were going on vacation or going into hospital to have a minor operation. The tears came later—hot, flowing freely and with abandon. I went back to the cell after my friend left and tried to answer a deluge of questions from those detained with me, though I didn't have any satisfactory answers. The contents of the pack of Marlboros were soon shared out between us. Then I fell asleep for some minutes and was visited by that complicated dream in which I come back to my apartment and find Shireen, my aunt Husniya, and Abdel Aziz apologizing for leaving me in the lurch.

Others apart from Abdel Aziz escaped the trap when the case was still in its early stages, and all the non-Egyptians—Arabs and non-Arabs—were released. I know there were more than ten of those. Some of the Westerners refused to go without their Egyptian companions and insisted until they managed to rescue their friends.

The police picked up dozens of men during the campaign, which lasted for several days in early May. The climax came in the early hours of May 11, 2001, two or three days after Abdel Aziz and I were arrested near Tahrir Square. The vice squad raided a large Nile boat, or floating nightclub, that was said to let gay men hold parties there every Thursday. It was called the Queen Boat, or Queen Nariman's boat, and the case became known in all the media as the Queen Boat affair. The media were careful to repeat the word "raided," which I just used unconsciously myself, although in fact the police did not raid anything. They just stood in the darkness on the riverbank and waited to pick off men who were leaving. They loaded them into trucks and, when the trucks were full, drove them to several police stations to empty the detainees into the cells, and then went back to pick up more as the night progressed. Apart from the ones on the Queen Boat, they picked up about twenty people from various public places—streets and squares. They even went so far as to arrest people from their homes and places of work, with the help of informers such as Hayatim. It was my fate to be among the twenty picked up in the street, after Hayatim noticed me by chance while he was driving around in the police van with the head of the vice squad.

That young voluble lawyer might have sensed that a major operation was underway, so he didn't press too hard to get me out with Abdel Aziz, or maybe it was because he had accomplished his basic mission when he plucked his clients' son from the lion's mouth. Maybe he advised Abdel Aziz to leave his friend to his fate. Wasn't his mother a famous actress? He must have important acquaintances who would get him out of trouble unscathed. "Didn't you call his wife and reassure her?" the lawyer probably said. "You also called that Prince guy, whom he sees as a father figure. There's nothing more we can do, believe me. Even visiting him in the police station could land you in big trouble." In the police station I heard some strange talk suggesting that for some reason the case was of interest to circles at the highest level. Don't ask me how or why, because even the devil himself couldn't imagine what those people were cooking up.

He must have said something like that, and Abdel Aziz was persuaded or was worried about his reputation and his future. A few weeks after the start of the case he left the country to work in the United Arab Emirates, all of a sudden and with a proper work contract. He stayed out of the country until the furor died down and those around him forgot that he had been friends with someone accused of debauchery and contempt for religion in the case which attracted massive publicity.

Abdel Aziz went home that night and left me there, dreaming of the fairy-tale prince who would come back to save me on his winged white horse. My hopes faded little by little and an invisible fist tightened its stranglehold on my neck with every day that passed.

8

EVEN BEFORE RA'FAT, AND BEFORE I started peeping at the penises of urinating men, I often imagined some man, a man I made up out of my fantasies. I tried to bury myself inside him. I curled up into a ball on my bed, as tightly as possible. I wanted to make myself so small that I could slip inside my imaginary man, settle down there, and live the rest of my life inside his skin, pretending I was him. On a few occasions this man was my father.

At the beach in Alexandria one summer my father and I went to take showers at the end of the day. He took off his tight striped swimming trunks and I, aged seven at the time, had a clear view of the shriveled brown bulge lurking among his pubic hairs, which were growing again after a recent trim. With a surprised smile I had a close look at his penis while he was aiming a powerful stream of urine into the round hole in the corner of the shower cubicle. His penis had extended a little with the flow of urine. I took hold of my own little hamama and tried to imitate him, but only a few feeble drops came out and fell right between my feet. He noticed that I was looking back and forth between my hamama and his elongated penis. He gave a little laugh. "Don't worry, Hannoun, when you grow up it'll get bigger," he said with confidence.

There is still something vivid about this old memory that I can't dismiss, however hard I try. Even now I enjoy the sight of a man urinating, not in the sense that it excites or arouses me, but as a game that we enjoyed in our childhood, that we look back on momentarily as adults with a smile of sympathy, nothing more. I may have been a little confused by the difference between my appearance and my father's appearance. My white complexion was different from his deep brown. He had thick body hair while I was soft and smooth. Maybe all this sent me a message that I wasn't associated with him, didn't look like him, and would never be a man like him. But before he could help dispel these delusions, he died.

I remember we were sitting in front of the television on one of the rare occasions Father spent the evening with us at home. In a variety program they showed a dance performance by Gene Kelly, whose name I discovered later. He was wearing a sailor's uniform and singing and dancing with two other men also in sailor suits as they roamed freely around town, singing "New York, New York." I no longer know what it was that enchanted me about this number, which only lasted a few minutes. Was it their dancing, their perfect timing, or their trim bodies in uniform? I went up to my father and told him straight out, "I want a suit exactly like that one for Eid."

A few weeks later, on the first day of the Eid al-Adha holiday, he stayed out till morning at an Eid party and came back in very high spirits. He woke me up himself, though I had slept only two or three hours because I'd stayed up in the hope that I might last till the morning. He waited while I got up and had a shower so that he could dress me himself in the white sailor suit, the only piece of clothing he ever made for me in his life. I put it on and started dancing in imitation of the foreign singer: "New York, New York."

Then he went into his room to sleep after the long night out. He kept Mama with him for some time before releasing her, and I noticed that Grandmother Sakina was going "tsk, tsk" and mumbling something incomprehensible when Mother came out. He slept until a little after the call to noon prayers, and in the meantime I had gone out in the street and back dozens of times. I was out with one of the neighbors' daughters, who was a few years younger than me and followed me all the time like a frightened kitten. Sometimes I amused myself by styling her hair as if she were a doll.

Then we heard Mama screaming from the bedroom, and she came staggering toward Grandmother, who was sitting with me watching a play called *Minus Five*. "Ahmad's not answering me! Ahmad's dead! Your son's dead!" she shouted.

I felt she was accusing her of something, as if Grandmother had taken my father's soul. At the sound of the scream a red balloon slipped out from between the fingers of the neighbors' daughter and made an unpleasant screeching sound as it suddenly deflated, bouncing left and right until it was empty and collapsed into a lifeless blob on the carpet. Grandmother had spilled a bowl of lupin beans she had been holding. She jumped to her feet with her long stick and began to call out in a voice that was completely new to her: "Ahmad, Ahmad, Hamada, the stew's ready, up you get, Hamada, come and have lunch with us."

The neighbors' daughter fled in tears. I wished I could go with her, but I was frozen to my spot on the sofa. I could hear their screams growing louder, but I didn't dare go near my father's room. I just stared at the television screen as Marie Munib asked Adel Khairy, "What have you come to work as?"—just as she had been asking him before the screaming started. And he repeated his same answer time and again: "A driver, madam, a driver."

For years to come, the terrifying face of Chamardel Hanem in that play would remain the image of death as far as I was concerned, and for even longer Mama refused to celebrate Eid al-Adha in any way. Whenever someone gave her Eid greetings, she would say, "No one's to congratulate me on the anniversary of Ahmad's death. Understood?"

Eventually she went back to celebrating the feast like everyone else and gave up the trips to the grave on the morning of every Eid, and I realized then that she had forgotten him and was trying to make me forget him too. She had put her memories of him with his remaining clothes in a small cardboard box on the balcony. Until then she had put a piece of his clothing in front of the Quran reader she summoned on every anniversary of her husband's death. The man would read two long sections of the Quran for my father's soul, which in some sense was still clinging to these clothes. As soon as the sheikh left the house, the sadness ritual was over and she went back to the Eid: she might put some lipstick on, hurry to turn on the television, or suggest some place we could go together to pretend we were enjoying the holiday.

After my father died, Mama rented out the workshop and I would visit every month to collect the rent. The place was slightly changed on every visit, as if reflecting the changes that were happening in my life and to my body. The workshop merged with the men's suits workshop where Ra'fat was a cutter, and he always seemed to be waiting for me. We started standing together and chatting on the landing or outside the building. He gave me my first puff of a cigarette. I took two puffs and handed it back, trying not to cough and annoyed that he was laughing. He spoke to me about masturbation and how pleasurable it was, and once he took my hand when the others couldn't see and put it on his hard penis. I pulled my hand back and looked away. Just touching that hot thing between his thighs unnerved me and made me feel limp. He said he had the key to the small fabric storeroom behind the elevator on the ground floor and that we could go in there alone for minutes at a time. I refused and hurried away. In the street I took deep gulps of air to get my breath back and I checked the rent money in my pocket every two minutes for fear I might have dropped it.

Ra'fat seemed to be the only person I had left from the world of my father and my grandfather; the only person who took an interest in me or spoke to me. At home my mother was completely self-absorbed, consumed by the necessities of living. Even Grandmother changed; she started to swing rapidly between her old imperiousness and a new attitude of meekness and weakness that was alien to her. All her ailments ganged up on her suddenly, and she was completely senile within a few years. She stayed in bed, gave up all her weapons, and began to act friendly toward Mama, addressing her as "my girl" and giving her one piece of jewelry after another for her to sell and spend the money on household expenses, so that she wouldn't leave us and go out looking for work. She spent years either in bed or on an old Turkish sofa next to the window, twiddling the dial on the radio, moving from one station to another. She hardly ever left her room and seemed to be waiting to join her son as soon as possible. In the end she obtained what she desired. When the ugly face of Chamardel Hanem made its next appearance, I no longer saw it as an unwelcome guest that had arrived without an appointment, but rather as an old friend. Mama and I tried to pretend to be sad for only the first two days, and when she had sold off the last of Grandmother Sakina's jewelry she had no other option but to go back to her old line of work, and in that Aunt Husniya was willing to help her.

I started staying away from the dreary house, and unconsciously my legs took me to the workshop where Ra'fat worked, even when it wasn't time to collect the rent. One time Ra'fat came out to meet me, rattling the keys to the storeroom. We made sure no one saw us as we sneaked in. I went in first, my arms crossed on my chest, and he joined me a few minutes later. He took my head in his hands and smothered me with kisses, planting them everywhere, hungrily, like someone gobbling down food without chewing. We didn't do much, but at any rate I finally discovered kissing, at the age of thirteen or maybe a little more. Ra'fat's mouth tasted nice despite the strong smell of cigarettes. I dared to fondle his penis, which was coiled up between his thighs, and he soon took it out. It was softer and warmer than I had imagined, and whenever I played with it, my own erection hurt me. I couldn't tell where his body ended and mine began.

Every time after that he pressed me to do more. I would resist and hurry off, and fear held me back however much I shared his urge to play. I felt as if we were prisoners in that cramped space of no more than three square meters, surrounded by troubling voices outside. My breathing was irregular, and I begged him to finish so that we could leave, although I enjoyed him holding me. I often imagined that my father had not died and was still working in the workshop upstairs, and that he would suddenly break down the door and discover that I was sullying myself with this young man who looked like a handsome devil.

Ra'fat ejaculated and tried to restrain his panting. Then he rubbed his shoe into the semen to smear it into the dust on the tiles and hide any trace of it. Adjusting his clothes, he listened awhile till there were no footsteps to be heard, then slipped out first through the half-open door. He waited again before gesturing to me through the gap in the door, and I would hurry out without looking behind me. In the light of the hallway I checked that my clothes had no stains, and along the way I kept wiping my mouth and face as if his kisses and his saliva had left some faint trace that might expose my secret to the world.

9

I GET CONFUSED AND IRRITATED whenever someone asks me about the first time, as if it had some special value. Often I respond by asking what they mean by the first time—the first fantasy, the first petting, the first kiss, or the first time I touched a naked body? Everyone has an infinite number of first times. Of course the person asking would specify that he meant going the whole way, and at this point I would bring up Ra'fat. I had his story at the ready: I had refined it and polished it over time, and I remembered it like an old song that tripped off my tongue without me having to think.

I was about sixteen years old, with a horrible pubescent mustache, and my voice was suddenly so gruff that I didn't recognize myself when I spoke. I kept having excruciating dreams, in which I writhed with men of every color. I woke up to find my underwear wet with sticky patches and washed them in warm water in the washbasin in the bathroom because I was embarrassed that my mother might work out what they signified, but she was too detached to notice anything, including that mysterious force that was reshaping me inside and out. She went back to acting and won some real roles thanks to Aunt Husniya's efforts on her behalf. My aunt was now Husna the singer: her star had risen a little and she had left the third-rate nightclubs behind her. She recorded several songs for the radio, and the future seemed to be smiling on her, though she herself took no interest in any future or any past. I used to hear my mother warning her about time and the consequences of loose behavior with men and telling her off in the crudest terms for taking various strange drugs such as opium. The elder sister's only response was to make light of it, to laugh and sing. I hated my aunt at that time because she had snatched my mother away from me and sent her off to studios, where they painted her face so that she could stand in front of the camera and pretend she was some other woman. She flitted from one lie to another at the speed of lightning and in her short breaks she would kiss me, give me some money, look at me for a moment as though she thought me strange, and quickly disappear again.

I was a plump adolescent, and I talked to myself in the emptiness of the spacious Abdin apartment. However much I turned on the television and raised the volume, however much I sat scribbling my sad thoughts in my secret notebooks or imagined invisible friends I could speak to about the pains in my soul and how everything made me feel I was suffocating, I could still smell the loneliness that followed me from room to room. Then Ra'fat reappeared after a long absence. He came unexpectedly at noon on a day that was so baking hot that you wanted to take off all your clothes and get right out of your skin to escape the oppressive humidity. When I heard a knock on the door, I was simultaneously joyful and terrified.

I was puzzled when I saw him standing at the door chewing a smile. I had stopped visiting him in the workshop a long time ago and had almost forgotten him. They would send me the rent money with one of the errand boys. He said hello, and told me he had brought the rent for Mama and that he wanted to convey a message from the owner of the workshop. I said she wasn't at home. He let himself in, sat down on a sofa, and asked for a cup of tea as he took a packet of cigarettes out of the pocket of his lightweight checked shirt.

In the kitchen I stared at the water that didn't want to boil and remembered our furtive meetings in the storeroom. My whole body tingled as if an army of ants were on the march. I felt that if we repeated here what we had done there, maybe the world would come tumbling down, or maybe the ceiling would crack open and the sky appear above us. I was wondering if he would try to have sex and I didn't know if I would be able to resist him.

He drank his tea and we pretended that everything was normal. We were playing the roles of guest and host in an embarrassed silence. When he offered me a cigarette, I shook my head and thanked him. He asked me how school was, and as I replied I glanced up at a picture of my father on the wall behind him.

"I'll be starting the first year of secondary school next year," I said.

"You've always been clever, Hani."

When he'd drunk the last drop of tea and put out his cigarette in the same large seashell that my father used to use, he stood up and came over to sit next to me on a seat that wasn't big enough for two.

In my room I saw his body complete and wholly naked for the first time. It was more beautiful than I had imagined. He had little hairs all over his dazzling white skin, in patterns that enthralled me. I moved my head back a little, simply so that I could look at him as he continued to kiss every part of me that he could reach with his full lips.

It was the first time a man had ever penetrated me. The pain was mixed with terror that my mother might suddenly arrive and with the pleasure of finally possessing a man. I didn't at all feel that something inside me had been broken or that I had lost something of value, such as dignity, honor, or manhood. In fact, I felt quite the opposite, as if I had recovered something I had lost; as if a fracture had healed, like a broken doll lucky enough to have found someone to put the pieces together again and bring it back to life, so that now it could talk, move, dance, and sing.

After ejaculating breathlessly, he laughed, or rather suppressed a little laugh that was almost a gasp. Then he got up from on top of me, flushed and bathed in sweat, smiling coyly as he hid his genitals with his hand. He came back from the bathroom a few minutes later, and I was back in my underclothes. I noticed a strange expression on his face, as if he felt a little sorry for me or as if he had won a contest that had gone on between us for years but was embarrassed to have won and didn't know what he should do with his victory. He dressed quickly in light clothes and stood in front of the fan with his eyes closed for a while, then combed his hair with a black comb that he always kept in his trouser pocket. Then he turned toward me and blew me a kiss. It was a final touch, one that I would later grow used to.

"I must fly," he said with a smile.

Before I opened the door for him, I gave him a tight hug, and maybe at that moment I hoped he wouldn't go, that we would repeat the performance, just so he wouldn't leave me alone. I kissed his lips very slowly and said something naïve. I don't remember what exactly, but maybe I said, "Be sure not to leave me, Ra'fat."

He laughed his little laugh and kissed my cheek lightly, then turned the door handle slowly and left. I heard his footsteps jumping down the staircase impatiently, like someone who had finally been set free.

A few weeks after Ra'fat's first visit, he finally spoke to me about his previous experiences. We were standing outside the Kursaal Cinema one hot Sunday afternoon, drinking Coca-Cola and smoking, when he pointed to a spot not far off and told me that in that very place he had first met the middle-aged man who invited him to watch a film with him and later taught him every pleasure that two men alone can enjoy.

When he met this first teacher of his, Ra'fat was still a complete novice, but the older man could see his potential and took him under his wing. Ra'fat said the man was like a sponge that soaked up every drop inside him and was never satisfied. He was ugly, with an obviously hunched back covered in horrible hair. Ra'fat left him about two years after they met; he missed an appointment and the man didn't know how to reach him. After giving up hope of contacting Ra'fat again, the man started looking for others in the usual places, and a few months later Ra'fat caught sight of him with a young man close to Ramses Square.

He abandoned his first coach, but didn't abandon the game itself. He discovered a vast but clandestine world of hunting grounds where he could play the game, and he started exploring that world with finesse, relying on his recently discovered qualities as a handsome stud, and on the experience he had gained with the hunchback. He learned how to test the vibes around him like a seasoned explorer. He picked up on lustful looks and took advantage of the men who gave them, in the darkness of cinemas, in public toilets where the janitors were complicit, or between safe walls if he was lucky enough to make a good catch. He had sex almost absentmindedly, maybe imagining that he was sleeping with a woman. What mattered was to ejaculate and feel relieved. He scarcely ever made a habit of kissing the men, and if he did, it was just a fleeting kiss without opening his mouth.

Ra'fat wasn't very talkative. It was I who did the talking, in the hope that I could loosen his tongue, while he listened, smiling and distracted. I would tell him about the books I was reading, about the poetry I was trying to write, hoping that he would ask me to read some of it to him, but he didn't show any interest. He would smoke and nod his head, always maintaining that sly smile of his, while he slipped into his clothes one after another and then I suddenly realized that he was ready to go. I suppressed my desire to go out with him because I had come to anticipate the ready excuses he would make for evasion. I managed to entice him out from time to time by inviting him to the cinema or to have lunch out. I noticed he was tense and uncomfortable on our few excursions together, and whenever I tried to hold his hand or put my arm around his waist he quickly moved away, looked at me reproachfully, and made an extra effort to eye the girls around him, like someone fending off unspoken suspicions.

Then I started offering sacrifices to my living idol: little gifts that lay within my means. Once I gave him an embroidered shirt, once a real leather belt with a fancy metal buckle, and I gave him some underwear when I noticed he had holes and tears in his old pairs. He would accept my gifts with a pretense of annoyance: "But why did you go to the trouble? It's me who should be giving you presents!"

Then he would kiss and hug me, and I felt I had triumphed over him despite all my doubts, and I would plan to write a poem about a boy who bought love.

Between writing in my notebooks and reading books, away from Ra'fat, my mother, and everyone else, I was making something else out of my loneliness, something that might seem reassuring and stable if only for some passing hours, before boredom got the better of me and I longed to speak with anyone, even someone imaginary. I would split in two and speak to the other Hani. On the one hand, there was the adolescent lover who waited anxiously and impatiently for his handsome boyfriend to arrive. He would look out from the balcony to the end of the street, then come back inside and examine himself in the mirror, searching for a hair on his upper lip or on his cheek that the razor blade had missed; or he'd throw a glance at the bowl of fruit or of sweets, or touch the bedsheet to check that it was clean. On the other hand, there was Hani the innocent; the good, well-mannered boy who didn't act like the devils who played hooky and stood on street corners harassing girls. He did his schoolwork without anyone nagging him. He put his dirty clothes in the old-fashioned washing machine that you had to fill with water by hand, and waited to wring them and hang them out himself. When the ironing man sent the clothes back he put them away in their places in his wardrobe and the wardrobe of his mother, who dropped in on the house as if she were an occasional guest. I became more than one person. I was myself, my father, my mother, my brothers, and my whole family.

From time to time I would feel guilty, or frightened that God would hold me to account and punish me, so I would wear myself out by praying, fasting, and crying. I prostrated myself every day at dawn, determined to do penance and vowing not to go anywhere near Ra'fat or any other man. I got up in the dark to do my ritual ablutions and went to perform the dawn prayers in the beautiful and historic Jumblatt Mosque, which was not far from our house. After prayers I read the Quran for a while, ignoring glances from other members of the congregation, who knew what kind of work Mama did and some of whom may have heard insinuations from our neighbors that I wasn't a real man.

I would walk a little in the streets, which were deserted and unusually quiet at that hour, glorifying God and asking Him for forgiveness. In the freshness of the early morning little tears would drip from my eyes, like beads from a broken necklace, as I whispered the words of the Khalil Gibran poem:

Have you taken to the woods like me, away from palaces,
Have you followed streams and climbed rocks?
Have you ever bathed in perfume, and dried yourself
with light?
Drunk the dawn as wine in ethereal glasses?

I imagined the streets of Abdin transformed into wide-open fields, populated by none of God's creatures but me as I followed the streams and climbed the rocks. I would walk until the first light of day broke, relishing the taste of remorse in my mouth as if it were the sweetness of faith and praying that God would also restore my mother to His grace, even if that meant I had to leave school and work in some manual trade.

Sometimes, for periods of ten days or two weeks, I could concentrate on my schoolwork and produce prolific amounts of inane poetry that rambled on about the secrets of the universe and the smile of dawn. In other phases, which would suddenly appear and then slowly wear off, my whole system would be in disarray for some reason. A thick, dark liquid would seep into me, bringing discontent, laziness, or a brazen desire to rebel. I would skip dawn prayers and sleep in, then miss school and find fault with my mother during the little time she spent at home. I seethed with resentment toward her and toward everything, and I would say insulting things to her when she was about to go out. She would glower at me, then leave without answering. She didn't have time to waste on me.

During these phases, I managed to elude Ra'fat. I once stayed away from him for a whole month, sustaining myself in the meantime by remembering his defects, his ignorance, and his coarseness. I looked back at the things I had done with him with delicious disgust. Then I saw him one day standing outside my school, waiting for me to emerge. I was flustered and embarrassed, as if it were my fault that he had made an appearance in bodily, visible form in broad daylight. He came up to me as sprightly as a cocksure dandy. He greeted me with a smile, struck up a conversation, and offered me a cigarette. I pushed his hand away and glanced around me, but didn't look at him. "What do you want, Ra'fat?" I asked.

"I just want to see you and make sure you're okay," he said. "You're like a brother to me now, Hani. Or maybe you see it differently?"

Despite my confusion and anger, I noticed that his arrival lit up something inside me. I was glad to see him, glad that he had come to my school, glad that there was someone who took such an interest in me that he would come looking for me even if I had avoided him. I told myself that it wasn't sordid lust that had driven him to come, because there are plenty of other bodies and he could obtain one whenever he

46

wanted, but he had come looking for me and had waited for me. Maybe love was not just a little word in the notebooks where I recorded my thoughts.

I walked with him like a captive, but told myself that I could attract him, not just the other way round; that I could persuade him to repent, fear God, and forget the terrible sin that the devil had enticed us to find so attractive. But I was too embarrassed to talk to him about sins and the devil's enticements. I was tongue-tied, and neither of us spoke as we walked away from the school and toward our house, and then from the front gate to the door of the third-floor apartment, and then to the living room, and then to my bedroom, where I stripped naked and submitted.

10

ONE DAY I WENT TO win Ra'fat back, after lectures in the Faculty of Applied Arts, where I had recently enrolled. I hadn't imagined we would be separated all this time just because he had suddenly gotten married. I couldn't believe he would disappear so casually, without saying a word, after all the years we had been together, even if we had met up only sporadically during that time. The building in Adli Street seemed smaller and more cramped than I remembered it, and of course less stylish and less clean. Only a few years had passed since I had last visited Ra'fat here. The place retained its old sway over me. I thought I could hear my father and his friends laughing behind the workshop door, and I felt a pang of fear that he might appear at any moment.

The bridegroom came out of the workshop with an embarrassed smile, but his smile soon disappeared after he shook hands with me. Flustered and impatient, he said it was no longer appropriate for me to come to the workshop because everyone there knew that my mother had sold it to her old tenant long ago, and some of them had suspicions about his relationship with me, and now he was a married man. I said I had had to come because he had mysteriously disappeared for months and I just wanted to make sure he was well. Staring at the floor, he again told me in a whisper that, as I knew, he had married his brother's widow and he wanted to bring up his brother's orphaned children and go straight. I almost laughed when he reminded me of what I had said about true repent-ance. I didn't know what to say, and when I finally spoke I had to suppress my emotion. "So you don't want to know me any longer?" I asked.

He was about to say something, but held back. He looked at me as if he had remembered something trivial that he was about to forget completely because of my unexpected visit. He asked me to wait a minute and went back into the work-shop. I stayed on the landing, avoiding the looks of curious passersby and asking myself what I was doing there.

Only a few months after his elder brother was killed in a brawl in their neighborhood, along with three other peo-ple, Ra'fat's father had decided that Ra'fat should marry his brother's widow so that the children wouldn't be brought up by a stranger. It was clear that Ra'fat welcomed this conven-ient marriage, which didn't cost him a cent. He moved out of his parents' apartment on the ground floor into his late brother's apartment on the second floor. It was a profitable arrangement, but I often wondered how anyone, however hard-hearted he might be, could replace his brother and move into his bed and home so easily. But then I said that maybe he felt they were one person and that this was what his dead brother would have wanted if he had been asked. This is something I will never understand, not just because it belongs to the world of men, with rules that are obscure to me, but also because I've never been lucky enough to have a brother.

Ra'fat came out a few minutes later with his arm around the shoulders of a short, plumpish young man with pimples on his face and thick coarse hair that looked like an enor-mous helmet on his round head. The young man was smiling in embarrassment, like someone who suddenly discovers that people are furtively taking photographs of him. Ra'fat intro-duced him to me by a name that I forgot as soon as he said it, a name with the letter *h* in it, maybe Yahya, Muhyi, or Ham-ouda. Ra'fat said this was his colleague and friend and that he had wanted him to meet me for some time. Then he leaned over toward me and added in a whisper that the young man would be at my disposal at any time.

The familiar smell of tobacco in his mouth hit me, and my tongue was in knots. I buried my eyes in the floor tiles, unable to take in what he was saying. An autumn breeze blew, bringing with it a whiff from the urinal not far off, the same urinal at which Ra'fat had stood playing with his penis years ago, while I sneaked peeks at him when my father and his friends weren't looking.

He must have been boasting about me to this colleague of his and maybe to other people for ages. He must have told them how highly I esteemed him, and that I never denied him anything he asked for. Maybe he complained about me in exasperation, saying he had become bored with me and tired of my insatiable appetite and the way I was pursuing him. Who knows? His colleague, Mahmoud, Hammad, Hamed, or whatever, must have long hoped to have a relationship like this one, and maybe he had begged Ra'fat to take him along with him when we met, and to sit alone with me, if only once. This was finally his chance to make the most of the used goods, as if I were just an undergarment that an elder brother handed down to a younger brother when it was too small for him or when he had bought a new one. I was reminded of Ra'fat accepting his brother's widow without hesitation; she might be more precious or more important than an old piece of clothing, but in the end she was just something that the males inherited or passed on for free to their work colleagues, as he was now doing with me.

I came round from my daydreaming to the rough voice of the rotund young man, who was repeating what Ra'fat had said about how he would be my very best brother and friend, and how I only had to try him once and I would never forget him. As he spoke he rubbed his hand rapidly between his thighs. I turned around, braced to make a move, then dashed down the old wide stairway. Outside, the sharp autumn air took me by surprise and my eyes stung a little. The street looked blurred, like a thin screen dappled by shifting light and shade.

I started walking quickly and aimlessly. I hardly saw anything around me. I cursed myself, mocked myself, and wondered what exactly Ra'fat had done wrong to make me seethe with so much rage. What exactly was my problem with the offer he had made? Hadn't he behaved generously and with good intentions? He wanted me to carry on playing the same game, though with a new partner, another man, just a male who was willing to play, so what was my problem? What difference does it make whether your partner is called Ra'fat or Hamatto? Whether he's tall and thin or short and fat? What's the difference between us and stray dogs? They might be better off, because they don't lie and they don't have to make up false names for things.

I started looking around me, as if I were looking for someone who might suddenly notice me among the crowds and the bustle, and who could answer my questions; someone like that venerable old man with the white beard who appeared to the hero in old films whenever he was in dire straits. The old man would give the hero hope and good tidings and help him solve the riddle. Sometimes I could imagine such an old man when I came out of the Jumblatt Mosque after dawn prayers, but for now I knew it was a lie no different from the lies I inscribed in my notebooks about the unity of the universe and the music of heaven.

As always the streets of central Cairo were packed with cars and people of every color and variety. There were men all around me, in the crowded buses, on the sidewalks, in the restaurants and coffee shops, gathered together at bus stations, hurrying eagerly to work, or just loitering to kill time. It struck me that endless possibilities lay ahead of me. Why should I cry over a man who had come and gone? I could find thousands of alternatives, and each one of them was bound to have his own smell and taste and touch. Each one of them would have his own tone of voice, his own way of laughing, his own story, however inconsequential it might be, and his own unique facial expression when he reached orgasm. So why should I imprison myself in adolescent fantasies? At that moment I felt I was coming out of a long coma, and I wanted to try out all the men in the world, almost without exception. What was to stop me? A door inside me opened to reveal a monster that had been trapped. It was hungry and started to howl for food.

That same day I picked up a man from the street for the first time. He was middle-aged, bald, and thin, and his suit looked too big for him, as if he had lost half his weight since leaving home in the morning. We exchanged glances at the bus station close to Ramses Square and understood each other's intentions. I soon found myself in the offices of the law firm where he worked and to which he had the key. There was no one else there at the time. I gave myself to him on a threadbare carpet that scraped against my body and my knees, which were pressed against the floor. His firm hands held me tight at the waist as if he were worried I might escape his grasp and run off. I didn't enjoy anything about it, but I just wanted to try, to break a barrier, to take revenge on myself and on my insignificance and fragility. I was a doll, made of cloth and straw, that had suddenly realized it was just a doll and that after this nothing could hurt it, however many pins they stuck in it and however hard they pulled its hair; a doll now lying half naked on a dirty carpet, with a thin stranger urging it to get dressed quickly before anyone took them by surprise.

It was not a passing fit of madness or just a reaction to the abrupt end of my relationship with Ra'fat. It was a sign of how my life would be for many years to come. I tore up that man's phone number and forgot him as soon as I left the building. He was just the first in a long line of phantom men, faceless and nameless, who plied my body and whose bodies I plied, with no illusions and no demands other than the impulse of the moment.

I learned the art of the hunt through practice, without a teacher. I learned how to make eyes and read the reaction on men's faces. I learned how to slip through the crowds once we had made contact, either ahead of my prey or some distance behind, until we were somewhere relatively safe. I learned how to sneak a peek at the penis of the man standing next to me at the urinals, awaiting his reaction, or how to make eye contact with men rubbing themselves in the crotch as a signal. I picked up university students and staff and met men who gave their bodies to those who wanted them in exchange for a meal or a small sum of money. I found bus routes that were known to be crowded and served as meeting places for gay men, some of whom took the bus only to cruise. I played the game in my room in the Abdin apartment, in dozens of unfamiliar rooms, and sometimes in public places. I tried some dodgy Turkish baths, where gay men met and sometimes flirted.

I started going out cruising whenever I felt the urge, rarely meeting up with the same person more than once. Even when that crazy period of my life was over, I continued to meet men I didn't know and wouldn't remember. Some man might stop me and remind me who he was, claiming we had done it together at one point. A man might say, "We went to my place in the clinic. Don't you remember when I examined you and gave you an injection?" or "I'm George, the bartender in the hotel in Dokki, Mr. Hani. You wouldn't let me leave the room for three hours. How could you forget?" Those were the ones I ran into again by chance, just a random sample from a sea of bodies. I submitted to the currents, which took me where they wanted, like a beautiful floating corpse.

Voraciously I started to explore the nightlife of the city and the creatures of the night. I found out more about the other persona that came to life inside me as soon as evening fell. That version of me grew and gained strength with the years. He lost his shyness and went out with his face uncovered. I saw him reflected in the reactions of every new man I slept with, and in my imagination I saw him with a headdress of painted feathers, decorated with strings and chains of beads, crystals, diamonds, sequins, and pearls. He wasn't so much a person as a character in a music-hall dance, a circus performance, or a moving cabaret of flesh and blood. Only superficially did he look like other people.

I began to attract men like me wherever I went, and a small circle formed around me. They were my courtiers and I was their queen. They started to call me Hanushka. I was no longer embarrassed about Mama's work, as I had been previously. In fact I boasted about it, and when I spent lavishly on my nefarious coterie, I would tell them, "Say a prayer for Mama, girls."

I deployed my old talents—fooling around and making jokes. I made sarcastic jibes at everyone, my friends and the men who played the role of male bees, who pursued me as I ascended until only the strongest and most patient of them could reach me. I was now Hanushka, an insatiable vampire that refused to settle down with any one catch. I would sleep with them once or twice, just to try them out, and then I might throw them as castoffs to the girl who was nearest. I didn't get involved, I didn't hang around, I didn't want to know anything about the other person or hear his stories. I only wanted his body, his warmth, the sound of him groaning or grunting at orgasm. Just sex, a guest with few demands, a plaything destined to be erased from my memory. And the show went on.

The joker went back to his mirror at the end of the day. I went back to a bedroom where I was alone in my nakedness. I might feel a slight thrill for some brief moments as I took off my clothes and made ready for bed near to dawn. It felt like I was Mother as she took off the accessories that went with the characters she was playing. I wasn't really Hanushka: that was the right role for me, but it was just a role, no more and no less. Perhaps I identified with the role more than I should, so much so that I no longer knew who the real Hani Mahfouz was or how to go back to being him when I wanted. I had many versions of him. It's true: they were all based on the original, but they were not the original. They weren't me. They were all masks, with nothing behind them. A void that was terrifying but that gave me pleasure. In these brief moments, I might write a few lines in my diary before putting it back in its place in a locked drawer, where I would forget about it for weeks or months, until I again had a wave of doubt. Just a few passing moments when the star, the celebrated artiste, the man-killer, lost the plot as she walked through the dark wings behind the theater stage. But as soon as the lights fell on her face she immediately went back to the role she had been assigned, because the show must go on.

11

WHILE THEY WERE TAKING US into the holding cell at Azbakiya police station, one of the informers or policemen came up to me, pulled a strand of hair that was hanging down at the back of my neck, and gave it a violent tug, jerking my neck back until I was looking at the horrible ceiling. "It's the first time I've seen this whore, though she looks like she's been around," he said, addressing his colleagues half seriously and half in jest.

"Let go of me, you animal!" I cried involuntarily, in a strangled voice.

It was the kind of thing that lovers might say lightheartedly during foreplay before bouts of frenzied lovemaking, and I had no idea what was coming. The next thing I knew, a heavy hand had landed on my cheek, forcing my whole head to the side. As my head swung back, for a fleeting moment I caught sight of two large tears falling in slow motion from my eyes. When I came to once more, curled up on the floor of the cell, I vaguely remembered they had persuaded a man to lay off me and stop kicking me, and someone had said it would be a shame if the shoes he had just polished got dirty kicking someone as foul as me.

When they closed the cell door on us, some of the detainees looked at me as if I were a madman, and some knew instinctively that I had no experience with police stations or detention, and so I was going to have a hard time. Some of them volunteered advice but I couldn't hear anything. I was just enjoying the sensation of the tears running down my cheek, which was throbbing with pain. The bouts of crying came and went unsolicited and undesired. I prayed to God, silently and in embarrassment, as I tried in vain to gain control over my trembling limbs.

Prince hadn't yet been able to reach me or hadn't yet greased the palms of the policemen or warders with amounts that exceeded their monthly salaries, so that they would at least leave me alone and bring me food and cigarettes. I was not yet inured to the beatings, the insults, and the humiliation, and I hadn't yet noticed or made friends with Karim Saadoun, one of the men in my batch of detainees. He would be with me in the nightmare for many hours before I realized he was there, and only later would we start what became our ritual of exchanging stories.

Time crawled at a different pace in prison. It moved so slowly that there was room in each minute for millions of thoughts and emotions. I no longer remember how long we were held in Abdin police station, without knowing anything of our fate, or how long we stayed in Azbakiya police station at the mercy of Hassan Fawwaz and his officers as they took morbid pleasure at our expense. I only remember the stifling, claustrophobic atmosphere, the disgusting smells, and having to stand embarrassed in the corner to urinate into a plastic bucket that was overflowing with shit. I vividly remember the taste of the first small cup of tea I drank in prison, after about two days without any food or drink other than dirty water. Some of the policemen supplied us with tea through a small hole in the window grille. A transparent hose passed through the hole—a hose that two days earlier I would never have willingly touched with my hand. The thin end of the hose poured the tea into a plastic bottle that we held on the inside. The bottle buckled and shrank from the heat with each round of tea, and ended up about half its original size. Despite my disgust, I would take a used plastic cup and drink from it. How wonderfully refreshing the first mouthful was! It felt as if the blood, which had previously stopped running through my veins, was now flowing happily and unconstrained.

I learned that the body has its own priorities, and I learned to take note of all the little insignificant things that matter to the body, such as a sip of hot tea or a drag on a cigarette, until my day became dominated by a long succession of such matters—food, tea, sleep, and relieving myself. In the absence of such urgent concerns, we would revert to more important matters—the disaster that had struck us, the case against us, the scandal, and what they would do with us in the end. But for much of the time a piece of bread with cheese was more important than anything else, and I would have been willing to put up with as much as the others around me if only I hadn't had bouts of asthma, sometimes accompanied by heart palpitations, only to remember suddenly that I hadn't taken any tranquilizers or antidepressants for some time.

Over two or three days they summoned us one by one and played a game with us along the lines of "Admit that you're a queer and we'll let you go," but none of us ever went anywhere, no matter what we confessed. Hassan Fawwaz had a small recording device to record our confessions as evidence before we were referred to the prosecutor's office or before we were transferred to the medical examiners to confirm the oral confessions. Fawwaz was constantly surrounded by two or three men who were more like rhinoceroses than human beings. I couldn't imagine that outside that place they had homes and families and maybe children they loved and cared for.

In a glass-fronted cabinet close to his desk, Hassan Fawwaz had a real black whip, which he used for the first time on Karim Saadoun. When the whip was about to land on his head, Karim automatically raised his hand and the tip of the whip wrapped itself around one of the fingers on his left hand, breaking a blood vessel or something like that. When he came back to us it kept bleeding for a long time, even after I ripped my shirt into shreds and wrapped some of them round his finger several times. The blood didn't seem strange in our surroundings, but Karim kept looking at it in amazement. He noticed I was having trouble breathing. He studied my face for a while, and then asked me my name.

We were all beaten in Azbakiya police station: those who confessed, those who held out, those who said they were tops, and those who said they were bottoms. They weren't too rough with me—just two or three blows. I was willing to admit to anything they read out to me. They asked me to take off my pants, and I thanked God that I was wearing white underwear. I knew that if they found anyone in colored underwear they beat them and humiliated them especially brutally, on the grounds that this was irrefutable evidence that they were effeminate. They laughed throughout the process and their tone of voice was surprisingly triumphalist. With each new pervert that stood in front of them for them to play with, their sense of their own virility seemed to rise, until it reached stratospheric levels.

Unlike Karim, I wasn't whipped, but there were fists waiting to punch me as soon as I went into their room. The bully among them landed a punch in your stomach and held it there for a few moments, like a massive truck unloading its cargo inside you. Then he came at you again, and you felt that it would never stop and you would never breathe normally again. Then the next blow came, and then the next, on your back, or a quick, stinging slap on the back of your neck, bringing you back to the real world and making you forget the stone sinking into your stomach as if it had never happened, and you were surprised to discover that, like pleasure, pain has no known limits.

Unconsciously or unthinkingly, I told them what they wanted to hear: "I'm gay, passive and active."

They asked me to repeat what I had said with the recording device switched on, after the beatings had stopped. My voice had calmed down a little and was now quite close to my normal voice. Other people had repeated this phrase under the impact of the beatings, without understanding what it really meant. After coming back bleeding, someone had asked me, "Does 'gay' mean you give or you take?"

At the end of the process all of us were preoccupied with the screams of pain from damaged parts of our bodies. Those pains continued long after we were referred to the prosecutor's office, and were then renewed in the "welcoming ceremony" at the Tora prison. I stayed close to Karim, wearing just a vest with white braces over my pants. I wept in silence, a silence that drowned out the sound of my thoughts amid the wailing and the crying. Then the cell door opened and an officer stood there, looking handsome and kind. We hadn't seen him before. "I'm not going to lie to you," he said with a serious face and in a sympathetic tone. "Yours is a very serious case. I want you to be strong and prepare for what will happen."

Then he rushed off without lingering even a few seconds to face the flood of questions and entreaties that everyone pressed him with. His apparent sympathy merely added to our alarm.

At that moment I began to have a serious asthma attack. I looked around for help of any kind. Suddenly, amid all the sobbing and the suffering, Karim spoke out from the corner where he was lurking. Pointing his bandaged finger in the air, he said, "You're our witness, Lord!"

He was staring at the ceiling with wide-open, startled eyes, as if he could see something none of us others could see.

12

IT WAS THE LONGEST YEAR of my life. I was fully convinced I was out of prison only when I stood naked under a hot shower a few weeks ago, in the bathroom of this room in the Andrea Hotel, which belongs to our elderly friend Prince—to be precise, at dawn on Sunday, November 18, 2001.

The release procedures took place in exactly the spot where the nightmare had begun: Abdin police station, which isn't far from the place where my whole life had started—our old house. The policemen at the station didn't believe that I really couldn't speak. They thought it was a ruse, and if Prince, the lawyer, and Abdel Aziz hadn't been there, they would have kept messing with me until they grew bored. That might have happened to others who were not of immediate interest to anyone. I came out of the police station with my friends, breathing with difficulty and panting like an animal wandering in the desert, despite the tranquilizers Prince had given me as soon as we came out. That man doesn't forget anything, and without him I would have been lost.

Under the shower that day, I ripped the small adhesive bandage off my forehead. It hurt and I could feel the stitches underneath. I remembered how I had injured my head in the prison truck and started crying again. They may have been tears of joy, simply at discovering that I was alone once more. At last I had no one at my side and I was far from my cellmates, the warders, the handcuffs, the jail, and the cage where we defendants appeared during sessions of the trial.

Maybe this is the only real freedom—having the chance to be alone.

I found some of my old clothes, which Prince had had sent from my house several days earlier. I grabbed them, hugged them passionately, and buried my nose in them. I lost my balance and had to sit on the ground in front of the open wardrobe. At that moment I saw, quite still in the corner of the wardrobe, a black spider so small he might just have been born. I found myself talking to him without moving my tongue or lips. I told him I was no longer afraid of him and his kin, as I had been when I was young. I had lived alongside all manner of insects for months in prison, and I would often wake up with them on my skin. I reached out to him. At first he moved away, but when he had no other escape route he started to climb up my wrist. I caught him with my other hand and put him on my open palm. I thought for a moment, looking at him, and then trapped him in the drawer of the nightstand. I imprisoned him. That way I wouldn't be completely alone.

My new prison was a room in a four-star hotel, with air-conditioning, an en-suite bathroom, a television, and a dressing table. I tried not to look at the dressing-table mirror most of the time, to avoid the stranger who threatened me with his deathly looks. I took pills and slept for hours, and from time to time I got up to eat and take a long shower. I might flick through the television channels in the hope of chancing on a film or a series that Mother had made, so I could hear her voice and see her face—her frowns and smiles and the sparkle in her eyes.

In the first days after coming out of prison I didn't leave the room. Prince and other friends took turns looking after me. They all wanted to check up on the man who had survived the carnage. Our friend Dr. Sameeh visited me several times, emphasizing that I shouldn't take too many pills and that I needed to rest and avoid any excitement. All of them spoke, while I said nothing. I could answer only with a pen and a piece of paper, and I always saw from their eyes that they felt sorry for me and hardly recognized me. They seemed to be asking themselves the same question that was never out of my mind: Where had Hani gone? Where was their old friend? Often I pretended to be asleep, just to be alone, and I would tell myself that all this was pointless, because you're finished, Hani, and also that it was no use taking a shower every few hours or rubbing your body vindictively with soap. They have succeeded in defiling you from the inside forever, and not even a torrent of pure water could wash their finger-marks off your body.

In order to prove that I wasn't defeated, or to postpone admitting it for as long as possible, I took Dr. Sameeh's advice and decided to go out one night, at least to stretch my legs. I saw the delight in Prince's smile when he saw I had gotten dressed and had prepared to go out for the first time. Later, when he had grown used to my nocturnal sorties, he continued to keep an anxious eye on me. Maybe he was trying to guess the thoughts in the head of his speechless friend. Maybe I left the hotel every night only to escape his excessive supervision and protection.

I walked hesitantly at first, stepping forward as if stepping back. Despite all the crazy noise in the city center, everything was wrapped in a terrified silence, the silence of a child who has been caught red-handed and can hear only his blood throbbing in his ears in expectation of severe punishment. I walked with my eyes on the ground, like someone looking for something he has accidentally dropped. I watched my feet move ahead of my body, dragging me forward almost against my will. I saw them busy with their little dance on the sidewalk or on the street. Once I felt that they were tame animals trapped inside my socks and shoes. Like a blind man who never takes off his dark glasses, although he only goes out at night, I didn't know where they would lead me. I had a clear sense that my feet were a living thing; maybe the only part of me that was still alive. I rarely looked up from my feet, maybe thinking I would lose my way if I lost track of their movement, if only for a second. I rarely looked up to glance around me. What might I see? People. More people than necessary; people of different kinds, shapes, ages, and appearances, and wearing a variety of clothing. Words, calls, whispers, and lewd remarks. The world disguised itself in the form of people in order to walk and forget, never turning to look behind.

The more I went out, the farther I strayed from Behler Passage, where the hotel was, and every time I stayed out a little longer. My feet hurried along, as if they knew where we were heading—a final haven where they would have room to breathe and relax, and where one of them could tell the other of its pains and hopes. Then one day they took me to a small working man's bar in the Alfi district, where I had my first taste of beer in many months. Prince had been pressing me to join him in gatherings on the hotel roof, but I hadn't taken up his invitations and didn't feel I was yet ready to face my old world again. In that bar, a few weeks ago, I freed my feet from their captivity and exposed them to the air under the table. Then I picked up my pen and wrote the first sentence that wasn't addressed to someone other than myself.

"My name is Hani Mahfouz," I wrote, "and I was an only child, pampered by everyone, as if my mother were the sun and my father the moon."

I look at this sentence with gratitude now that other lines and whole pages have followed in its wake. Without it I could never have untied my tongue on paper, and losing the power of speech would have been a two-headed monster. The words came sparingly at first, and my inability to speak gripped my hand and prevented it from moving. I made do with this sentence for days, until I learned how to move on and found what I wanted to say, to myself, to Dr. Sameeh by email, or to some unknown person I imagined reading my words many years after my death.

The sky gave me a gift with a smile yesterday. I was looking for any of Mother's work on the television channels, to watch before going to sleep toward dawn. I was surprised to find an old serial of hers, in which she played the part of a divorced woman with a son called Hani. Maybe the director deliberately suggested changing the son's name in the script so that it would seem more natural when she called him, when she played with him, or when she cried after the father obtained custody of the son. That night I saw my mother and heard her calling me "Hani, my dear," even if it was just a colored picture on a cold screen. I fell asleep as soon as the serial ended, as contented as an unborn baby in the darkness of the womb.

13

WHEN I SAW MOTHER ON screen for the first time, sharing a hot kiss with an actor in one of her beach-and-swimsuit films, my stomach turned and I almost vomited. I was no longer a child and I knew that it was all acting through and through, but she was still my mother, and that handsome man wasn't my father.

When she woke up late that day I didn't speak to her, and I expected her to ask me what was wrong, but she wasn't interested. Then I realized I was making too much of it, and I decided instead to provoke an argument with her. That afternoon I went up to her on the balcony as she sat like a queen in her maroon bathrobe, drinking tea, smoking, and looking through magazines. I sat down opposite her without saying anything, until she looked up at me with a smile.

"Mama, I've decided to smoke," I said.

She chuckled, handed me a white Marlboro, then sent me to fetch a wooden box inlaid with mother-of-pearl from her bedroom. When I handed it to her, she took out a silver lighter and gave it to me.

"Look after it, my dear," she said. "It's a keepsake of Father's."

Her eyes wandered for a moment, between the trees and the birds, as if she was remembering Ahmad, her only man. Then her smile returned and she went back to reading, or pretended to do so.

Most of the time she seemed as remote as the lantern of a lighthouse, flashing and fading on the far shore of my dissipated lifestyle. I watched her bloom like a rose as, over time, her efforts bore fruit beyond all expectations. Major directors seemed to have suddenly noticed her talent and the unaffected nature of her acting, and had given her more important roles and more space. She had a role in a major religious film about the Prophet's military campaigns and played a village chief's tyrannical wife in the series *Saqiyat al-ayyam*, which achieved unprecedented success as soon as the first episode was broadcast in the month of Ramadan. It was as if her place had been left vacant until she, and she alone, was ready to fill it. When I watched her, I wavered between admiration, envy, and irritation.

We had moved to the Garden City apartment in my second year in university, and she sold our old apartment when she found out that I was still going there in the company of certain friends. That alarmed her. Maybe she thought that, like Aunt Husniya, I had been caught up in the wave of drugs. She questioned me at length and wasn't convinced by my assurances, even when I swore on the Quran, so she took me to the doctor. I felt insulted that she didn't believe me, but she was reassured, at least as far as drugs were concerned, and it was I who started the periods of estrangement that might extend for weeks. I was seething with indignation for no obvious reason, and I was always expecting that a fresh surprise would bring another pillar of my life crashing down on my head. I might have been worried she would find a man other than my father, other than me, and then the fragile bond between us would have been broken.

I wasn't excited about the new apartment at first, despite the large rooms, the expensive furniture, and the fact that Gamal al-Din Aboul Mahasin Street was quiet. I missed the Abdin area and the Jumblatt Mosque, and I often went there after college to walk around awhile before going home.

I spoke to her more in my diaries than I did in real life. I wrote nice, friendly words about her, and I meant to say them to her at the earliest opportunity, but the words would slip my mind as soon as I saw her. Under pressure at work, she would sometimes snap at me. I started hearing phrases such as: "What more do you need to make you succeed in life?", "I go through hell every day so that you can live well," and so on.

Then, without warning, she tried to recreate our happy old times together: she would come to me to ask what I thought of a new dress, or to drag me out of my room so we could watch the first episode of her new serial together. She was trying, I must admit. Only now can I imagine the extent to which she too was trapped in her loneliness, on the other side. And then, to her long list of worries were added the problems of Aunt Husniya, who over a matter of a few years had lost her place on radio and television and had gone back to third-rate music halls.

Some years later I heard her telling Mother how she was singing at a party in Suez organized by some security agency, as was usual at the time, and they had notified all the singers taking part that they should not sing for more than half an hour each. The instructions went in one ear and out the other. She was in the mood and wanted to sing her heart out. When her turn came, she sang until her allotted time was up, very much to the delight of the audience, which was calling for encores. The next singer was standing in the wings, waiting to come on. The organizers had to turn the lights out on her and bring down the curtain, and then they dragged her off the stage by force as she continued to sing what was her most successful song at the time, "Mil-askari al-asmar ya ghulbi." She didn't give in easily, and while they were dragging her off she went past the woman who was going on next. Aunt Husniya reached out, grabbed the woman's wig, which stood atop her head like a tower, and tugged it off. "You mercenary whore with your phony voice! You goat!" the woman shouted, so loudly that the audience could hear.

After that incident she didn't dare go near the radio building, and she no longer appeared on television or at official government celebrations. She went back to her original audiences of cabaret drunks, laughing and having a good time, as if she were watching a comedy film about the life of some other woman. Her ribs were visible under her thin clothing and her beautiful eyes turned into dark hollows in a gray face. The lovers and admirers disappeared from around her. During her frequent financial and medical crises, her only refuge was the home of her younger sister. Whenever I saw her with the doorman behind her dragging her large suitcase, I was distraught and locked myself in my room. I hated the weeks or months she spent with us recuperating, and the longer she stayed the more isolated I would become.

I discovered at this time that my loneliness was no longer a rock I had to carry around day and night. On the contrary, it was my only real companion, a mirror that did not trap me inside it but set me free to fly at will whenever I wanted. The presence of Aunt Husniya denied me this freedom and upset the measured equilibrium Mother and I had created. Husniya behaved like a woman who walked around naked in broad daylight and didn't care that she was naked. Her presence ruined the atmosphere at home, with silences, secrecy, and locked doors. Her inane laugh might ring out at any time of day, sometimes for no reason. She wandered from room to room half naked much of the time, and wanted to talk to anyone, even the maid or the doorman's wife. She would stop singing one song, only to start on another. When she had recovered and was bored of the house of ghosts, as she called it, we would wake up one morning to find she had gone we knew not where. Then I would take a deep breath and close the doors and windows again, as if afraid of the slightest draft or the feeblest ray of light.

When I flunked my second year in college, it was an alarm bell that woke Mother out of her reveries, but she didn't know what to do. She tried to talk, to be friendly and give advice, but it was no use. Then she took me to a small beach house in Agami that she had recently bought. For some days we tried to restore the affectionate relationship of the past, but she spoiled everything when she got it into her head that I needed a father, a man who would live with us at home, and that was all there was to it. After much hesitation and much hedging, she revealed her idea to me, as we were drinking tea on the balcony at sunset. She hinted that she had turned down many offers of marriage and that she had no desire for men, but she might do it if she felt that it would be in my interest.

For a moment my natural inclination to make fun of the idea almost won out, and I thought of reacting by saying that I agreed, as long as her new husband was willing to let the two of us share him. But I restrained myself as usual, shrugged indifferently, and took another cigarette. "If you want to get married, get married," I said in a provocative tone. "You're a free woman, but there's no need to use me as an excuse. I'm a big boy now and I don't need a father or a . . . ."

I didn't complete my sentence. She looked off into the distance, then gathered the hem of her long silk bathrobe, stood up, and left the balcony. We managed to avoid the subject till the end of the short holiday, and we didn't return to it once we were back in Cairo.

The second alarm bell was louder: I started to have sudden panic attacks when I was reading, eating, or watching television. I felt something gripping my throat, my heart would race, my limbs would shake, and I felt I was about to die. The doctor I visited with my mother referred me to a psychiatrist, who prescribed me some pills. I visited him often, for a long time, and I had fun tricking him by mixing truth with falsehood in the ridiculous sessions of analysis. But I gave in after a while and told him about my nightmares—the old nightmares about spiders and the new ones in which I saw myself completely naked among everyone I knew.

I didn't even think of telling him about my secret inclinations for men. I was sure he was submitting regular reports on my mental state to my mother. After a while I started getting used to the panic attacks. I even began to like them in a way. After them I felt that I had died and then come back to the world, or like someone who has been punished in some strange way and then emerges washed and new and ready to commit more mistakes and sins.

Sometimes I woke up in a panic long after midnight, maybe after one of the spider dreams or my other dream, in which I'm late for an important exam. I'm gasping for air, standing by the open window. I knew at that moment that I wanted someone to hug me, so that I could dissolve completely into his embrace. Sometimes I remembered my father and recited the first chapter of the Quran for him, and then for some reason I ended up cursing my mother, my aunt, the psychiatrist, and everyone else, and thinking that death was the only possible and logical solution to all the shit that was landing on my head and that I carried around with me in public while pretending I was normal.

Then I went back to praying and sobriety after I discovered a beautiful little mosque close to our new house. Sometimes I performed the dawn prayers there, and then went for a walk in the neighborhood, breathing in the freshness of the morning and admiring the design of the elegant buildings. I watched the sky as it slowly took off its dark veil and decked itself out in cheerful colors. But I never felt anything like the warm pleasure I had experienced a few years earlier, when I imagined someone appearing out of the void to change me completely.

I imagined him as a friendly, venerable old man who I would meet one day after dawn prayers. With just one look at me he would understand. He would see right through me, see my shameful secrets, then come up to me and put his cool hand on my forehead, and with that one touch he would expunge every sin and every defilement. Within a few seconds all the odious memories, with the phantasms and fears they evoked, would melt away, and the sky would regain its old bright colors.

It was a pleasant distraction, a harmless sedative, but it did not fill the hole that had opened up inside me and that was growing deeper by the day. I knew that kind old men like this existed only in naïve films, and even if one day I came across one I would probably try to seduce him. I would offer him quick sex and tease him by asking him if he was still up to it, but he would run away from me, because mythical old men of this kind don't have real bodies and the most they can achieve is a cheap smile, a smile of impotent commiseration, like those exchanged by patients in a ward for hopeless cases.

14

I DIDN'T HAVE TO WAIT long before I came across my kindly old man, but he was very different from the way I had dreamed of him. I didn't meet him after dawn prayers. He wasn't dressed in white robes and he didn't have a halo around his head. He came up to me in a place full of steam and naked bodies seething with sexual desire. He was Prince Aktham, who became my godfather and who still holds me protectively by a silken leash.

On my exploratory excursions I had found my way to a working-class Turkish bath not far from Ramses Square. It was an old building that may have belonged to the Ministry of Antiquities, and it was almost sunk below the surface of the earth. It was frequented by men seeking to bathe and have a massage, while we frequented it for other reasons. For us, it was a place to meet people and cruise. Not much happened inside, although the staff were complicit. Two men might find seclusion in a dark corner for a while, but only desperate men would bring their encounters to a conclusion there.

My first time there I was amazed and bemused by the naked bodies, the inquisitive stares, and my strange sense nonetheless of familiarity with such an environment, as if I had experienced it before. With time and repeated visits I started to talk and laugh and sometimes exchange kisses and light caresses with strangers, who felt protected by the almost complete anonymity. Before going I would usually pluck up courage by drinking several bottles of beer in some downtown bar and then, in the outer hall of the hammam, I would abandon my clothes, my name, and my whole life. I went in stripped of everything but my desires, unsteady on my feet because it was hard to move in the heavy wooden bath clogs, covered only by a wrap around my waist.

I might have caught sight of Prince before that night, with his hair dyed fiery red at the time and his extraordinary attachment to a kind of elegance associated with past eras. He was never without his hat and cane. He aimed quizzical glances at me whenever he saw me in one of the places we frequented. He seemed to expect me to appear in front of him and perform rituals of loyalty and obedience. I would ignore him, and he would merely blow the smoke from his thin brown cigar in the air, and maybe smile or wink at me. But on that evening in the hammam he reached out and held me before I fell into a trap that someone had laid for me.

The trap was a massive dark-brown man; everything about him was bursting with obvious virility. We had made eye contact, and then he came over to me and started a conversation. Prince saw us whispering to each other and understood the game. I was going to go off with that giant to his apartment, which he said was nearby. The man went off to change ahead of me and later, before I too went to change, I felt a cold hand on my shoulder. I turned around and recognized at once the elderly man who was trying to act young. He looked into my eyes, shook his head slowly, and whispered a single word that rang like a bell: "Danger!"

Then he took me by the hand and we sat outside the steam room, where he stretched out, lit a cigar, and told me that the man I was about to get involved with was a thug who had made a profession of selling his body to men, then started cooperating with the vice squad as an informer, and now made a living out of blackmail by threatening either to expose the men to their families or hand them over to the police. "You shouldn't go off like that with just anyone, Mr. Hani," he said in a deep voice that would suit a broadcaster. "You're a well-brought-up lad and your mother's a big actress and there are lots of bad guys, here and everywhere, and for them you're a wonderful opportunity for blackmail."

I believed him without hesitation and he inspired me with trust and reassurance. I wasn't surprised that he knew me so well, because he was Prince. I stayed by his side as if hypnotized until he decided to go. We agreed to meet again soon and I felt that I had come across a real school and that I should join it immediately. I also realized that he wasn't stupid or boring, as I had thought, maybe because he looked rather like a feudal lord who had escaped from a wax museum.

Only two days later I was sitting with Prince at a table that was always reserved in his name at a strange place called the Cobweb, a restaurant and bar that sometimes provided live music, on the ground floor of a building in Zamalek. The decor was weird and depressing, like old castles in vampire films, but it was an ideal place for whispering gossip, telling secrets, and taking lessons from Prince. In our first meeting there, because of the name of the place, I told him how, when I was about six years old, a small spider had dropped onto me while I was sitting on the toilet seat. It landed on my neck and quickly slipped into my pajamas. I screamed, sprang up, and, my bottom half completely naked, ran to my mother and grandmother. "A spider! Help me, Mama! A spider, Mama!" I shouted.

My mother and grandmother had a good laugh at me that day. But the story didn't end there; it had only begun. I told Prince that since then I had started to see spiders constantly in my dreams—spiders of various shapes and sizes, either one big spider or many small ones running toward me. The storyline in the dreams might vary, but the spiders were a constant. In my subsequent meetings with him, I told him about the panic attacks that I had, about my relationship with my mother, about how studying made me feel stifled, about my contempt for myself because of my homosexual tendencies, and my fear that I could never be attracted to a woman, however hard I tried. The words just poured out of me whenever I was alone with him, when I didn't have to share his table with beautiful faces and there was no party underway with jokes and songs. He attracted all kinds of people, us and others, grown men, young men and women. He was very much like the head of a Sufi order, followed by disciples wherever he stopped, and he never begrudged his advice or an answer to any question on any subject. He was far from modest and was unwilling to admit his ignorance on any matter. To my eyes at the time he seemed to be a walking encyclopedia, especially on anything that mattered to us, the "luvvies," as he was in the habit of calling us.

He taught me to be careful and hesitant, to watch where I trod and not to throw myself at any available man, to sample, compare, and choose. I learned how to separate my public social life from my secret life with its impulses and adventures. I learned how to be ambitious, and I started to think about the future, almost for the first time. I was no longer embarrassed to buy condoms at the pharmacy and I never had sex without one, because Prince's stories about acquaintances who had contracted AIDS kept ringing in my head. He took me and others by the hand, to lead us through the murky jungle of desire, where we did not know which fruits were poisonous and which animals were predatory. At his table in the Cobweb I formed real friendships with others who had the same inclinations. I broke off contact with my old group of friends and looked down on them as worthless and vulgar. Now I knew how to enjoy wine, music, and men, while listening to Prince's life story, which he didn't hesitate to retell whenever a new guest joined his ever-open table.

Prince had inherited most of his wealth and connections all at once from his brother, who was seventeen years older than him and who died before Aktham reached the age of thirty. His brother was the great songwriter Elhami al-Alfi, who never had any children and who adopted his brother as his son, business manager, and private secretary. Young Aktham had no significant academic qualifications or any evident profession, but his social skills were obvious. He spoke many languages and knew how to smile, flatter, and move in artistic circles as if he were in his own bedroom. Not content with that, Aktham had dreams of performing himself. He felt he was born to be a star in the world of music and song. He tried to convince his elder brother that he had a good voice but the composer was sensible enough never to play along with his delusions. He consoled Aktham by saying, "Your real talent is in your ears, Aktham. With them you can tell diamonds from dross. Don't forget that I often take your advice on a new tune or the voice of a singer." Elhami wanted him at his side and hoped that Aktham would forget his dream of singing one day and abandon his passion for men. Once Elhami despaired of him and said, "Do what you want, but without scandals. As long as you live among people with your dignity intact, no one has the right to ask whether you sleep with women, men, or cats."

Maybe he gave him that advice toward the end of his life, after the last obstacles to candor between the two brothers had come down, as the great lyricist lay ill in bed in London. It wasn't his first medical crisis. His desperate attempts to have children, by trying every possible form of treatment, had not left his body unaffected. He had a disease that was unknown even to the Western doctors at the time. It started to emaciate his body with every hour that passed, and within a few weeks he was reduced to a skeleton that a nine-year-old boy could have lifted. Young Aktham was the only person at his side when he passed away in the late 1970s. He was the one who held him up as he went to the toilet or looked out of the window. He was the one who played him old recordings to remind him of his greatness. He was the one who listened to

81

Elhami's last performance on the oud, when his arm was as thin as a stick, with fingers like needles holding the plectrum.

In those final days, the elder brother finally yielded to Aktham's old wish and wrote a song for him. That was the birth of "Lightly, Lightly, Love," which I would hear Prince sing innumerable times and which he refused to sell to any singer or to allow anyone else to sing, as if it were the only real thing he had inherited.

15

"You do know, Hani, that your mother's still young and desirable and she has a right to enjoy life?" Prince once said, holding my hands after taking me aside in the Cobweb. We were standing in a small, gloomy corridor. It was a bitterly cold night in January. I had recently recovered some of my psychological poise and, miraculously, had managed to focus on my studies enough to reach the third year of college, without that keeping me away from Prince's late-night gatherings or from short-term, carefully considered relationships from time to time.

I read between the lines of Prince's remark but pretended to be stupid and asked him to explain what he meant. Without evasion he told me he had learned that my mother had entered into an informal marriage with Adel al-Murr, a director she had worked with on several occasions. He was about sixty and had a wife from a well-known family and some grown-up sons.

I pulled my hands out from between Prince's warm palms. "She's free to do whatever she likes," I said, looking at a picture of a disgusting hairy spider on the corridor wall.

"Exactly. Well said, Hani. If you'd like to talk to me later, don't hesitate," he replied.

I didn't go straight back to our table with him. I wanted to be alone for a while. I stood in front of the mirror in the bathroom in a daze, not knowing what to think. What should I be feeling now? I wondered. I looked at the lines of my face in the mirror. I clearly took after my mother, and if I looked carefully enough she would appear from behind the mirror and answer my questions, and my heart could rest easy.

I went back to them and drowned my worries by drinking. I danced wildly that night, and when my speech was slurred and I couldn't think straight a friend gave me a lift home. In the elevator I saw my face again and I slapped the mirror several times, as if trying to sober up the drunk inside it. "You're happy for her," I said to myself. "Don't lie. There's no need to act upset."

I knew she wouldn't be back from the theater until about four o'clock in the morning, so I sat up waiting for her. I didn't have any specific intention other than to talk to her. I had finally come to terms with a certain rhythm in our relationship, and any change that threatened to upset that rhythm would throw me off track and revive my old fears. I didn't expect her to renounce men, when I was messing around with men of every kind. We were like an image and its opposite, even in appearance. While I ate and got fatter, she stayed slim. While I wallowed in languor, dependent on her for everything, she scurried about with extraordinary vigor, defying her age and her health problems, moving from a movie to a television series to a play without a break to take a breath, except to ask a fleeting question about household matters, how Hannoun was, whether he needed anything, whether he was doing well at university, and whether he was studying. She also found the time and energy to bear the burdens of her elder sister without grumbling. She covered the cost of her sister's treatment in expensive clinics, at a time when the fashion for addiction rehabilitation was in full swing and movies about drugs were in vogue. Aunt Husniya never hesitated to try out anything new, however poor her health or however close she was to her inevitable end. One day at dawn a taxi driver brought her to the house after finding her semiconscious in a street in Giza. She gave the driver her sister's address when she came round, and managed to say a few words.

Mother handled the initial shock adroitly. She put her sister in another clinic and kept the story under the tightest of wraps. Even so, some newspapers got hold of the news and published it. My mother completely denied it, threatened to sue the newspapers if they didn't publish a retraction, and won. Then, in several interviews or telephone calls with the media, she said that her sister had given up singing years ago, started wearing the hijab, and devoted herself to worship. She said she spent all her time in devout seclusion, seeing only her family and close friends.

I followed this seedy drama with tacit derision while pursuing my own destructive lifestyle. The only thing that stopped me going completely mad was my love for my mother, and maybe a strange fear that she might lose hope in me and give herself away to one of the men who came knocking on her door. That's what she did in the end, and I felt I had been relieved of a secret burden. Yet where did that anger come from that drove me to wait up for her, wrapped in a blanket, chain-smoking, and switching from one television channel to another? I would fall asleep, only to wake up when she came back near dawn and touched me, saying, "Go and sleep in your bed, my dear."

I looked at her in a daze. Her beauty was harsher than that winter's cold. She took off her gloves and her black fur stole, and unhooked her earrings in a trice. I tried to come to my senses, to remember my anger and irritation, but all I could do was whisper in a sleepy voice, "Congratulations to the bride."

She stopped a moment and looked at me as if trying, without success, to recognize her son in me. She looked away and went off to her bedroom. I stood up and walked after her, drawn by an invisible thread. At almost every step she took something off and threw it here or there—her handbag, a hairpiece, a necklace, anything. I felt she was doing this deliberately so that we could retrace our steps out of the forest, like Hansel and Gretel in the fairy story.

While she took off her coat in front of the wardrobe and looked at me, her nose protruded in a little gesture of disgust, a reference to the fact that I smelled of whisky. I looked into the distance and tried to gather my thoughts without thinking about the drinking, which we had argued about before. I couldn't tell her I thought she was betraying me with her marriage. The only objection I could find was that the marriage was unofficial and secret. "It's better for all of us this way," she said, looking me up and down and taking off her clothes one by one.

"But it's all so furtive!" I said.

"Adel and I haven't committed any crime, Hani."

I was annoyed to hear her saying his name for the first time, and I didn't know what to say. I waited while she went behind the screen, wrapping a thick gown tightly around her body. "I was going to tell you, but at the right time," she said. "Adel is a respectable person and he cares for me."

"You never told me you needed a man," I whispered, almost speaking to myself.

"I'm tired. Where are my cigarettes?"

I lit a cigarette and passed it to her. She took a long puff, then exhaled the smoke slowly. I could hardly see her face for the smoke. For five minutes or so, she launched into the longest monologue I had ever heard from her in all those years. She told me she was tired of everything—of work, the house, the scandals about her sister, my dissipation, and the way I avoided her. For years she had been taking on more than she could bear, and she always had to behave judiciously and with great poise in front of other people, and she had to stand firm in the face of smooth talk and attempts at flirtation, both overt and covert.

I sat on the carpet at her feet and she started to run her fingers through my soft hair, as she used to do in the old days. She admitted that on many occasions she had cried herself to sleep without knowing why. On other occasions she found herself wishing for strange things—wishing that she had died rather than Ahmad and that he had brought me up and taken the responsibility, or that she had swapped places with her sister and that she was adrift in her own realm, doing whatever took her fancy. For the past few years Adel al-Murr had been her only friend and her refuge in times of adversity, willing to listen to her worries. He hadn't concealed his feelings from her, and she had finally decided to award herself a rest before it was too late, rather than feel remorse for the rest of her life.

"And me? Why don't you talk to me?" I said, looking up at her.

She was about to say something, but held back a moment. First she took another puff on her cigarette and gave me what seemed to be a reproachful look, or as if she hardly recognized me. "There were things it wouldn't have done to talk to you about, and also I was worried about you. I worried about making you even more confused," she said.

I jumped up and stood facing her. "I'm not confused!" I shouted in an offended voice. "I'm well now, better than before."

"I know. I know, my dear."

A silence fell, and Mother stubbed out her cigarette, then looked at me earnestly. She asked me again who had told me about her marriage. I didn't know why that mattered to her so I told her calmly that it was a friend called Aktham al-Alfi. As soon as she heard the name she sprang up, as if the hem of her robe had caught fire. "Prince?" she asked.

I had expected that Mother would know Prince, but I hadn't expected her to flare up like this.

"I heard you'd made friends with him, but I can't understand what a student of your age would find in common with a degenerate old man like him," she said.

Faced with her outburst, I stammered, mumbling vaguely about him teaching me to appreciate music and introducing me to musicians and important people. I wanted to hide the other thing by any means possible. She dismissed what I said and told me she wasn't willing to take risks with the most important person in her life. She ordered me to break off relations with him immediately.

"I'm sorry, I can't," I said. "Prince is a friend, and just like my father."

"Your *father*?" she shouted, with a vehemence that struck me as excessive for a newly married woman. "May God have mercy on your soul, Ahmad Mahfouz. Never say that again. The whole world knows that Prince guy is a pervert. Understand?"

"What does that mean?" I asked, maybe to be especially disputatious or because pretending not to understand would avert her suspicions as far as possible.

"I mean he's a faggot. Okay? Understand?"

She used the derogatory term without thinking, and at that moment something changed in the whole world, something very small but fundamental and permanent, as if the world had dimmed slightly, in a way that no one could tell unless they noticed that little lamp in the sky go out.

I looked away from her, and when I dared to look back, I saw she had come a little closer and was staring at my face quizzically and suspiciously. Moments later she tried to put her suspicions overtly into words: "Don't tell me you're . . . ." She didn't complete her sentence, and I didn't stay around to hear her say it in full.

I decided to leave home immediately, with no plan and no arrangements. After crossing the threshold, but before closing the door behind me, I came back inside when I felt the cold outside. I quickly picked up the thick woolen coat she had bought for me on one of her trips to London. Then I slammed the door, lodging a final protest before heading into the dawn chill in the street.

16

As THE THIN LAYER OF mist that surrounded everything cleared, I started to breathe the fresh and invigorating air. In Qasr al-Aini Street I noticed a coffee shop in an alleyway that was still accepting customers at this hour. The first sip of coffee jolted my head and I wondered what I was doing there and whether I should go back home to bed, and if I did go back how I would punish her and show her how angry I was. How would it be if people were born without fathers or mothers? I didn't think that would be too hard for the creator of this complex and ingenious universe to arrange.

Before finishing my cup of coffee I remembered that I had an old friend living nearby, a young Nubian called Omar Nour. I had met him again by chance about two months earlier, not far from the coffee shop, and after some hesitation I went off with him because I wanted to discover him. After taking the ancient elevator to the top floor of the building, we walked up a spiral metal staircase to the roof, where he rented a tiny apartment—a bedroom, a bathroom, and a living room that was in fact smaller than the large bathroom in our apartment.

As we drank tea at his place he started talking about politics, the state of the country, and things I had never taken any interest in. I nodded, pretending to be following him, while I looked around absentmindedly, looking for anything beautiful in his house and finding only reproductions of Picasso,

Matisse, and Juan Miró paintings. After two sips of tea, I was bored with sitting there and with his prattle, which reminded me of those discussion programs on television. On that occasion I took my leave of Omar, because I felt uncomfortable and embarrassed at the way he lived. He assured me that his door would always be open to me, and in order to set the right seal on this invitation he kissed me on both cheeks and brought his lips very close to mine. I smiled to myself in the elevator and told myself there was no harm in putting him on the list of reserves, because who knows?

I suddenly decided to go to his place that morning, maybe to punish Mother or simply to get away from her for a while. I dragged myself to the apartment block, my eyelids drooping. I was yawning at regular intervals, and all I wanted to find at his place was a clean, warm blanket.

Omar's family had been our neighbors when we lived in Abdin, and we used to see each other on the way to school—where he was two years my senior—or in the mosque at Friday prayers or outside the European-style bakery in the evening. He was always tall and thin and smiling like an idiot. Then we left Abdin and I forgot him. We remembered each other immediately when we met once in the Hurriya coffee shop. We exchanged greetings and told each other what we'd been up to. Most of his group of friends were artistic, political, or in journalism. I wasn't very comfortable sitting with them, but he often joined my group of friends. He joined in the conversation intelligently, gradually let down his guard, and by subtle signals began to disclose to me that he had ambiguous tendencies and wavered between desires for women and for men. He seemed sensible and serious, despite the politics that had turned his head. On the surface he looked like a completely normal man. Nothing in his clothes, his gait, his body language, or the way he spoke suggested that his sexual inclinations were uncertain. Even so, if one watched him closely for a while—his delicately featured face and his deportment in general—you could detect something pliant in his glances and gestures, something suppressed like a shy orange glow under the surface of his soft brown skin.

He opened the door, rubbing his eyes. I thanked God that he hadn't gone out early, because I had an insanely urgent desire to sleep. He recognized the person standing in front of him, smiled, and stood aside to let me in. Waving me inside, he peppered me with greetings. Nothing had changed in the place since my only previous visit, but I was grateful to have four walls around me, and for the breadsticks and the tea he made on a small one-ring stove. It reminded me of the tiny old Primus stove that my grandmother Sakina was so proud of owning. She told the world she was outraged when she found out that my mother had sold it to the junk man. "Do you remember my grandmother Sakina?" I asked Omar, who looked calm and slightly puzzled. He suddenly laughed so much that he choked on a mouthful of tea, and started to cough and wheeze until his chest cleared and he got his breath back.

Still laughing, he said, "May God have mercy on her soul. Several times she gave my mother hell for bizarre reasons."

After a short conversation about our old days in Abdin, Omar realized I had come to stay for some time, so he got up and fetched a thick, warm, apricot-colored woolen cloak. I came out of the bathroom and found him rolling a joint. At the time I didn't like hashish, and on the few occasions when I had tried a puff or two it made me feel nauseous and reminded me of my panic attacks. I was "aqueous," as we call people who like to drink. I respect alcohol's magical power to rid the spirit of fears and worries and relax the body, so that it dances and leaps into life like a bird in paradise. Even so, when he hesitantly offered me the joint, I took it in the hope that it would make me sleep deeply despite being in a strange bed in a strange room. After the first puff, I said straight out, "My mother's finally started to suspect me."

We started laughing again, although my eyes were wet with tears. Omar came close to me and patted me on the shoulder. Omar was a friend to me then, even if only for a limited time. He was my friend as much as it mattered because he patted me on the shoulder and pulled me toward his slim body, which was warm and comforting. When I tried clumsily to share some of my confused thoughts with him, he pressed his lips to mine and shut me up completely.

I spent two days in Omar's apartment without leaving it, and I liked the seclusion, especially in the hours when I was alone, when Omar went to work at the magazine and the world fell still and I could hear my thoughts clearly. He would soon be back, impatient as a newlywed, bearing bags with basic necessities, as well as beer and hashish. I felt a slight pang of vanity at his impatience and his simple joy at having me stay, as I knew I didn't deserve all this and that he might hate me if I told him some of what I thought of him.

I decided to go home on my third day as Omar's guest, out of pity for my mother, and also because I was simply bored by the place. I missed my comforts—hot water in the shower, my clean clothes, soft sheets, and the many little pillows that I always hug in my sleep. I may have been bored with Omar too. Despite all his affection and kindness, after a while even his interest in me and his solicitude for me became stale and artificial. He pretended I was his partner, and on that basis tried to please me in every possible way, although he doubtless knew deep down inside that that was not what I was. We pretended to be satisfied with the gentle, pleasant sex that we had over and over, like two buck rabbits that think they can have children if they try hard enough, so they exhaust each other to no avail.

I told him I had to go home before my mother went mad with anxiety. He said he had been expecting me to come to this decision when I was ready, although he was happy I had stayed with him. He insisted I promise to keep in touch with him, at least so that we could carry out some joint projects we had dreamed up over those two days. We were to read and discuss certain important books, and I would show him some of my old poems and writings. I might get enthusiastic about writing again. I promised him all that, insincerely. Inside I felt contempt for his naivety and innocence and his dream of a decent world for everyone, even those who would stone him to death if they found out his secret.

Later I traced my aversion to him to its origins inside me. He was honest. He lived almost without masks or roleplaying. He lived as he wished and as he chose. He had clear principles, even if they were strident—a word that sounded strange to me then, and maybe still does. He was still in journalism school and working as a stringer for independent magazines and leftist newspapers, living almost at subsistence level. But he didn't have nightmares or panic attacks. He spoke without thinking and laughed heartily for the simplest reason.

After I left him on the third day we met sporadically, sometimes by agreement and sometimes by chance, but we never slept together again. Our affection for each other was unaffected, however. Sometimes he would drag me to meetings of intellectuals and artists, seminars and discussions, though I never managed to get used to them. Most of the people there didn't have Omar's simplicity and honesty. They spoke a lot but did very little. They always tried to disguise their real selves, living on coffee and cigarettes, and beer and hashish in the evening. Omar introduced me to a novelist who was said to be important. At a party in that old writer's downtown apartment he kept looking at me, smiling and nodding. When I got up to fetch a beer he followed me into the kitchen. He came up behind me and hugged me, and his breath smelled horrible. I slipped out of his grasp carefully to avoid making a stupid scene in front of the other people, but he grabbed my hand and put it on his pants over his penis. I grabbed one of his testicles and squeezed until he squealed and pushed me away, muttering, "That's a real faggot"—the same horrible word that had blighted the world for me after I heard my mother say it, the word that sent a shiver down my spine whenever I heard it in the street, even as a lighthearted insult between friends.

I didn't bother to tell Omar what had happened, but just left without offering an explanation, and I didn't go back to meet those friends of his after that party. However, I didn't lose my relationship with Omar himself. I was grateful for the beneficial effect he had on me, because he had encouraged me to start reading again, this time with the appetite of a hungry man who discovers a tunnel under his room leading to Wonderland and becomes addicted to going down into that underground world almost every night, at least to give myself some relief from the domestic dramas and the frenzy of running after men. I left the real world behind me through beautiful novels, and identified with the personalities of the protagonists in my own world. I began to discover new books by myself, without recommendations by Omar, and because I was good at English I read books that hadn't been translated into Arabic. I realized the extent to which translation diminishes our enjoyment. I dug around until I came across many books about gay people, including short stories, sentimental romances, and sexual adventures. Although the amount of material available was not enormous, it was enough for me to access this other world, which was so far beyond our wildest dreams. The most we could hope for was to read about this world or see it on screen. Books started to proliferate around the house like cobwebs, although I was careful to get rid of books I had finished reading, unless they were masterpieces. I'll never forget that it was Omar who gave me the first novel I ever came across where the hero had homosexual tendencies. It was a Japanese novel called *Confessions of a Mask*. I forget the name of the author. I started reading it during my brief stay at Omar's place, and he gave it to me while I was preparing to

94

leave. Then I found it dull and thought the hero was strange, so I didn't even finish it when I was back at home.

When I left we exchanged a long kiss at the door and I took off the apricot-colored cloak that was steeped in my smell, to go back to my fine clothes and my English coat, which had been hanging on the wall all this time like a European tourist stunned into immobility by the slums of Cairo. I felt a double joy: that I had been able to get away from my mother, if only for two and a half days, for the first time in my life and without her knowing anything about where I was, and that I would finally be leaving Omar's place, despite his generosity and the slow-burning sexual pleasures we had enjoyed together.

17

W<small>ALK</small>, H<small>ANI</small>. D<small>ON'T STOP WALKING</small>, or else you'll freeze up and be done for. Move fast, like someone being chased, running away from all the stories, the old and the new, the same stories you're chasing when you write. By day you describe scenes from your past as honestly as possible and at night you erase them and imagine yourself as another character, a stranger to yourself, so you try to behave as this stranger. A perfectly normal man, like all these people. Are they really normal? What are they hiding behind those faces and those skulls? What is a normal person in the first place and what do they look like? Are those people who tormented me and humiliated me normal?

Write, Hani. Write. Don't stop writing. That's what Dr. Sameeh advised me to do, after I sent him some of your writings over the past few weeks. He also said he was reading them with great interest, lapping them up. As he reads, he imagines my voice, which he knew for ages before I lost the power of speech. He imagines me saying aloud what I wrote.

I also imagine my voice sometimes. I hear it repeating phrases in my head. It might sing one of the songs I hear in that little bar where my feet take me almost every evening. I was there two days ago, when one of my aunt's songs was broadcast and I heard a discussion about her among some of the regulars. What they said was a mixture of truths and untruths, but one of them referred to the son of her sister, the actress Badriya Amin, and said I had been arrested about a year ago in the big case of the perverts on the Queen Boat.

I was terrified. For a moment I thought they knew who I was and were addressing me obliquely by insinuation. Miraculously, I kept my fear under control and refused to get up and leave. Or maybe it was the fragile courage of alcohol. Then I invited them to a beer and told them by pen and paper about Husniya and the myths about her. I denied what they had said about Husniya's nephew. I wrote about her as if I were writing the script for a movie on the life of the late singer. On pages torn out of my notebooks I gave them scraps of the truth. I didn't say I was that nephew or that the worst periods in my life had been when Aunt Husniya came to stay with us. I didn't say I had carried her body out of the bathroom to put it on her bed, after she killed herself with an overdose.

I said I'd write about all this in the morning in my room, where the calm contrasted with the frightening voices in my head. I'm writing now in the quiet and warmth of the hotel room, but I'm still out of breath, like a man running from a pack of rabid dogs.

Whenever my mother came back from visiting her sister in the clinic, she would cry and say that her heart bled for her and she no longer knew what to do. The only time I went there with her, I found my aunt fully alert and focused, and it was painful to hear her begging me to persuade Mother to set her free and take her away.

"I'm better now, Hani," she said. "The doctors here are only interested in money. Make your mother take me out of here, my dear, please. I die a death here every day."

My mother finally took pity on her and discharged her. Or maybe it wasn't so much pity as the need to have her sister by her side. Aunt Husniya settled in with us and went through a meek and obedient phase until the comic drama resumed between them. I left the house to them most of the time, or kept to my room, leaving it only to go to the kitchen or the bathroom. I left them in their own world, while I busily wove the tent of my loneliness day after day. I studied, I read, and then I drowned in the seas of the Internet, which I had recently discovered and which became my companion in solitude for years. I met people and chatted and watched pornography from every country in the world, lounging on my seat like a pasha, smashing the rocks of my lust by masturbation after masturbation, without wanting to go out and find a real man who would give me only the transient delusion of gratification.

Although I tried to ignore them, it was difficult to avoid the two old ladies completely. I would catch myself looking at them furtively from a distance. Growing old had made them more alike than they had ever been—almost twins. Husniya was the pale, ravaged version, while Mother was the fresh, wholesome version, but the underlying appearance was the same. Mother reduced her acting commitments to a minimum, maybe out of concern for her health, which wasn't as good as it had been, or so that she would have time to play with her elder sister, who had ended up dependent on her charity.

All they had left to do was rummage around in their bag of memories. One of them would pull out whatever her hand happened to find there—maybe a rose, maybe a scorpion. I'd find one of them kissing the other on the cheek, or I'd be woken up by the sound of them quarreling over who was the star. Both seemed to be embarrassed that they felt sorry for each other and obviously needed each other, so they projected their emotions into poisonous attacks on each other. That was after my aunt abandoned the veneer of submission and self-absorption, within a few months of coming to live with us, and recovered her old vampish spirit.

My aunt made sure she reminded Mother all the time that she could take credit for bringing Mother back into the theatrical world and introducing her to directors and actors, after she had gone off and gotten married and everyone had forgotten her.

Mother wouldn't take this lying down. She would respond by making fun of my aunt's supposed talents, her degenerate taste in men, and her consumption of too many drugs.

My aunt would flutter her eyelids and say, "Some people know how to live well." Or else she would kiss her own hand back and front, and say, "Well, thank God, we've had our fill and had some crazy fun. I've never denied myself anything."

Then it would be my mother's turn to remind her how she had picked her up off the street unconscious and how there were many people like her sleeping on the sidewalk and eating from the garbage cans because they didn't have anyone at their side to feel sorry for them and look after them.

These contests would go on, quietly or feverishly, for days on end, until they dragged in my father and the incident when he groped my aunt, and he often received his fair share of their malice. Whenever I caught scraps of these conversations, I felt sick and my head spun. I no longer knew where I was or what time I was in. It felt like we had gone back to the Abdin days, to Grandmother Sakina and her Primus stove, but this time we had lost all our innocence and compassion. Or it was one extended moment that took on different forms, though it was without doubt all the same vulgar drama.

I had to get out of the house until they went to sleep. I took refuge with Prince in the hotel he had bought in Behler Passage downtown after the Cobweb was sold and converted into something else. When I got tired of spending the evening with Prince in the roof garden of his hotel, I went looking for Omar in the Hurriya café or the Stella bar to talk about books, the state of the country, and the way we were ostracized. He told me of his big plans, none of which ever came to fruition. He would tell me about the few brief sexual adventures he had had. I would tell him about mine, and we discovered we had lost our old appetites and could go weeks or months without a successful sortie. He said it was strange and amusing that people had the idea that we had sex all day and all night. They didn't think we were like other people, obliged to study in order to succeed or to work in order to eat and live, or that we also took an interest in public affairs and the state of the country. According to them, our only interest in life came down to sex. I didn't tell him that we sometimes seemed that way to them, and sometimes to ourselves, because the problem of sex was insoluble. Maybe if they accepted us and we accepted ourselves, we could see the many things that we and they had in common. But usually I just listened to his long monologues in silence.

In the meantime, I continued roaming the streets, especially after I graduated at about the age of twenty-five, when I faced a massive void. I wasn't cruising: walking the streets at night had just become a diversion, despite the crowds and the noise, or maybe because of them. I developed a habit of spying on people, taking snapshots of them in my head, especially in those moments when they escaped the hell of their daily lives: a middle-aged man, for example, leaning on a windowsill, watching the world beneath him with disappointment and discontent; a girl smiling dreamily as she looked at a dress in a shop window and tucked a strand of hair under her hijab; a well-dressed man bending down to tie his child's shoelace as the boy held his father's ear as if to tell him off for behaving badly.

I thought of buying a camera and taking real pictures, to keep myself busy. Maybe I would take it up as a profession, but I thought that would ruin the pleasure and reveal me to the victims of my spying. I thought I might also become a writer if I worked hard and concentrated, but I soon admitted to myself that I didn't have the patience to sit and write, even for just an hour. I thought of acting, and said it would suit me better than anything else. My life was dominated by daydreams. I saw myself as a movie star in the spotlight, surrounded by gossip about why I wasn't married yet. Then I would come to my senses when I remembered I was plump and prematurely balding, an appearance that might qualify me to play roles as the hero's gluttonous and amusing friend. I was sure that the artistic life was the only life I could imagine for myself . . . but what art should I choose? I had no idea, and intentions and fantasies were as far as my efforts went.

I went home reluctantly in the end, exhausted from roaming the streets, to catch up on the same old soap opera between the two sisters. Our maid, Umm Ibrahim, had started following the drama with interest as it unfolded, and she would brief me on new developments while I had a bite to eat at the kitchen table.

"Mrs. Badriya threatened she'd send Mrs. Husniya back to the clinic. Then Mrs. Husniya threatened to go on television and tell the whole story," she said.

Then my mother started wearing the hijab and took very few acting roles—basically mothers or women in historical or religious serials. She felt she had gained new ground in her war with her sister, and her criticism of her took on an unfamiliar religious aspect. If my aunt put an old hairpiece on her head, or slipped off during the day to do her face or try on a fur coat and jewelry, my mother would seize the chance. First she would give Aunt Husniya her fill of ridicule, then suddenly switch into a short sermon interlaced with verses from the Quran, sayings of the Prophet, and traditional adages. My aunt's usual response to all this was outrageous laughter, or else she would spread her arms wide, shake her sagging, shriveled breasts, and sing her an old song: "Who are you singing to, handsome? We're the ones who invented love songs."

The appropriate last scene in this tawdry and tedious drama finally came when I had to break down the bathroom door to find my aunt stretched out in the empty bathtub, her eyes wide open as if she had finally seen that extraordinary thing that had managed to elicit a look of surprise from her.

Her body was heavier than I had expected and she was a strange color, ashen but turning blue. Everything happened surprisingly quickly, as if I were watching a movie in fast motion. It ended as suddenly as it started, without me knowing what had happened. I never found out how the heroin reached the house, given that she hardly ever went out. I suspected Umm Ibrahim for a while, until I remembered the short, fat nurse who had met her in the clinic and who visited her regularly after she came to stay with us.

My mother managed to keep the details of her death under wraps. The show-business press took some interest in the old singer Husniya Amin, or Husna as her fans called her, who had recorded only a few songs for the radio and had appeared as a singer in one or two movies more than twenty years earlier. Some television and radio stations played whatever songs of hers they had on hand, possibly out of respect for her sister, the talented actress.

At my aunt's funeral I saw a handful of old show-business people, and for a fleeting moment I thought about Mother's funeral and what it would be like. Who would attend? Where would I be? What would I do then? My imagination didn't come to my aid in any way. I couldn't even imagine Mother being dead, with me standing as I was standing then, receiving people's condolences. I couldn't breathe properly, my chest felt tight, and I started looking around for her, as if her existence were under threat, as if she might be taken away from me at any moment. Then I saw her in the distance, her face radiant against the black of her clothes, sad and broken but tough and robust, shaking hands with the mourners and bowing her beautiful head. I told myself that Mother wouldn't die. I had to have faith. I had to believe it. This was something about which there was no doubt. She would not die now, or soon, or even in ten or twenty years. Until that day came, I would have to be ready, to train myself to imagine her death, otherwise I would go mad when her moment came.

The first time I saw my face in the mirror after my aunt's funeral, I found that little hairs above my ears on both sides had turned white, and that my baldness was on the advance again. I also remembered that I had no job and no real life separate from my mother's life and that the last time something I'd seen in a dream had come true was many years earlier and it had been trivial—just a pair of red socks that I liked, one of which had gone missing, and I dreamed it was stuck in the bookshelf behind *Of Love and Other Demons*, and in the morning I found it in that exact spot.

I felt that something was bound to happen, something was bound to change, even if for the worse. When I was about to cry in front of the mirror, I pulled myself together and whispered to myself, reproachfully and imploringly. "You've grown up, Hani," I said.

18

KARIM SAADOUN WAS THE PERSON standing next to me in the hallway at the police station when the policemen came with the handcuffs. He was the first person I was handcuffed to. The first time handcuffs close on your wrists, it comes as a surprise, and despite the distress and the sense of constraint there is also a sense of relief and resignation. You feel as if you no longer have to think or make any decisions for yourself. Suddenly you go back to being a child, holding your father's or mother's hand, submissive to them, except that at that moment the state was the father, the mother, the guardian, and the omniscient god.

I caught sight of Prince outside the police station as they herded us toward the police truck. In my excitement I raised my free arm, waved, and called out to him. He hurried toward me, jostling past some of the people who had heard that their relatives or friends had been jailed. Just seeing him restored some of my peace of mind, after the days in Abdin and Azbakiya police stations, which had stretched out like a whole other life. When I saw him I felt confident that my old world was not a delusion, that it still existed and continued uninterrupted, and I mistakenly believed that I was only a hair's breadth away from being set free.

I deluged him with questions and he answered me quickly, having noticed the impatient tone in which I was speaking. I was out of breath and he was looking with dismay at the spots of blood on my undershirt, my pale face, and some slight bruising on my shoulders. He told me that Abdel Aziz had called him to tell him I'd been arrested and was being held at Abdin police station for some unknown reason. Then he had disappeared and turned his phone off. Prince had called my wife to reassure her, claiming I had suddenly gone to Alexandria and had turned my phone off. He evaded her questions and he didn't feel she had believed him. As I was at the door of the truck, he handed me a bag with food, water, cigarettes, and packs of tissues. With tears in his eyes, he said, "Don't worry, Hani. You're not alone."

I tried not to believe him, but I did believe the tears in his eyes. As they piled us on top of each other in the back of the truck, I thought to myself that it wasn't Abdel Aziz who had finally come out of his hiding place and dared to admit his true feelings. It was Prince, who had spent his whole life looking after us. God seemed to have breathed into him the spirit of a kindly mother, and if he abandoned me, the government's handcuffs that I had on might then seem less cruel toward me than most people.

"Is that your father?" asked Karim.

"My friend," I said, short of breath and suppressing my sobs. "Like a father to me."

"Okay, please don't cry, for my sake," he whispered slowly.

As we pulled away from the Ramses area, the other detainees in the truck behaved like grief-stricken mourners at a funeral. They realized that the case against us was not going to be dismissed lightly. It was going to be a genuine sexual offenses case, with documents, prosecutors, medical examiners, and whatever was needed. They broke into weeping and sobbing because some of them had seen their families and were ashamed to be seen, or maybe it was just seeing the light of day and getting away from the stuffy cell, where we hadn't been able to tell night from day for the past few days. We had with us an emaciated man as tall as a beanpole, with a large bald head. They called him Said the Skull. He moved slowly, leaning his long neck forward and always dragging behind him the man who was handcuffed to him. After a while along the way, Said looked out of a small hole in the truck, and then gazed around at our faces with his hollow eyes. "It looks like they're going to take us straight to the detention camp," he announced in his husky voice. He seemed to enjoy frightening and tormenting us.

Everything seemed to have been prepared in expectation of our arrival. The only thing missing was our physical presence in front of the prosecutors, to stitch up the case against us in their documents with the black eagle letterhead. The prosecutor who ordered us detained, initially for questioning, did not notice the bloodstains on our clothes. He wasn't interested in the beatings we had endured or the injuries that were visible on all of us. When some of us asked him to record that we had been beaten and abused and that our confessions in Azbakiya police station were given under duress and torture, he behaved as if he couldn't see or hear. My consternation at what was happening was comical compared with the calm acceptance by some of the detainees. At first I never ceased to be amazed by people such as Said the Skull or Mohamed Sukkar, Karim's friend who was arrested with him when they came off the Queen Boat. They handled the disaster with resignation, as though it were an act of God, maybe because some of them had nothing to lose anyway. They lived precariously all the time, as was evident from the face of Mohamed Sukkar: his cheeks had two long scars left by a sharp razor, or maybe two razors working together simultaneously, held by a man who was expert at disfiguring faces.

On one of the occasions when we were handcuffed together, during one of our many journeys to or from the prosecutor's office, he told me how he had appeared before Hassan Fawwaz several months before the rest of us, in the winter of the same year, when Fawwaz had arrested him and some other men and had fun with them for a few days, then turned them over to the prosecutor, who set them free.

"They poured icy water on us in the middle of winter to stop us getting a wink of sleep night or day, and in the end they brought in a bunch of kids high on drugs and let them loose on us. They told them, 'Those fags are all yours.' One of those kids had sex with me against my will. He didn't want to. It was just so that they would send him home. He took out his anger on me and kept pounding me like an idiot, and however much I screamed or begged for help it was no use. In the end I lost consciousness, and they left me till I came round again."

He and others told me stories whenever I sat next to one of them or when we were handcuffed together, maybe because I didn't speak much because of my breathing problems, and they imagined I was willing to listen, or maybe because they wanted to win my sympathy and persuade me to help them in some way, or maybe each of us was trying to say his piece to anyone he found nearby at the time. Karim was different. He only spoke when necessary, and he only told stories if you asked him to do so inside the main cell, but only Karim's stories helped to keep me going. He seemed to read what was written on my face throughout our detention. He saw that I needed soothing. He felt my pain with an intuition untainted by anything around us. With time I felt that this young man was related to me by blood, like my son or my brother.

Something in Karim's face caught your attention at first sight—a secret something that meant you could never get your fill of looking at him. At first you thought that if you looked at his features long enough you would find the answer to your question and the mystery would be solved. But as you kept looking, the question remained unanswered. His face was almost completely round, with a clear, pale complexion and dimples in his cheeks, which were like sunken points when he was silent. When he smiled, laughed, or spoke, the dimples were even more obvious, like tattooed marks on each cheek.

His hair was jet black and thick, neither soft nor coarse, and his eyebrows were bushy, joined by a thin line of hair over the top of his nose, which made him look even stranger. He had rather full lips that always seemed to be pouting, as if he were about to kiss something, or upset, or giving a sign that he knew nothing about some question. As if to say: "How would I know? I'm handsome and that's enough." Sometimes, between bouts of breathlessness and weeping, I would look at him admiringly, but without desire. Prison had killed off all desire, but not my unease when face to face with the mystery of beauty.

Over the coming months in detention, I went to sleep to the sound of his endless stories, and when I woke up I found him next to my bed, alert. "You slept well, thank God," he would say. "Shall I make you a sandwich?"

Then I knew that God existed and still loved me and was taking care of me.

In the interrogations, we were surprised by the questions we were asked. They were questions that had almost nothing to do with the reasons why they had rounded us up. They asked some of us if we were members of a group called God's Proxy on Earth, or what we knew about "the Kurdish lad." Had we attended religious meetings on the roof of the house of the principal defendant, Samir Barakat? Had we attended same-sex weddings as part of the group's rituals? It was clear that the charge went beyond merely having illicit sex regularly, and included blasphemy and forming a secret religious group. We concluded they had decided to lock us away at any price and remembered the case of the Satanists a few years earlier. Some newspapers announced simply: "More than fifty members of a Satanist group arrested: engaged in perversions and took pornographic pictures." They also said they were "arrested while engaged in indecent acts, naked in the main hall on the Queen Boat, at a party celebrating the wedding of two young men, God forbid."

I read all this after I came out of prison, among the cuttings that Prince had collected with help from some of the lawyers. He proved he was not just an old man who was trying to be young and who seduced young men with his money, connections, and charisma. He could have gone into seclusion and lain low to protect his reputation and fend off the accusations, of which there was no shortage, but that wasn't his style. He was a stubborn fighter, even as he approached the age of seventy. He jumped into action in every possible direction, meeting lawyers and human rights workers, Egyptian and foreign, and working together with our friend Wagdi, the theater director, one of whose best friends had been arrested on the Queen Boat. If Wagdi hadn't been too ill to go out with him that evening, he would have been among those arrested too. Wagdi started sending out statements like a maniac to anyone he hoped might help, until some international human rights organizations took notice and started to follow the case, with condemnations and publicity, but this happened when it was already too late. The documents had been prepared and they had tightened the noose around us.

The whole motive for the case might have been to take revenge on Samir Barakat, or more precisely on his family, and to tarnish their reputation by association with him, all because of a disagreement with another important family. They had raided Samir Barakat's house about a month before they began their drama with us. They impounded all his files, pictures, and books, then summoned him to collect his belongings, and he hadn't seen daylight since. Before his arrest he had been under surveillance for weeks. Then they interrogated him blindfolded for two weeks, under the most appalling psychological conditions. God alone knows whether Samir, who was pampered and well brought up, broke down like me under the pressure, the humiliation, and the physical torture and confirmed whatever they wanted him to confirm, or whether he really did have strange religious delusions.

They claimed he had suddenly told them, without any obvious context, about having a dream or a vision, as the official papers put it, about fifteen years earlier. He still remembered the dream, in which he saw the Prophet Muhammad receiving a visit from a young fair-skinned lad, and the Prophet said that this Kurdish lad would appear on earth and exact revenge on the whole world—Jews, Christians, and Muslims—simply because they hadn't tried to stop the Turks attacking the Kurds. What did the Turks and the Kurds have to do with us? It might have been Samir's fantasy after a heavy dinner or it might have been the brainchild of an unknown writer in the state bureaucracy, who suddenly gave free rein to his suppressed literary talents and started to compose dozens of pages about the God's Proxy on Earth movement. Anyway, that ridiculous dream would be at the core of the case that would shake Egypt, annoy the world, and destroy the lives of some of us.

At first I didn't understand anything and didn't know how to answer when I was asked about the Kurdish lad and the God's Proxy organization. I was indeed in another world. I was stammering so much and having such trouble breathing that I couldn't put together a whole sentence that made sense, and I was willing to sign anything they wrote as long as they would let me go back to the cell to have a rest. Other people admitted they had homosexual tendencies in response to questions about whether they had made planes or missiles, and these were people who couldn't read or write in the first place. In effect, they wanted to say, "We're just gay, so take pity on us and don't make us out to be terrorists."

Now I like to imagine that talented civil servant who sat down and let his imagination run riot as he looked down at a blank piece of paper and then, like a novelist of genius, wrote the twenty-nine-page booklet, several copies of which they claimed to have found in Samir Barakat's house. He gave his book the title *God's Proxy on Earth: The Religion of Lot's People and of Our Prophet and Guide Abu Nuwas.* I hadn't known that Abu Nuwas was one of the "luvvies." I later read some research papers and other documents that included references to this bizarre literary work. I remember the titles of some chapters: "Our World," "Why Lot's People?" "Our Religious Law in Summary," "Gay Hymns," "Commandments and Prohibitions." The booklet included words of advice, such as "Satisfy your partner so that he won't leave you." Now I can smile or laugh when I read such words, as I see the nightmare from afar, as if it were a horror movie, relieved that I've left the darkness of the cinema and the grip of fear and entered the light of the street and the familiarity of ordinary life.

One of the police reports said Samir Barakat confessed that he had set up something called "The Proxy of God, the Lord of Hosts," and one of his colleagues at work, a man called Mustafa, had built a prayer room for this organization on the roof of Samir's building. They arrested this Mustafa and impounded 893 of Samir's photographs that showed him in indecent poses with men and boys. In the investigations no pictures of naked men or men having sex appeared, and one of the things that Samir's family told the representatives of human rights groups was that he was an amateur photographer whose work had appeared in several galleries, and that he was religious and had been to Mecca on pilgrimage.

I had seen this Mustafa shouting at Samir in the hallway in the court building. "You've ruined me, along with yourself. May God take revenge on you!" he said.

"I'm in the same situation as you!" Samir shouted back tearfully from afar. "Don't wish me ill. That's unfair."

A few weeks later I heard Samir Barakat shouting in the courtroom in front of the journalists: "We're victims, the victims of a grudge match between two big families."

At that moment I remembered the story of King Solomon and the ant in the Quran. Amid the sweaty bodies of the men in white clothes packed into the defendants' cage in the courtroom, their faces covered with handkerchiefs or white undershirts, with slits cut for the eyes, I tried to remember the whole verse. I crawled between their feet until I reached Karim, who was busy reciting in a whisper from a small Quran he was holding. "Do you remember the Ant chapter?" I asked him in a trembling voice. "Do you remember the verse where Solomon laughs at what the ant says?"

Karim nodded behind the handkerchief hanging down over his face and then, in his sweet voice, whispered the verse into my ear: "And then, when they reached the Valley of the Ants, one of the ants said, 'Ants, go into your homes in case Solomon and his troops crush you unawares.' And Solomon smiled in amusement at what the ant said, and said, 'Oh Lord, inspire me to be grateful for the blessings You have bestowed on me and on my parents, and to do good works that please You, and include me by Your grace among Your righteous servants.'"

19

THE ROOF GARDEN AT THE Andrea Hotel, the Thursday night gatherings, and a life of fun and happiness, flitting aimlessly like a wanton butterfly sated with sweet and poisonous nectar—all this could have gone on forever if I hadn't met Mina Gamil at the right time.

The hotel had been our constant refuge ever since Prince had bought it. It was on the top three floors of an old building in Behler Passage, just steps away from Talaat Harb Square. On the roof there was a restaurant, a bar, and a small square in the corner, slightly raised off the floor, for those who wanted to dance especially on Thursdays, the only night when Prince let go a little, forgot his role as manager and owner of the place, and became just a customer like all the others around him. Often he would send for an imported bottle of something from his private wing in the hotel and chill out, constantly surrounded by young men like flowers. Then he would pick up his oud and start singing. The music might go on until the break of dawn on Friday.

It was also on a Thursday night that I met Mina Gamil for the first time. Prince had told me that Mina was looking for a suitable partner to set up an interior-design business. We had an appointment with him in the early evening, before the usual noise began. He arrived a few minutes early, and my eyes lingered on him for some moments. I was drawn to a slight squint in his left eye. It was an almost imperceptible defect but somehow it lit up his face. His black hair was parted to the side like a well-behaved schoolboy's. Prince had told me about him on the phone and indicated that he was one of the "luvvies."

Prince briefly made the necessary introductions and went straight to the subject of the proposed partnership. When Mina spoke I was surprised by how serious and dignified he was. I thought that maybe he didn't want to mix business and pleasure right from the start. He had a reasonable amount of money, but not enough to make a good beginning, and he was looking for a young man who wanted to go into business and who had some familiarity with the nature of the work. He mentioned Prince's account of my previous work, and since I remembered my work experiences as failing for various reasons, I accepted his complimentary remarks in silence. I raised a glass of beer as a toast to him and looked into his strange eyes. He raised his glass of water and smiled a fragile smile. We exchanged telephone numbers and made an early appointment to discuss the details, and he soon indicated he was ready to leave. Prince invited him to stay, since the evening had hardly begun, but he declined, saying he had other commitments. I sensed he was uncomfortable with the ambiance. He confirmed our appointment before going, and when we shook hands I pressed his hand gently. He didn't react in any way, but headed briskly for the elevator.

"Why's he so serious?" I asked Prince.

"That's exactly what you need," he replied enthusiastically.

He said that Mina's seriousness would encourage me to be focused and committed, and that the company would be our company and so I wouldn't face the same problems I had faced in previous jobs. All I had to do was provide my share of the company's capital, then go along with Mina step by step so that we would succeed and so that my life would have some meaning, instead of spending it wandering around aimlessly. He elaborated on this theme in a short sermon, saying that although life appeared to be empty it was in fact full, but with traps that could lead to ruin at any moment.

Two or three days later I met Mina in the À l'Américaine café. As I prepared for the meeting I tried to find a balance between a pragmatic demeanor and a sense of levity and play, but his quick glance at my orange shirt warned me that I had veered too far in one direction. We didn't go into details of the partnership directly. We spoke a little about Prince and about many of the people he looked after and whose lives would be harder without him. Mina said in passing that he hoped Prince would settle down with someone faithful, instead of moving rapidly between short-term partners. This hope of his irritated me, maybe because it smacked to me of criticism of Prince's promiscuous lifestyle, a criticism that would also apply to me, even if Mina didn't know much about me. I defended Prince's lifestyle and explained candidly that I thought freedom and being uninhibited were preferable. With a calm that would often irritate me at the beginning of our relationship, he said that freedom might work for some time, or perhaps early in our lives, but after a while we fall prey to loneliness and need something deeper than quick, easy sex. That thing need not be love. Call it what you like: something close to empathy; finding someone you can talk to without embarrassment or fear.

I thought that what he said was romantic and foolish. I had turned that page long ago. I believed in flesh and blood, nerves and muscles, and nothing further—no feelings, emotions, or any of that. I saw all such things as delusions made to deceive adolescents and naïve people through novels, movies, and songs. But I didn't have the energy to get into an argument with him, especially when I saw that he wanted to turn the conversation to the crux of the matter, which was our business plan.

I liked his idea, which was simply that we should specialize in interior design for new shops and cafés in malls and upmarket areas. When we realized we could raise only a modest amount of money to start with, and of course after consulting my mother, who agreed to lend me a reasonable amount, I asked him why we shouldn't restrict our work to very small businesses, because the owners didn't have enough money to commission well-known companies and because they had a greater need to exploit every inch of their limited space. There wouldn't be any major competitors harassing us, and with good advertising and modest pricing we could gain ground specifically in this market. When I suggested this idea, I noticed for the first time since we had met that his view of me was changing, as if he had discovered that he'd hit upon just the right partner. Then we rented an apartment as an office, furnished it quickly, and set to work. We gave the company an English name, Free Space, at the suggestion of Prince in a daytime session in the roof garden.

I found I faced a real choice for the first time, a choice I had to make alone rather than in the presence of everyone else. After I graduated, until I met Mina, I had worked in several places, mostly in jobs that came to me through Mother or Prince. The jobs were all more or less connected with my special expertise in drawing and interior design. Once I had designed sets for television programs, and once I'd worked as an artist in a company that made animated movies. That went on for years. I started each new job enthusiastically. I wanted to prove myself, and so I would wake up early and take care of my appearance, avoiding garish or conspicuous clothes. But within a few weeks, or months in the best of cases, the enthusiasm would wane and it would end in disillusionment. They would dismiss me politely when they felt it was no use having me with them, or else I would stop work one day, out of irritation or disgust at their stupidity.

This time was completely different. I stopped staying up late and began to start the day early, sometimes to prove—to Mina at any rate—that I wasn't a lazy, pampered mama's boy.

At first we relied on our personal connections. We had small colored flyers printed and we distributed them wherever possible. Mother's connections brought us our first clients: one of her friends decided to open a hairdressing salon for her daughter. The second client came through Prince: an adventurous gay artist had decided to open a workshop to print cloth and clothing with designs requested by the customers. Gradually other clients showed up, and we found the days passing rapidly because we were so inundated with work that we often forgot to eat.

The experience was a challenge for Mina as much as for me, because he had long wanted to be independent of his uncle's company, especially after rumors of his sexual inclinations came up as a result of a failed love affair. The other party had pursued him in an attempt to threaten him with blackmail. I came to know Mina well, and I discovered that beneath his serious, staid exterior there was a soft core. I noticed that under his dark suits and heavy shoes he sometimes wore shirts and socks that were all colors of the rainbow, so I suddenly remembered that he was one of the "luvvies." I once caught him singing along in a low voice to an old song coming out of his computer: "If I had my way, if anything was up to me, I could buy you an island and a silver yacht, if only, if only . . . ."

"My God, you have a better voice than Muharram Fouad!" I shouted at him mischievously.

His face lit up with a shy smile.

After Mina's gay tendencies leaked out, his brothers silently kept their distance, except for one brother called Atef, who lived in Naples with his Italian wife and who continued to support him. Whenever I heard Mina talking about "my brother Atef," I felt a sudden yearning for a sympathetic brother of my own. He said that Atef believed in individual freedom and thought that everyone had the right to have sex in whatever way and with whomever they wanted as long as they didn't hurt anyone else, and I was left with a twinge of something like envy for

Mina. Once when we were coming back from an evening in the roof garden, emboldened from drinking, I held his hand in the elevator, kissed and licked the palm, and looked into his eyes. He stroked my cheek lightly, then moved closer and kissed it quickly and lightly, like a bird pecking.

He asked if we could sit in his car awhile, and in its dark warmth, glancing from me to the quiet street and back, he told me he loved me very much, like a beautiful brother that God had given him to compensate for the brothers who had ostracized him, although they lived only a few yards away from him. But he wasn't attracted to me and he had promised himself long ago not to have sex with any man without an emotional attachment, because he was worried he would forget how sweet those feelings were if he slept with every available person he met, yet he didn't criticize anyone who did so as long as that gave them fulfillment and relief.

I listened to him with mixed feelings and looked at his kind and handsome face. Then I kissed him on the cheek and left, intending not to try ever again. I went straight home without going cruising, though I was very much in the mood for sex. The desire waned over the days as a new face took shape in the mirror—a new and unfamiliar version of Hani; a version that was more at peace and more confident about himself and the whole world. If my mother hadn't constantly insisted I get married, I would have said that this was the happiest period in my life. Then came a shock from an unexpected quarter, after Mina returned from a two-week vacation as the guest of his brother Atef's family to tell me bashfully that he wanted to wind up the company as soon as possible. In Italy he had met an attractive middle-aged man, half Moroccan and half Italian, who had lived there almost since childhood. The man had turned his head, so much so that my partner had decided without hesitation to go to Italy and live with him.

Mina told me he had abstained from sex and been as celibate as a monk for ages, and whenever he masturbated to pornographic sites on the Internet, alone late at night, he felt empty and degraded, and sometimes he cried out of embarrassment and self-pity. On some occasions he felt that he needed psychotherapy because of his inability to do what other people did and he thought that his hope of finding the right partner for life, after the ordeal of his first and only love, might have upset his psychological equilibrium permanently, because after that he wouldn't allow anyone to be intimate with him. He told me that all these fears evaporated as soon as he exchanged a few words with the Moroccan man, a shopkeeper who spoke broken Arabic and was always laughing when he spoke. From the first meeting, it was obvious that they had an unusual rapport, and the man invited Mina to dinner the following day. Mina agreed hypnotically, although he knew nothing about him. At the third meeting, when he went to bed with him, Mina discovered that he could still give himself and allow himself to go with the flow. He said he had often heard people say they had been born again, but until now he hadn't believed them or understood what they meant.

His eyes were shining with gratification and enthusiasm, and I felt as if he were telling me one of those fairy tales that end in a magic kiss, and they live happily ever after and have loads of children. That was a story I could only observe or listen to, always from a distance and always happening to others. I gave my friend a hug and wished him well. Then I asked him to tell me more about his knight, maybe so that I could escape my own crisis and turn a blind eye to the phantom of my loneliness, which stood waiting in the corner with a morbid, vengeful smile.

20

"ALL THAT'S LACKING IS THE right girl."

That was the expression that Mother never stopped repeating in various forms, for years and years. It was the yoke that tightened around my neck every day. After separating from her husband and then giving up work completely, she now had time for me. It was she who told me about her divorce, showing no signs of regret. On the contrary, she looked cheerful and free and smiled as if she were saying, "Here I am, yours again, all yours." I wasn't happy with that. In fact, I might have been frightened and annoyed, and I said to myself that she no longer had anything to distract her from me and from her insistence that I get married. After a while she wasn't satisfied just to talk. She started proposing names to me and inviting me to go with her to family meetings. I took care to avoid them by any means possible. The last ambition of her life was for me a frightening ogre, the existence of which I had long ignored. The old methods—prevarication and making excuses—were no longer working.

I hadn't been unaware of her suspicions about my sexual inclinations since that cold night when she asked me to stay away from Prince. In front of her I always had to act as though I liked women, without ever being certain that I had succeeded in deceiving her finely tuned antennae. I left boxes of condoms in places where she might find them—condoms that I really did use, though for completely different sexual activities. It was like living out a detective story, leaving a trail of evidence that proved I was guilty, in the hope she would believe her son was a normal man like other men and that his aversion to marriage was just a question of avoiding responsibility and clinging to a life of freedom and frivolity.

She called me to her bedroom one morning before I could escape and go out. She didn't broach the subject of marriage. On the contrary, she said she was thinking of moving to Saudi Arabia to live out the rest of her life there, especially as one of her actress friends, after retiring years earlier, was living in Madina with her husband, an Egyptian preacher. She had stayed with her for a time after her first post-retirement pilgrimage to Mecca. I saw what she said as a veiled threat directed at me, as I couldn't imagine living without her. She was my remaining proof that I wasn't completely alone, that I wasn't a branch cut off a tree that no longer existed, and that I hadn't fallen from the sky, like rain on the ground, naked, screaming, and unprotected—though that was of course something I had wanted when I left home and stayed with Omar Nour a few years earlier. Then I started hearing long phone conversations between her and her old friend in Saudi Arabia, as they talked about details of her stay in the city. I stole Mother's passport, hid it in my drawer in the office, and hoped she would soon forget the whole subject. But she didn't forget. She kept insisting and threatening to get a replacement passport, and saying that she would go as soon as possible. Our arguments became a daily ritual that could occur at any time.

When Mina asked me to wind up the company and buy his stake in it or find another partner, I realized that it isn't easy to stop irritants when they start to seep into your life through some crevice, and in the end they may sweep you away like a deluge, leaving you drowning in misery. When I realized it would be difficult to find the right business partner to replace Mina, I swallowed my pride and made overtures to my mother again. I told her everything candidly, except for the real reason why Mina had decided to leave. She made it clear she was willing to help me immediately, but on one simple condition—that I at least get engaged before she signed the check. I had expected anything from her except for this bargaining with my life. I hated her and was so appalled by my hatred that I was willing to deny it completely by any means possible, even by submitting humbly to her demand.

In the roof garden, I laid out all my concerns at Prince's table, and he advised me to go along with her game for some time because an engagement could be broken off for any one of a thousand reasons, and even if I got married, the option of divorce was always available. I also consulted Omar Nour, telling him everything. He said that maybe the time had come for me to come out of the closet. He said my mother was an actress and understood the world and wouldn't reject her only son because he didn't like women, and if that was impossible then I should let her go wherever she wanted, or I should go, escape her and her world, and try to make for myself an independent life; that I should take a house where I could live with someone I loved, instead of having brief encounters in the office after working hours or in other dubious places. He said that if I didn't escape now I might forever lose the chance to save my skin.

Unlike Omar and some of the other "luvvies," a tendency to disobedience was not one of the qualities I could boast of, yet inside me there had always been a kind of secret and repressed rebelliousness with a disfigured and distorted face, because I aimed my weapons at myself, wavering between a false and baseless sense of superiority over others and pleasure in humiliating myself and forcing myself to yield to any gust of wind that blew my way. What could I do when faced by the storm that was my mother, who harassed me night and day?

In the end I took Prince's advice and, like a radar antenna, I started looking around for a victim or maybe a partner in the farce in which I meant to play the lead role. At that point I noticed Shireen. She had already been working with us for about a year, and she soon became like a sister to Mina and me. Since he wasn't inclined to chitchat or clowning around we spontaneously excluded him from our little circle, which had regular sessions every morning for gossip and jokes, before we lost ourselves in the bustle of work. It was this brother–sister relationship that encouraged me to think of Shireen as a fiancée—just a fiancée—in the hope that I could persuade her to play this role for a time and then we would separate while preserving our friendship as it was. Then I dismissed this idea completely, because it involved humiliating her.

She had told me a little about her troubled background. She had grown up in her uncle's house after her father died and her mother remarried and moved to Libya. Her mother came back some years later, old, rich, and alone after her Libyan husband had died. She asked to have her only daughter back. She wanted to take her away from the only life she knew, from her uncle and aunt and their children, who were now like brothers and sisters to her, especially Asma the youngest, whom Shireen had helped to bring up and who was like a daughter or sister. She refused to go back to her mother despite the money and comfortable lifestyle her mother tried to tempt her with. She saw her mother as a stranger, and even her accent made her laugh. I was aware of these problems, which had recently flared up, and I thought that maybe getting engaged would be an escape plan for her too, or a temporary respite for us both. After initially dismissing the idea, I ended up asking to marry her, a few weeks after the humiliating offer Mother had made.

I remember we were in a shopping mall in Nasr City, supervising the interior design work in a flower shop. Shireen was talking to me about work matters and I wasn't paying attention to what she was saying. I was staring at her but not hearing a word. Slightly embarrassed, she touched her nose and face in case I was looking at something she hadn't noticed. Then she said, "Ground control to Hani."

"Tell you what, Shireen, why don't we get married?" I replied, out of the blue.

The worker closest to us stopped what he was doing and turned to look at us, his mouth agape. Because she had a cold, Shireen was wearing layers of woolen clothes in warm, cheerful colors and her nose was redder than a beetroot. I had suggested marriage as casually as if I were offering her a cup of coffee. She thought I was joking as usual, so her surprise didn't last more than a few seconds and I didn't notice that at first she thought I was serious, at least for a moment.

"Why not?" she replied in a serious tone. "Are you free tomorrow?"

The swarthy worker laughed inanely as if he were watching a comedy movie. We both glowered at him and he went off, covering his mouth with his hand. It was a naïve and awkward moment, but it led us unwittingly to a shared destiny. In the meantime I was staring at her red nose, which had a tiny beauty mark at the tip, as if I had just discovered it was there. "Very well then, tomorrow it is," I said.

We were half serious, half joking, but at the end of the day we agreed to take a short while to think it over, to be sure that our mental faculties were sound. I had no need to give it lengthy thought, because I knew that if I hesitated for a moment, I would back out and run off forever, so far away that no one would be able to find me again, not even myself. That's what I wish I had done.

21

I PLAYED MY NEW ROLE as well as I could, smiling amiably to hide the kernel of fear that was growing inside me. Emboldened by the enthusiasm of my mother and Shireen, I became further entangled. When I saw how happy Mother was, everything else ceased to matter, and I told myself it was no problem that I was doing this only for her sake, even if it changed my whole life. I said "maybe"; I said "perhaps" and "whatever," and I pressed on into the soft sands that slowly engulfed me with every passing day.

I found even Prince encouraging me, saying I wouldn't be the first or the last gay man to get married, either under family pressures or to avert suspicion, or even simply because they wanted to have children and a family like anyone else. I reconfirmed what he already knew—that I had no sexual desire for women in any way, unlike some men who are bisexual. When he found me wiping away a flood of tears I couldn't control, he stood up, came over to me, put my head on his chest, and started to pat me on the back. He was as close and sympathetic as Badriya Amin the great actress was distant and heartless, yet I forgave her whenever I saw how her smile had recovered its old magic and her voice its vigor, and how her laughter rang out like a woman trilling in joy on a festive occasion.

After the procedures for winding up the partnership were complete and Mina left for Italy, I didn't have the courage to break off the engagement, maybe for fear of the effect the news would have on Mother, or maybe out of concern for Shireen, who was like a child going to the amusement park for the first time. She would finally leave her uncle's house and be safe from her mother harassing her. She would dress up as a bride and have a husband, a house, and a family. I would be deceiving myself if I thought she saw me as the knight of her dreams. In fact she may have suppressed suspicions she'd had about me since her first day in the company. Asma, her young and sensible cousin, advised her to consult her heart. Shireen even prayed to God for guidance in making a choice, and decided to try her luck. Marriage for her was a necessity, a means to achieve fulfillment and a normal life now that she was over thirty and had started to put on more weight than she should. Above all, my social status was an opportunity she shouldn't miss. I admit all this now, but in the carnival atmosphere a naïve sense of elation turned all our heads and drowned out our fears and suspicions for a while.

When I came to know Shireen properly, not as a colleague at work or as someone to have innocent fun with, I discovered a rare human being. Her concern for those around her outweighed everything else inside her. She couldn't bear to see anyone worried or in a bad mood and would give of herself out of kindness until she restored that person's smile. Sometimes I felt that she was as similar to me as a sister would have been, and at other times I mistakenly imagined that I loved her, but not in the way that men love women. Maybe I loved her ready wit and her easy laugh, the way she plunged into life with simplicity and confidence, but my body wasn't on fire when I was close to her and my fingers didn't tremble if I touched her hands. Something else developed between us, very far from the delusions of love: we were like traveling companions and the responsibility I had assumed was an easy burden, something that seemed serious on the surface but was really more like innocent fun. I liked the game, especially when other people started seeing me differently as soon as the engagement was announced. I seemed transformed into a superior creature, but the levity quickly took a serious turn, and when I saw the engagement ring on my finger one morning, I had my first panic attack for many years.

With the panic attacks, various forms of dreams about exams came back to haunt me. I dreamed I was terrified because I was late for an exam, or I would be sitting in the examination room staring at the question sheet but unable to read the questions or understand a word. If I did understand I couldn't find the right answers, and if I knew the right answers I found that my pen had run out of ink and I couldn't write a single word. In some of the dreams I was old, with a head that was half bald and half gray, and all the other people taking exams were little children busy filling in the spaces on their answer sheets. Then the spider nightmares began to recur, like a traveler who had long been away. My sleep at night was torn to shreds and my nerves teetered on the edge during the day. I felt like I was walking along some high ledge.

Prince drew up an emergency plan for me, and we started by consulting Dr. Sameeh the psychiatrist. Sameeh wasn't gay but he was close to our world and open-minded. Unlike most people in his profession, he didn't see homosexuality as a disease that needed treatment, though he didn't deny that we faced pressures that prevented us from accepting the truth about ourselves and living with it. He advised me to think, not once, not twice, but three times before submitting to the test of marriage. When he realized there was no way back, he taught me some relaxation and breathing exercises and recommended I do them every day for at least twenty minutes. Then we moved on to some imagination exercises. I had to imagine myself with Shireen, laughing and playing and touching each other. Then we started kissing and fondling and getting into various sexual positions until the fantasies aroused me. I wasn't convinced, and maybe he didn't believe in these experiments himself, but we went ahead with them till the end. Then I had to start approaching Shireen physically to sustain these fantasies. When I first stole a kiss from her, I saw her make a strange smile and a look that was somewhere between surprise and relief, as if she were saying, "At last, you idiot." Then we shared another long kiss and I felt a very slight degree of arousal, and I told myself exultantly that God was capable of anything.

Then we had to move to the decisive stage of the plan—having full intercourse with a woman. Dr. Sameeh moved out of the picture and it was time for Prince to play his part. He took me to see a woman he knew called Aunt Kima. Her real name was Camelia but because she liked Rushdi Abaza the actor so much, she adopted the name Kima, which he repeats often in the movie *The Second Man*: "I swear by the life of Aunt Kima, and I never swear false when I swear by her life," he says in the movie. She was a kindly, well-dressed woman of the type that become broadcasters on Egyptian television. I had to choose the lucky girl from a catalog of photos on a computer. Aunt Kima, Prince, and I went to view the pictures. We were laughing and making silly comments about the girls. I chose a girl with coarse features, but blonde with blue eyes, and with the body that was most like a man's. The girl, Amal, arrived late for our appointment the next day and when she arrived she looked as if she'd just woken up. That first time didn't last more than a few minutes. Amal did everything necessary to excite me and maybe Aunt Kima had told her confidentially what my problem was. As soon as I ejaculated I avoided looking at her and ran off to find my clothes in embarrassment at myself, at her, and at the pictures of nature scenes hanging on the walls.

During the month leading up to the wedding, I slept with Amal about twice a week. I cheated on Shireen even before I married her. I cheated on her only so that I could sleep with her without any mishaps. Amal, who was tall and broad, could hold me with her legs and arms as if I were her plump child. I thought to myself that if she hadn't had blue eyes and blonde hair, which seemed to be natural, she wouldn't have been able to make a living here with her giant body.

I was regaled with massive portions of seafood, pigeons, and other kinds of meat, and other supposedly aphrodisiac foodstuffs, besides vitamins and stimulants, just so that I could unload an essence of all this between Amal's legs. Every time, before throwing the condom into the little basket next to the bed, I had a quick look at it, examining the semen, its color, thickness, and quantity. I wondered whether this pathetic liquid would pass the test and produce the right answers. Or would the female spider lap it up nonchalantly before devouring me? I still had strong misgivings in spite of everything, because Shireen was a virgin—unlike Amal, a trained professional who did what was needed to make sure I performed well. I also had to give Shireen the impression I was the perfect man, confident about every move and touch, so that she didn't have any suspicions.

The Garden City apartment looked colorful, revived, radiant with the light of joy, new clothes, presents, and perfume. Everywhere Shireen and I received congratulations, good wishes, hugs, and kisses. I felt like a calf being fattened for slaughter on the altar of its mother and society for the sake of appearances. Whenever I looked in the mirror, my increasing plumpness reinforced this feeling. I imagined my soul, unlike my body, turning into an insubstantial ghost wrapped in white sheets, with sticky patches that started to spread like cobwebs.

22

ABOUT TEN DAYS AFTER I came out of prison, I told Prince I wanted to see my daughter, little Badriya. That was before I embarked on my program of therapy and writing, or dared to leave the hotel room in the evening on aimless rambles.

When Prince called Shireen and made an appointment, I was overcome with hesitation and fear. I was still hesitant when Prince's car was taking us slowly through the downtown traffic. I didn't know how I could face Shireen after everything that had happened. I had seen her only once during the trial, in the first session, a few weeks before the divorce took place.

We drove into Garden City from the corniche. Although I had been away no more than a few months, I was almost overcome by tears when I saw the familiar buildings of the elegant neighborhood and the trees in the streets. When we stopped in front of the building, I froze in my seat next to Prince.

"Would you like me to come up with you?" he asked.

I gave him a quick nod, grateful for his suggestion. While I was checking that my pen and notebook were in my jacket pocket, I heard the voice I loved to hear. "Papa, Papa!" it cried.

I turned and all my hesitation suddenly vanished. It was little Badriya, five years old, with frizzy hair framing her round head like a shiny black halo, waiting for me in front of the building and trying to break free from the hand of her nanny. Without a moment's hesitation, I opened the car door and ran to her, picked her up, and kissed every part of her face and head that my lips could reach. Although I tried to control myself, I broke into tears when we were in the hallway. Badriya just lifted the sunglasses off my eyes and wiped my tears away. "Don't cry, Papa," she said. "You'll get better and get to speak again. I pray to God for you every day. Not just me but Somaya too. Isn't that right, Somaya?"

"That's right, my dear," said the nanny as she pressed the elevator button.

As I carried Badriya into the lift, she sneaked a peek at Prince. "Who's that, Papa?" she whispered in my ear. "A friend of yours? Uncle Sallam is visiting too."

It was true—I was no longer Shireen's husband, so one of her relatives had to attend our meeting, or maybe Shireen's kindly uncle had something he wanted to say to me, accounts of some kind to be settled or an indirect apology for the method they had adopted when they sought a divorce. The elevator moved and Badriya didn't stop whispering in my ear about what had happened to her during my absence from the house, about the time she had spent with her mother in her grandfather's house, and about playing in the street outside with the kids there. She said something about one of the friends she had met there and laughed, and in her laugh I heard a distant echo of the laugh of my precious mother, Badriya the Elder—a laugh like the vague impression that remains from a dream.

Suddenly I found myself in the house, the house where I had lived for years, where I had eaten, drunk, slept, made love with my wife as much as my desire and willpower allowed, attended to my mother's comfort, and said farewell to her dead body. It was here that I carried my aunt's body from the bathroom to her bed, and read, drew, planned my life, listened to a thousand songs, watched hundreds of movies and shows, and laughed. Yes, I well remember that I used to laugh often on the slightest pretext. And where was that fat clown now?

Sallam, Shireen's uncle, greeted me and embraced me with a warmth that seemed strange under the circumstances. He patted me on the back with the affection of an aging father. He seemed to be giving me his condolences and I wondered who had died. Since I couldn't speak for him, Prince introduced himself, and Sallam's eyes lingered on Prince's face a little longer than necessary after the handshake, as if he were trying to uncover something hidden behind the red face with its protruding cheekbones and gray eyes under white eyebrows. He was trying to detect some stigma, a proof of guilt, and maybe he wanted to have a look at the man he had recently heard so much about.

He led us to the living room as if it were his house. Inside, pictures of Mother and other people who had passed away awaited me, beautifully arranged on three walls around us. Nothing had changed, and yet everything had changed. Prince took his leave, saying he would wait for me in a coffee shop close to the house, as we had agreed on the way. When he left I felt that my back was bare. I clung to Badriya as my only life buoy. I now realized who had died. It was me. It might as well have been my soul that had come back, after I was dead and buried, to have a last look at my loved ones and at the lost dwellings it had lived in. I wished I could close my eyes and then reopen them to find that everything had reverted to how it was just two years earlier—with me, Mother, Shireen, Badriya, and life like a children's song that began again as soon as it ended.

I looked at a large photograph of our wedding, and in a few seconds I remembered my terror on that day, when I resorted to furtive swigs from a hip flask of cognac in my jacket pocket. When they were taking pictures of us on the hotel balcony that overlooked the Nile, Shireen noticed the bulge in my pocket and asked what it was. I took it out and she drank a mouthful in front of her friends and relatives, and one of them let out a cheer. We were very much like circus performers on that day—having fun and clowning around with everyone. We danced with Fifi Abdou to Hakim songs, and we had dozens of pictures taken with dozens of stars and guests, and then went up to our suite exhausted.

Before the break of dawn we finally had sex. After two or more attempts I managed to take her virginity, drawing on my brief experience with Amal and by having fantasies about sex with some of the performers who had entertained us at the fake wedding party. Shireen's softness as a woman was more than I could bear. I was relieved to see the light-red drops of blood, though I also trembled in fear in case I had unintentionally injured her. She was gratified and forgiving, but I felt like a criminal lying next to his victim, who closes her eyes to hide her disappointment. Maybe my time in prison was meant to punish me for my crime.

Seated in our old living room again, I shied away from the future that was in store for me, and I couldn't take my eyes off a large old photograph of my mother on the back wall. Didn't she take part in the crime too, albeit with good intentions and with love? Does ignorance absolve us of guilt? Mother was smiling in the picture, standing there seductively and elegantly, holding a bunch of flowers, all of them white—flowers that hadn't faded for more than fifty years. Badriya noticed my glance, held my chin, and turned my head to face her. "By the way," she said suddenly, "I've finally decided. I'm going to be a famous actress like Grandma. So I'll be Badriya Number Two and she'll be Badriya Number One. What do you think?"

I quickly took out my little notebook and wrote her a message: "Badriya Number Two will be the prettiest and greatest actress in the whole world."

With artificial theatricality, Uncle Sallam read out to her what was written on the piece of paper. Then she tore the piece of paper out of the notebook and ran off, calling Somaya.

Then Shireen came in. I looked at her impassively, as if I didn't know her. She was wearing dark, modest winter clothes, a plain dark-blue headscarf, and no makeup. I knew it meant she was in mourning. Uncle Sallam left us and Somaya brought coffee and took Badriya, slightly resistant and grumbling, off to her room. I quickly wrote a message to Shireen: "I'll never forgive myself for anything that happened to you two because of me."

I looked at the piece of paper for a moment before I handed it to her. My handwriting looked shaky, like that of a child who has only just started learning to write. I shuddered as I saw Shireen struggling for words. In the past she had always had a ready answer but now she was stumbling to start a sentence. She stood up and pulled the sliding door closed, as if to cut us off from the rest of the world and everything in it. She came up to me without hesitation, stood next to me, and slapped me hard on the face. "Why did you get married?" she said, choking with tears. "Why did you have children? Shame on you, Hani. Shame on you."

The slap hurt me more than all the abuse and pain I had received in prison. Just to have her hand touch my cheek with such anger made me understand instantly everything she had put up with because of me, both before and after the scandal. Both of us cried in silence, far apart. Then she came over to me, took my head, rested it on her shoulder quite instinctively, and started to massage my shoulders as if she were now my mother, until we calmed down a little. When I took out my pack of cigarettes, she took one and lit it herself. "I started the moment it happened—a cigarette every now and then," she said.

Then she poured her heart out, inhaling the warm air from the room and turning it into the words she had stored up inside her over the previous months. She spoke about how she was forced to ask for a divorce, after my name and job were published in the newspapers; how she had taken refuge in her uncle's house for a long time, until she felt that the people here had almost forgotten the scandal. She said she had asked herself day and night whether there was anything wrong with her as a woman. And if there was nothing wrong with her, what had induced me to ask to marry her, if I didn't desire her? Then she said she didn't absolve herself of responsibility, because she had made a mistake when she ignored her suspicions. To her, I was an amusing interior designer, with a mother who was a famous actress, both comfortably off. "And me? In the end I'm nothing," she said. "My only assets are my tongue and my wits—wits that hadn't even helped me to discover that something wasn't quite right in the first place." Throughout our years together she had kept her suspicions at bay. She had turned a blind eye, ignoring all the feelings she had as a woman, as well as her intuition, which had never let her down.

She also said she had sensed my feelings toward Abdel Aziz almost from the first day, the day he got engaged to her cousin Asma. She felt that my state of mind had changed. My face seemed to light up with electricity drawn from Abdel Aziz and to go out when I was cut off from that source of energy. She felt it, and denied her feelings, months before the arrest and prosecution and before Essam, her cousin, revealed what he had seen Abdel Aziz and me doing together in Alexandria.

When I was arrested, the lie finally fell apart. She no longer had the option of continuing to deny it. Then Essam came out with what he knew and the picture was complete. Even so, she said, she had held out against them and refused to seek a divorce at first, but then she backed down out of concern for Badriya, who was guiltless in all this, and because she knew it was now impossible to go on being married, even if they acquitted me. On top of that she wanted me to hate her as much as she hated me, and so she obeyed them and asked for a divorce. She had wanted to slap me, as she had done just now, and only now could she forgive me. However guilty I was, I hadn't deserved everything that had happened to me, and because I was Badriya's father and would remain so, we turned the page quietly and I sincerely wished her well in every way, and we told Badriya that I had gone to hospital for treatment to recover the power of speech.

I came out of Mother's building toward nine o'clock in the evening, holding a cardboard box with some of my stuff. Quickly and awkwardly, I said hello to Saad the doorman and walked hurriedly toward the place where I had agreed to meet Prince, but when I arrived I couldn't find him. I looked left and right, scanning the faces of the customers in the coffee shop. I put the cardboard box down next to me outside the coffee shop and felt lost and short of breath. I didn't know if I should sit and wait for him or take a taxi to the hotel. In my breathlessness, I doubted I could lift my feet off the ground. I leaned back against the wall and tried to pull myself together. How would a taxi driver react if I wrote the address of the hotel for him on a piece of paper?

For a moment I thought of going home to Shireen, who hadn't let me go without setting my mind at rest, after unloading months of rancor, anger, and pain. I could go back and beg her to call Prince. Instead, I took out my old cell phone, which I had scarcely used since my release, but before I could find Prince's number and write out a message, my eyes filling with tears, I felt his hand on my shoulder. I started and my whole body shook. When I turned and saw him I wanted to insult him and punch him in the chest, but instead I threw myself into his arms, though we had only been apart for two or three hours. He said apologetically that he had had to move his parked car to make way for another car. I wasn't interested in what he said. I signed to him that we should leave the place fast—very fast.

If it hadn't been for Prince I would have been lost, now, in prison or over the years. He was always there, available, and all I had to do was call him and he would come. Even so, I would forget him for months when I didn't need him, and when I suddenly remembered him and dropped in on his haunts, his only reproach would be a critical smile. He was like a middle-aged uncle whose displeasure does not last long and who has recently had a visit from his nephew. No, he wasn't an uncle. He was probably the only father I ever had. Maybe he was that old man I had been looking for and whose appearance I had awaited as an adolescent coming out of the mosque after dawn prayers. The difference was that he couldn't recreate me out of nothing, erasing all my vices with a stroke of some heavenly pen. He couldn't and he didn't want to. He was still holding out against time, ignoring the impact of the years on the pride of an aging peacock, using expensive perfumes to fight off the horrible smell to which he had been condemned for years. He was still looking after his "luvvies" with all the influence, connections, and experience at his disposal, even if he had to wage wars he could have done without. If only I could just be like him, for little Badriya's sake—to be the kindly old man who dispels the gloom and offers peace of mind and a sense of security. But I was very far from being able to do that. All I could do was observe people and the world from behind dark glasses, and they seemed remote and unfamiliar, just like the scenes from my life that I'm dragging out of my memory and setting down on these pages.

In the cardboard box I had carried out of the house I found many photographs, including one of just me and Abdel Aziz on the balcony of the beach house in Agami. I don't remember now who took it. Was it a coincidence or had Shireen deliberately put it among those pictures? He had his strong arm around my shoulders and was smiling, arrogant in his self-confidence, while my face suggested a joy as fragile as an April fools' joke.

23

As soon as I saw him I was no longer myself. I remember that Shireen noticed the change in me from the first moment. It was at the party celebrating his engagement to her cousin Asma. "What's wrong, Hani?" she asked me several times.

I was usually the life and soul of the party on occasions such as this, dancing and encouraging others to dance. But as soon as I saw the groom that night, going into the reception hall surrounded by the pomp and noise of the bridal procession, arm in arm with Asma, I was transfixed. I found myself tilting my head and looking at this man as if he were some strange creature. I told myself that I was grown up and sensible, that I had already tried everything, but how naïve I was!

It wasn't hunger of the flesh, because the volcano inside me had subsided long ago and, as I entered my forties, all that remained was a slow-moving stream of lava. It might erupt on irregular occasions but it would soon die down. I made do with infrequent encounters I snatched in secret from time to time—quick transactions with men whose circumstances were similar to mine and who sought only a tranquilizer for their pain, without any commitment or complications. Then we could go back to sleep, confident that our public, respectable lives would stay on track. I thought I had reached dry land, but how naïve I was. I was terrified when faced with the strange monster called love that I had heard about all my life without ever meeting it. I had even come to see it as a myth, and I made fun of those who talked about it. That night the monster was as seductive as it was frightening.

Shireen and I reached home late that night, silent and a little tired. As I drove home absentmindedly, my body felt like a wreck, as if someone had dealt me a death blow. At home, Shireen checked little Badriya, then came back and stood there, taking off her hijab and her shiny black evening dress, which was rather too tight. I took a quick shower, and then went to bed in my nightclothes, carrying some old photo albums with me. One of them was full of pictures of my father in his childhood and youth, and I sat browsing through them. I was aware of Shireen's quizzical looks. I called her over, pretending I wanted to bring her in on a little mystery. "Come and look, Shiri," I said. "Isn't there a resemblance between Asma's fiancé and my father?"

She couldn't see the resemblance as clearly as me. I started pointing out my evidence for the similarity. I cited his square face, his broad forehead, the nose that was flared like Gamal Abdel Nasser's, and of course the bushy mustache that almost hid his upper lip. She played along, making jokey comments on my father's wayward youth and his love affairs and how maybe he had once climbed over the wall into the home of Abdel Aziz's big family in the southern town of Minya and left progeny there. Then she smiled, undid the top buttons of my pajamas, and said, "Thank God his only son turned out to be sensible, don't you think?"

When we made love I tried to finish quickly, but for some reason I lay trembling on top of her for ages. I couldn't shake off that strange feeling that had come over me. It was knocking on a door inside me with the urgency of a child trapped in a dark, cramped space. Sleep eluded me after Shireen slipped into her gentle, intermittent snoring with its familiar rhythm. When the sound of praying, hardly audible, reached me from Mother's room around dawn, I thought of getting up and eating something, in the hope I could then go to sleep. When I came out of the kitchen I saw Mother on her way to her bedroom, leaning on her stick. She was muttering some prayers she had memorized with as much skill as she had memorized her lines for the roles she had played in the past: "In the name of God, in the presence of whose name nothing can do harm. In the name of God the Protector, in the name of God the Healer, in the name of God, in the presence of whose name nothing can do harm on Earth or in Heaven, for He is the one who hears and the one who knows."

Her voice faded into the distance. For some reason I didn't try to speak to her or alert her to my presence. I stood there watching her small, patient steps, and repeated after her those words of her whispered prayer that I could hear. Where does strength go when it leaves us? How is it that beauty withers till nothing of it remains? Was this the tigress who used to inspire such awe and reverence in me? I didn't move until she reached the door of her room and shut the door behind her, and the flow of her prayer was interrupted. Then I fell asleep immediately, a deep sleep without dreams.

I tried without success to forget about the groom, but a few days later we were invited to dinner with the couple to get to know each other properly. We met in a fancy restaurant on the river in Zamalek that Abdel Aziz clearly visited regularly. I did everything I could to appear normal, but my tongue was in knots and the words stuck in my throat. I was even worried they might see this as a sign that I was displeased or bored with them. Shireen lifted the burden from my shoulders when she saw that I was unusually silent. She bombarded them with questions and advice for the future. I followed the conversation distractedly, commenting or intervening as little as possible, just enjoying listening to his resonant voice. I noticed for the first time that he pronounced his *r*'s rather like *w*'s, which gave him a certain boyishness that contrasted with his mature Upper Egyptian masculinity.

I followed their conversation about Asma's writings, which were one of the reasons she and Abdel Aziz had come to meet, in the context of his work as an editor on a newspaper that devoted a whole page to the opinions of young people, besides his many other duties and responsibilities. He seemed to be a rising star in the media world and he was conveying that impression through carefully studied references, while flashing a modest smile that failed to conceal his admiration for himself. I guessed he was over thirty, though I couldn't fix his age precisely, but he was definitely several years older than Asma. He came from a family of tough men with a violent history. I would discover later from Prince that his family had an extensive network, with its base in Minya and branches across the country. Most of the menfolk held senior positions or high rank in the army, the police, or the judiciary, and included businessmen who were pillars of the ruling party. But Abdel Aziz didn't mention that at the dinner or later, except briefly and to a limited extent, as if he were embarrassed to be associated with them and wanted to be forgiven for the connection.

He might have noticed the signs that I was nervous, or maybe he picked up one of my furtive glances at him. He graced me with a polite smile and opened a conversation with me on various unconnected themes—the nature of my company's work and the economic situation in general, and then ending up on football. Whenever I didn't show enough interest in pursuing the conversation, he stopped talking or turned to talk to his fiancée or my wife. I was careful drinking the expensive wine so that I wouldn't let slip any signs that might have consequences for which I wasn't yet ready. When I shook hands with him by my car, I looked into his eyes earnestly, as if entrusting him with a secret, but he didn't say anything. His smile tightened and he frowned, as if facing an enigma.

For days I went over what had happened at the dinner, what he had said and what he had done. Had he really given a suggestive smile to a young man who was serving in the restaurant, or had I imagined it? Damn the ambivalence of doubt! When and how could I meet him again, at least to try to change his impression of me? Then I would tell myself I had to get a grip. Now that I had taken the first step by deceiving myself and getting married, I had to keep going till the end. I no longer belonged to myself. There was Shireen now, and more important than either her or me, there was little Badriya.

I had never imagined that I would be able to feel like a father. When I picked up Badriya for the first time, an hour or less after she was born, I felt an aversion that was almost nauseating as I looked at this strange creature who was said to be a part of me. I completely avoided her for days and just watched her from a distance, while she was nursing or off and away on one of her sleep journeys, during which she grew at an astonishing rate. As she grew, her features began to take shape. A recognizably human hand the size of a postage stamp would suddenly appear from between the folds of her tiny clothes. At first out of a sense of duty, and then gradually out of curiosity, I moved closer to her and tracked her changing appearance and her strange convulsions during bouts of crying that I found harrowing. I was staggered by the amount of attention this pet animal needed in order to become a human being like the rest of us. In hindsight, I imagined Mother looking after me as a baby about forty years earlier, and I tried to gauge the amount of love that all those around me had invested in me. I even caught myself sometimes feeling grateful to Mother for forcing me to get married. That way I could experience the sense of extending into another body, one that was new and fragile. Eventually I plucked up courage and started to pick Badriya up again and again and rock her to sleep. I ended up singing to her one night while Shireen was taking a shower: "Her mother's beloved, oh my goodness, how I love her!"

When she gripped my little finger until she fell asleep, I almost cried at the miracle of creation made flesh before my eyes. This was another trap I hadn't reckoned on—a grip as fragile as cotton candy but as strong as a steel chain.

Again I was a man alone among women, and again I yearned to run far away before I suffocated on their numbing and familiar smells. I longed to smell the sweat of a man. That was my only salvation, or else I would turn into a real female and join their flock, to be surprised one morning to find my nipples producing warm milk like Shireen's breasts. Shireen's interest in sex had abated, as if in giving birth she had taken from me what she wanted, and that was that. This pleased me to some extent, but I was still worried she might have despaired of me completely, of me giving her a pleasure that she still expected. Sometimes we would revert to being the Hani and Shireen of old, the colleagues at work, and we would tell each other stories, reliving our lives from the beginning, up to the moment when we became attached.

I told her many things, except for the one thing that, if a man told his wife about it, he would no longer be a man and she would no longer be his wife. Maybe Shireen had long had suspicions without having the courage to name them. How often had she sensed it but denied it! How often had she felt that the man she was living with was saving his enthusiasm and his passion for something else or someone else other than her? Maybe throughout her years of marriage she had been mulling suspicions, and I had been missing her stealthy glances at me as I stood in front of the mirror preparing to go out, examining my complexion or the sparse hair between my eyebrows. Our eyes would meet in the mirror for a few seconds—four little question marks colliding and vanishing in the same moment. And we went on singing the song of fake happiness until Abdel Aziz appeared, like a highwayman in the dead of night.

24

IN THE SPACIOUS CHANGING ROOM at the bathhouse, I turned my cell phone off and put it in a little drawer with my wallet and everything else from my pockets. Then I locked the drawer with a key attached to a rubber strap that went around my wrist. I had come to escape the image of Abdel Aziz, disappointed that Prince couldn't understand what I was going through and was advising me to back off immediately. Prince tried to make light of the whole issue, saying I was obviously projecting my own views—that I simply desired this man and hoped that he shared my inclinations.

He was explaining in his highly modulated theatrical voice, speaking calmly and dismissively. He knew nothing of the turmoil inside me, of my need to find a straw I could clutch on to, of my constant desire to cry and scream. I had a sudden impulse to punch him in the face, with its taut skin and protruding cheekbones, maybe because what he said seemed too logical. I didn't know how to explain to him that this time was different, even if I had projected my own feelings onto others in the past and imagined that they had inclinations that they didn't have.

I needn't bother explaining something that I can't put in measured words, even when I'm talking to myself. I went along with what Prince said, pretending to be partially persuaded. Before one of his guests could come to join us, he suddenly put down his glass and looked at me. Without any preliminaries, he said that maybe this time was different from previous times. "Because this time you're playing with fire," he said. "He's the son-in-law of your wife's family. If it ever got out, it would be like someone burning his own house down to light a cigarette."

He stubbed out his cigarillo and made a dismissive gesture with his hands, as if brushing something away. "And there's no cigarette that's worth all that, believe me. I've smoked all kinds," he added.

I took off all my clothes and hung them on nails hammered neatly into the wall above a high bench. I wore just a piece of cloth wrapped tightly around my waist. Only now have I noticed that there's a ritual for going into the world of the Turkish bath: at the threshold we abandon everything that links us to the outside world, if only for a while. I feel I'm shedding a false persona that is weighed down by appendages and adornments. I lose my outer skin and appear as I really am, transparent, in order to enter a different, transitory world where I tread more lightly. I enter it naked, as if newborn. And yet I'm not completely naked. The loose cloth covers my private parts and the rubber strap around my wrist holds the key that will take me back to my public life. In the locked drawer I have everything I need in order to go back to the role that's been scripted for me, to the preordained pattern of daytime artifices and society's lies, to a clear identity, a name, and other keys too, more important ones—credit cards, cash, and little photos of my father and mother, of Shireen and my daughter. How can such a little drawer be big enough to hold a life almost four decades long?

Although I didn't frequent the place as often as I used to, several men glanced at me and recognized me. They were all on the run like me. They had shed their names, their dates of birth, their socks, and their underclothes, whether cheap or dear. They had come from fashionable neighborhoods or from shantytowns, from air-conditioned offices or from workshops smeared with oil and grease. Even after they stripped off, their bodies all carried marks that gave the outside world away—marks that couldn't be taken off and put in little drawers. A tattoo on the shoulder might remain from prison or from a visit to a fair—a tattoo of a lion brandishing a sword or a phrase such as "My Most Precious Mother." A man might retain a gold chain he is proud of and never takes off. Instead he leaves it hanging down on the soft skin of his chest. Another man might have a long scar on the side of his torso or above his cheek, or might even have the remains of an old suicide attempt on his wrists. Someone might be wearing a tight red pair of swimming trunks of the latest fashion because he's above putting one of those disgusting wraps on his body. The yellowed and decayed teeth remain, and the bad breath, alongside the soft faces and the glossy hair. We drag after us the world we have left behind, with threads that are still visible amid the steam swirling around us. In my case I brought with me the specter of a man called Abdel Aziz, who arrived out of nowhere to turn my world upside down. I could feel him prowling stealthily around me.

I reclined on my side on the marble platform around the fountain in the center of the inner room, resting my head on my hand and indulging in my private fantasies, biding my time before going up to the room with the hot plunge bath. A sliver of crescent moon appeared through the domed roof, so thin it might break if I looked at it too long. I imagined myself in the old workshop as it used to be, with Biba the owner and her lover, my grandfather Khawaga Mida, with the decorated tiles, the curtains, and the mannequins. I was holding a long gray feather with which I tickled the legs of the beautiful women as I slipped between them like a cat. One of them would panic; another would laugh. When one of them bent down from on high and kissed me, I found that she had turned into Ra'fat with his handsome smiling face, but instead of kissing me I was surprised to find him biting me on the cheek. It didn't hurt, but then I started to stretch and grow bigger, and then I ran till I reached the bathhouse, naked, where I was surrounded by naked men floating between the floor and the ceiling as if there was no longer any gravity. I checked their faces for someone until I finally found him—Abdel Aziz. We exchanged a kiss, which was like a dream within the dream, until he suddenly pulled away, like someone coming to his senses after being drunk for a moment. He looked at me disapprovingly, as if I had unwittingly committed some offense. Before turning and disappearing into the steam that surrounded us on all sides, he said something hurtful and cutting, such as "My God!" He shouted it out as if I were disfigured and repulsive.

I suddenly came around, to the cry of the old man who did the scrubbing and the massage. He was coming in from outside, and as usual he called out, "In the name of God, the Protector, the Strong, the Helper!"—obliquely announcing his arrival so that everyone would be on their guard and cover up a little. I heard him moving the heavy wooden door that separated us from the rest of the establishment outside. I felt refreshed by my nap and my dream, no longer drunk and in despair. Someone came up, sat nearby, looked straight at me, and smiled like an old acquaintance. He brought his freckled, fair-skinned face toward me and whispered, "Sleep well? Don't you remember me?"

How many times had I heard that question? How many times would I hear it again? Might I not put that question to Abdel Aziz someday soon? This must be the answer to the puzzle that had tormented me for the past few days. I wanted to keep hold of the dream before it dissolved in the steam. If I uttered a single word in response to this stranger, the last remaining trace of the dream would disappear. Now I was confident that it wasn't the first time I had seen Abdel Aziz, the bridegroom who was so thoroughly proud of himself and his own presence. It must have been the second time, and the first time was when we had that long drunken kiss, which we would relive together one day. Now I remembered, but did he remember?

"I'm sorry, but I'm not aware of it," I answered the blond man after a few seconds of distraction. Then I left him and moved away.

In my brief sleep, I saw you, Abdel Aziz, as if we had met here in this place or somewhere else smarter and cleaner, maybe in the sauna at the Nile Hilton. I saw you surrounded by steam, your swarthy brown body strewn with herbs and oozing with sweat. I was a little dizzy, maybe drunk or stoned. While dozing I remembered everything despite the years—a dazzling memory in the form of an old photograph. We exchanged a long kiss and you quickly disappeared from sight. You melted into the steam among the bodies that all looked alike. I now remember that I kept looking for you in the places I expected you to be, maybe because I knew you were mine and I was yours, and when I lost hope I denied my intuition and gradually forgot you among the bodies that came and went every night. Was that man really Abdel Aziz? Or am I confusing them now while awake, as I confused them while dreaming? There's no way to be sure, other than by trusting my intuition. I hurried back to my clothes and my other things, without even stretching out in front of the old man with bowlegs, for him to massage me as I like. I no longer needed anything from this place. I went out into the night, my mind more at ease. For the first time in years I walked until daybreak, smiling like an idiot. I knew I would pursue that man to the end of the world.

25

I MET ABDEL AZIZ AGAIN, and then again and again. The pretext I would use for contacting him had been obvious to me since that dinner—I would offer to help him and Asma prepare and furnish the apartment they were moving into when they were married. When I plucked up my courage and called him the first time, his voice sounded innocently grateful for my offer. It was the voice of someone unaware of the trap that awaited him, or maybe someone who was deliberately ignoring it.

Merely anticipating my meetings with him made everything different. I spent more time than necessary ensuring my clothes were in matching colors. I wavered before choosing a cologne, and I relished all this indecision. There was a spring in my step, as if I had lost at least half my weight. I suddenly loved life. I went back to joking with everyone, especially Shireen. I played with little Badriya as if I were younger than her. We would roll around on the carpet in her room as I tickled her, blew at the nape of her neck to make funny sounds, and nibbled her stomach till she almost died laughing. From time to time Shireen would throw a quick glance at me as I stood in front of the mirror before a meeting with Abdel Aziz. She observed silently and contentedly. She wanted to ask why I was suddenly and mysteriously so happy, but she held back. I don't know what I could have said if she had asked me. I might have lied and claimed that I was the happiest person in the world because I had everything that any sane man had ever dreamed of, and that was true but it wasn't enough. It wasn't the truth. I wasn't about to say, aloud, my face red from embarrassment and happiness, "I'm in love. I'm in love, Shireen. I love Abdel Aziz, the fiancé of your cousin Asma." I shivered with malicious pleasure when I imagined her reaction.

It was a happiness for which there was no justification as long as nothing obvious had happened, as long as I couldn't be certain. We only had brief meetings in public places or at his apartment in the Digla district of Maadi, with its bare walls and floors. Nothing happened, but I was anticipating events and my imagination was moving at a breathless pace, building up and knocking down, tracing possibilities and setting out plans and scenarios. Even so, just waiting for an appointment with him gave everything a different flavor and made me sing songs, imitating some singer or other to my little female audience— Mother, little Badriya, Shireen, and Somaya the nanny. I would stand by the kitchen door holding a ladle like a microphone and sing to them in a silly imitation of Samira Said's seductive style:

He said he came to me two days later,
Crying his eyes out, complaining of a new love.
He spoke as my fire burned; I heard him as my mind
wandered;
I kept silent, with my heart as a witness.
See how unfair it is, people?
Is that right or is it wrong?
Oh how my feelings were hurt—
These pains of mine are the hardest pains,
And I advise you to be patient, my heart,
Because his love turned out to be delusions.

Then I would bow absurdly low to their applause and cheers, pick up my jacket and keys, and go out. I would smile at the angry drivers around me, stuck at traffic lights that never changed, and they would think I was an idiot or that I was high. I bought all the garlands of jasmine from a girl who was selling them in the street and gave her loads of money, and moved on lightly through life as if I had lost weight without the humiliation of dieting or exercising.

As soon as I met him, I changed. I became another person. I had special powers like the strange creatures in science fiction movies. All my senses sprang into action and worked at full capacity. My eyesight was sharper, and I missed nothing about him, even if it was just a downy hair on his earlobe that was dancing in the wind, and I wanted to kiss the hand of the barber who had left it there when he depilated Abdel Aziz's ears. Yet I wasn't completely detached from reality. I knew when to speak and when to keep quiet, how to make a joke or a witty insinuation, how to tell him a story that on the surface seemed pointless and irrelevant to our conversation but still contained a suggestive element. All he had to do was come down off his faraway branch and take hold of a suggestive kernel, stepping toward my hidden little trap.

I wasn't prepared to listen to anything that might deter me from pursuing my course. I ignored every voice that tried to bring me back to reality, whether from Prince or from within me. At the height of my infatuation I heard about the murder of one of the "luvvies," and the wretched story shook my confidence in the exquisite dream that was taking over my life.

I read the news one morning like everyone else, and I learned more of the details through Prince later, in evenings in the roof garden. The victim was a ballet dancer from a well-known family and they found him at home, lying on a comfortable sofa in front of the television. Blood had spurted from the back of his head and on the wall nearby there was red patch that was turning black. I imagined the murderer holding his face gently to kiss him and then suddenly going crazy and banging the victim's head against the wall, time after time. I remembered the young man when I heard his name. I had seen him briefly several times. Once he had been dancing wildly in a discotheque on the Nile and another time it was New Year's Eve in Alexandria, when I was stunned by the white fur coat he was wearing. I was fascinated by the idea of a white coat that didn't have a single thread of any other color. That night I smiled at him and nodded. Clinging to the arm of a muscular young man, he returned my greeting.

As was usual in such cases, his sexual orientation soon came to light in the investigations, and they arrested all the gay men he knew, in his immediate circle and beyond. They held them for days without charge or justification, and subjected them to all kinds of abuse and pressure until one of them was willing to confess to anything. The news leaked out to the newspapers, which turned the case into a sensational drama about the perversion that is anathema to all religions, about imported phenomena that were alien to our society, and about the natural consequences of such an offense. The vice squad saw it as a promising opportunity and started to carry out random roundups of gay men or suspected gay men in all their usual places. It was in those days that I heard for the first time about the head of the vice squad in Cairo, a man who took special pleasure in hurting and humiliating gay men.

They would hold them for two or three days, then release them as soon as they were referred to the prosecutor's office. It rarely led to real prosecutions. Nevertheless, those who went through the experience told horrible stories about what they had endured in the police stations, about the insults, the beatings, the threats, and the pressure to work as informers for the vice squad. I heard the stories and ignored them. Maybe I thought that such things only happened to other people. I felt protected, but I didn't know why. Maybe Mother would protect me, just by being alive and having connections and money, or maybe my car, which I moved around in all the time, or the tall building I lived in. When I heard about this brutal murder I tried not to think about it, so that I could treasure my newfound sense of joy, and protect it from contamination by any frightening news I might hear. It was like blowing the dirty dust of the world off a chick's clean feathers. A few days later, the victim's fugitive lover returned from Marsa Matrouh, maybe because he couldn't forget the murder scene, with the blood, the victim's startled eyes, and the way that beautiful head had slumped into his hands. He handed himself in and confessed to his crime and that was that. The media didn't focus on the incident for long, perhaps because of the status of the murderer and his victim.

On one occasion Prince linked the murder indirectly to my relationship with Abdel Aziz, which was still in its very early stages. "It's a crime worse than murder when we try to change other people's natures to suit our whims," he said gravely. I gathered that two years earlier the victim of the murder had converted his young lover from the love of women to gay relationships, and that he had first met him as the fiancé of his elder sister's daughter. He managed to snatch the man away from her within weeks. The other man might have been a little curious but at the end of the day he wasn't inclined toward men. I could trace the outlines of the story from start to finish, and it wasn't a pretty tale. I kept imagining the extraordinary white coat spattered with blood, and it wasn't a pleasant sight. Yet I insisted on going all the way with Abdel Aziz, whether as murderer or as victim, it didn't matter.

26

I WAS WAITING FOR HIM, turning this way and that way, rubbing my hands and not knowing what I could do to be sure and then relax. I didn't know if I was the cat or the mouse in this game, but I wanted to put an end to it that day in any way possible. I started looking through my arsenal of secret weapons in the hope of finding the right one. I was ready for anything other than drowning, anything other than giving up and walking away from the beach defeated, without even paddling in the water. But my arsenal was completely bare, just when I needed it most. My weapons had vanished into thin air, leaving me defenseless to confront a youthful death. Looking at the office wall in front of me, I suddenly had a distant memory of a drowned boy's body washed up on the beach under the midmorning sun. The hair had hardly sprouted in his armpits and his upper lip was still smooth. That death was as beautiful as the dark man from Minya in his thirties, who had just come into my office in a formal white shirt and an expensive tie, with a broad smile under his thick trimmed mustache.

I started making small talk, in order to avoid saying the only thing I wanted to say. I didn't even know what I was talking about. I was just trying to distract his attention so that he wouldn't notice that I wasn't in my normal state and that when I looked at him I was thinking this would be my last chance to see his face or that I might never see it again at such close quarters, if he finds out, if I confess. My fragmented conversation continued, from my office to the elevator to his car. And all the time I was forcing myself to keep my eyes off him, off his mustache and the little triangle of hair under his lower lip, wondering how it would feel on my tongue. Then there was the cleft in his chin, a short, nearly invisible line that divided his chin in half. I looked away from him, then gave in and looked back to feast on the sight of his face. Surprising myself, and surprising him, I said, "Ever since the engagement party, I've had a feeling that I've seen you before, but I can't remember when or where."

I now remember the remark with embarrassment. It was such a cheap cliché, such a timeworn pickup line. I had often used it to pick up men but this was probably the first time I had used it sincerely. He kept nodding and smiling, without noticing the interrogative tone in my voice. When I stopped talking awhile, he said we might have met in a public place sometime, because it's a small world. I wanted to tell him it was both a public and a private place at the same time, and you were half-naked and half-drunk or stoned. And you took my lips in your lips as you went past me, without me asking anything of you or seducing you. You simply leaned toward me and kissed me. I can still remember the taste of your saliva.

I took my T-shirt off, pretending to find the extreme heat annoying. I was with him in the large apartment, which was now flooded with light after some clutter had been removed and before the new windows had been installed. We were swimming in a pool of August daylight, so I kept my sunglasses on. I wasn't wearing anything under the T-shirt and I wasn't shy about the shape of my breasts, which were like women's breasts, with round clove-colored nipples like two ripe grapes. Despite the light hairs here and there between them, my upper body was waxy white. I went up to him, close enough that we could smell each other or that I could touch his body gently. Then I moved away immediately, before my closeness might start to annoy him, and also so that he could see me and I could see him and notice every change, however small, that might reveal a change in his state of mind. With excitement I noted his unease as he fidgeted where he stood, not knowing where to lay his eyes, what to do with his hands, or where to stand, while I pretended to be busy examining the place. Then I would go up to him and maneuver him back against a wall or into a corner, as in some comical chase. I was in a crazy mood that day—it was drowning or nothing. I took off my dark glasses and exposed my eyes to the light. Everything was clear and dazzling but I stared fearlessly, with my eyes wide open.

We stood next to each other, smoking a cigarette at the open part of a large window facing the street. I put my hand on his shoulder and rubbed it for a while in silence, putting everything I wanted to say into my fingers. I sneaked a look at his crotch and noticed a bulge that suggested an erection, not a full erection as straight as an arrow, but there was an intention, an idea, a fragile bud. I felt reinvigorated.

Without knowing what I was doing, I found myself moving away from him, spinning like a dancer, then stopping suddenly in the middle of the large, empty reception room. I gave a long whoop of joy at the top of my voice. The echoes of my whoop died away and an embarrassing silence fell. I looked at his face, which was full of surprise and alarm. "What's up with you, Hani?" he asked.

I laughed. I didn't know how to respond. Between my nervous laughs I muttered something inane about the bridal apartment and how it needed at least one whoop of joy. His big brown face flushed, maybe because of the heat, maybe from surprise or anger, or maybe from excitement. His broad nostrils flared like an angry bull's. I had to physically restrain myself from throwing myself at him. The light was intoxicating too, and that was a new discovery.

He started acting evasive, glowering and smoking one cigarette after another. I approached him warily, as if quite unintentionally, and touched his arm gently as I spoke to him. The tip of his cigarette touched my skin for a moment, and I winced in pain. He shied away, stumbled on some cardboard boxes on the floor, and fell, banging his head on the edge of a column and injuring himself. A few drops of blood trickled out. It was a minor incident with no loss of life and no bad intentions on either side, yet it had many consequences. He sat down in silence and put his hand on the cut. I leaned over to examine the cut, fetched some water, and washed it, but it was still bleeding a little. He called the security people in the building and asked them to buy him something to bandage the minor injury.

I sat down on the floor next to him, my torso bare. I could smell his sweat, his perfume, his blood, and the smoke from his cigarette. He could also clearly smell my body, but he seemed uninterested, a little uncomfortable at this close proximity, focused wholly on the cigarettes he kept lighting. After some minutes of embarrassed silence, both of us said "I'm sorry" at exactly the same moment.

The coincidence was a surprise. He may have wanted to apologize for burning me with the cigarette end and I wanted to apologize for him falling over and hurting himself. Maybe we were apologizing for something completely different, something that it was no longer possible to avoid or ignore. We laughed, disconcerted by the little coincidence. Pulling himself together, he said, "You unnerved me and made me fall over."

"I fell first," I replied slyly.

He ignored my innuendo, and we sat there in silence until the doorbell rang. I opened it to find a tall, thin young man that the security people had summoned from a nearby pharmacy. He was carrying bandages and disinfectant and was ready for work. The man's laughing almond-shaped eyes jumped from one of us to the other, looking at my bare chest and the small amount of blood on Abdel Aziz's head. "It's nothing serious," he said, slightly puzzled by the scene.

He disinfected the cut, bandaged it slowly and carefully, and gave Abdel Aziz instructions, smiling all the time as though harboring a pleasant surprise for us. Before leaving, he stood between us hesitantly while he plucked up courage, and then out of the blue announced, "By the way, I'm a poet. Would you like to hear a poem?"

He didn't wait for an answer. He had already thrust his hand into the pocket of his worn and tattered jeans to pull out a folded piece of paper. He quickly unfolded it and proceeded to recite his lengthy poem till the last line. All I remember of it now is one line: "One day we will find out that we have run away from ourselves, only to find ourselves."

We laughed and laughed as we drove away.

27

I didn't hurry things along, despite my impatience. Any reckless step could have unraveled the web I was weaving before it was tight. I left him free to decide when and where we met. I joined him and Asma soberly on trips to look at furniture and choose wallpaper, curtains, tiles, and so on. I worked with good humor, proving to them that I was a valuable asset and that if it wasn't for me they would have paid many times more for materials that were not of the quality required. I took them to stores they didn't even know existed and introduced them to simple craftsmen who could do fine work with natural materials. In my mind I was furnishing a love nest for Abdel Aziz and myself, not an apartment for him and his fiancée, indifferent to whatever might happen in this melodrama after their marriage. Shireen noticed my unusual enthusiasm. "I don't remember you doing all this when we were getting married," she said.

She took the opportunity to ask for some renovations in our apartment too, and I agreed without hesitation. If she had asked me for anything else, I wouldn't have refused, because I realized that a happy lover is like a happy drunk, willing to cut off one of his fingers as he sings and give it to anyone who asks for it.

His tolerance of my overtures now seemed unjustified unless he was willing to reciprocate. Why else would he not rebuff all the coded messages I had sent him or the casual physical contact that I tried to disguise as the kind of contact that would be fairly normal between colleagues or friends, though in my case it was charged with the pangs of desire? Why didn't he say anything about all this? And if he was willing to respond, why did he look away? Eye contact was the only thing he wasn't prepared to face. Maybe he felt that acknowledging my glances and reading the message behind them would amount to an irreversible and irrefutable confession. I said words with my mouth, while with my eyes I told him: "You've been discovered. Try another trick," or "Why are you frightened? Let's try!" He was content to play along, complicit in my game, or maybe he enjoyed being the object of admiration of this effeminate man in his forties. No, not brotherly admiration, Abdel Aziz. You know desire. You must have come across the word on more than one occasion in your work as a writer and journalist.

I was overjoyed when I managed to make him laugh and could hear his nervous chuckle. He would throw his head back, close his eyes, and knit his eyebrows as if laughing embarrassed him or hurt him. We chatted nineteen to the dozen whenever we went out on an excursion, usually in his car, in a furniture showroom, or in a pizzeria we had discovered and that we both loved, along with other kinds of pastries and cakes. At every step along the way the list of things we had in common grew longer. I snatched them from the air like a well-trained dog. I knew that such things were the bridge that would bring us together. Not just the things we had shared since meeting, but our separate memories that we would have shared if we had met five or ten years earlier, or if we had grown up together and the love between us had grown as we grew. Where were we at the time of the 1992 earthquake? The first movie we ever saw in the cinema? The year of our final exams in secondary school? Amr Diab, Samira Said, and Angham albums. The first time we got drunk and ran away from home and stories of the bad company we had kept. And finally came our shared interest in astrology, one more element in the conventional friendship we constructed as the facade for another kind of friendship—one that as far as I was concerned included desire that was like a flame, hotter than the scorching August streets around us.

On one occasion in his car we sang together an old Amr Diab song:

I tried to stay away from you but I couldn't.
I tried to forget what happened between us but I couldn't.
I tried hard but my heart wept at me and drove me mad,
And I ended up lost in gloomy regrets, regrets that grew and grew.

When the song ended, and we had finished singing along with it, we broke into raucous laughter like a couple of madmen. I touched his shoulder gently for no particular reason, and he ignored the touch and took a deep breath. That was a precious moment that held the promise of everything . . . almost everything.

Then the music stopped, right in the middle of a crescendo, and Abdel Aziz disappeared. At first I thought he must have unexpected commitments, that everything would get back on track sooner or later, and we would resume our outings and our meetings. But the separation grew longer day by day, without any reasons stated. Eventually there were no longer any appointments he could cancel and the calls from him stopped completely, all within a matter of a few days.

I felt betrayed and thought he had decided on his own that the game was over. From Asma, through Shireen, I heard excuses such as "Because he's very busy these days, Hani," and "He's going to a workshop in Germany soon and he's getting ready," and then came the final blow: "He feels that he's been too much trouble to you recently so he decided to have an interior designer finish off the apartment." Been too much trouble? It was like a massive slap in the face when I had my hands tied behind my back. Did he suddenly feel he had gone beyond the proper limits and that he had been too accommodating toward this clown? Had he fallen into a trap unnecessarily? I wanted to understand, but I refrained from contacting him, not out of pride so much as because I was worried I might put an end to the brief interlude by creating an embarrassing scene. Maybe I held out hopes of another chance, of explaining, of a door or window that would suddenly open in the black wall I faced.

My hope was a disfigured child, born old and malevolent, who sat with me every night and shared a drink in dark, noisy bars that I frequented only after I had already started to get drunk in other places that were clean and respectable. In these cheap places I could smell my father on the clothes of the customers. It didn't matter who dragged who into conversation, or what stories I made up for them every night to explain my sighs of anguish when I heard the songs of Umm Kulthoum. When there was a stranger at my table or I joined someone else's table, the disfigured child followed me like my pet and never stopped talking, strewing possibilities and hypotheses in my direction and making insinuations in a hoarse voice: maybe he's depressed, maybe he needs time to come out of the closet and admit his sexual orientation. Don't underestimate a decision such as this, Hani. Not everyone has the courage to live with their various inclinations. The world is full of prisoners. In fact, the world is a big prison.

However much I told that disfigured child to shut up, it wouldn't obey, so I sang with Umm Kulthoum and invited strangers to another round of beers, all the time resisting an urgent impulse to get in touch with him and abuse him or beg him, asking for another meeting. I only succumbed once, when I sent him a message with a line from a song that was playing in the bar: "Who can I go to, to save me from your injustice?" I simply put the question to him, and the next morning I regretted it so much that I wanted to hit myself with a shoe. The disfigured old child was with me on the bed and wouldn't stop saying, "Maybe he's gone to Germany, as they said, and when he comes back and sees the message and imagines the torment and pain that lie behind it he will relent and confess and get in touch with you. He might, perhaps, maybe . . . ." And however many pillows I put on the face of this hideous creature and however hard I tried to suffocate it, it never stopped pestering me with whispered suspicions.

I was lost. Unthinkingly, I drove to strange places that were far from my usual itinerary. Or I would stand in the elevator for minutes without pressing any button and without noticing, until other people called the elevator up or down. I floated in a void without a compass and was hardly ever sober. Despite some doubts, the certainty that was born on that day in their apartment never flagged, not for a moment.

I couldn't suppress my pain anymore. Fighting back tears, I told Prince. He took me to his little office, which was always full of surprising smells from exotic countries I couldn't identify. My eyes teared up when I heard my voice mentioning Abdel Aziz's name as I tried to put what had happened over the past days into coherent words. The whole thing seemed too trivial to distress me in this way. I was irritated by the way Prince looked at me; he seemed to be saying, "Didn't I tell you? Didn't I warn you?"

When he finally spoke, he said, "Our friend, this Abdel Aziz, even if he really does have genuine inclinations, has decided to continue with the lie, and if your overtures have unsettled him, he doesn't know how to react. Should he come out of the darkness of the closet into the light that you have revealed to him and confront his desires, or should he stay as he is for the rest of his life, and tell himself he'd rather be safe than sorry?" Prince advised me to forget the whole subject, and the sooner I forgot it the better for everyone. He also prescribed moderate doses of partying and pleasure.

I acted on his advice, but the doses I took were not at all moderate. I plunged into sex and drinking like a rabid dog, as though a phantom were pursuing me—a phantom so tame and beautiful that it was hard for me to run away from it. And then, once when I was drunk, I went off with a young man I imagined had a distant resemblance to Abdel Aziz. I picked him up, or he picked me up, toward dawn in a third-rate nightclub, and then I forgot myself and took the risk of going with him to a cheap hotel that he knew. In the taxi that took us there, I remember that I called him Abdel Aziz and started asking him where he had been hiding for so long. He just laughed.

As soon as the door of the hotel room was closed, he started beating me up and took all the money I had on me, including the coins, as well as my cigarettes and my cell phone. I wept and begged him to leave me the lighter, because it was a keepsake from my father. I bowed and tried to kiss his hand. He didn't notice it was silver and he threw it onto the toilet seat. I hurried over to pick it up and he saw me off with a kick in the ass and a final pledge that he would purge the country of faggots like me.

I tried not to attract the attention of the young man at the reception desk but the way he looked at me suggested that he understood everything. He went back to focusing on the television screen, which was showing a Robin Williams comedy. I left the hotel frightened and lost, but luckily I came across a kindhearted taxi driver and told him I had been mugged and that I would pay his fare and more when we arrived. He took me to the office, where I found some money in a drawer of my desk. As soon as he left, I finally burst into tears in front of the bathroom mirror and slapped my cheeks, almost drawing blood with my fingernails.

28

IT WAS BADRIYA'S BIRTHDAY PARTY. I left the children and retired to the balcony on the pretext that I wanted to smoke, taking my coffee with me. I slumped into a rattan chair like a corpse. I had turned into a depressive old man overnight, since the robbery incident, which Shireen had heard about without the embarrassing details. My vigor was sapped and I stayed home, managing the company solely by phone calls. Shireen put up with my mood swings with a patience that embarrassed me on some days and was so unbearable on others that I wished we could have a furious argument and insult each other. I looked at the people walking along the street under the building, laughing and chatting on their phones, and I wished them all a slow death.

Little Badriya came onto the balcony with a cloth puppet over her right hand. Imitating the voice of a cartoon character that I didn't recognize, she said, "Everyone wants Hani. Come on, Hani! Come on, Hani!"

Another child followed her, and then two more, joining her in her chant. At first I smiled at them and was about to throw away the cigarette and join them, but I felt too lazy. Suddenly I was terrified of these little creatures with their faces painted in bright colors to look like animals. Their high-pitched shouting and manic enthusiasm frightened me. I imagined they had been sent from hell to torment me. Calmly I told them to go away now and said I would join them shortly, after I had finished my cigarette and my coffee, but Badriya started to lead them in another round of ever more frantic chanting: "Come on, Hani! Come on, Hani!"

"Enough of that!" I shouted, without thinking what I was doing.

A silence fell and the other children scurried off the balcony in alarm, while Badriya stood looking at me in amazement for a few moments. She suddenly shuddered and screwed up her face as if she were about to burst into tears. I threw the cigarette away and was about to get up and hug her, but she disappeared in a flash. She didn't want to talk to me despite all my attempts and, in tears, she stayed in her room with Shireen.

The atmosphere was completely ruined. I took my car keys and fled the scene of my crime. After driving around, I ended up in a hotel bar, far from everyone. In a mirror behind the counter I saw someone I didn't recognize, though he did look like me. I told my lookalike in the mirrors behind the lines of bottles that I shouldn't allow myself to poison their lives any more than I had already, so I should keep away from them. I told myself that my little outburst that day might be followed by things that would be more dangerous to the little girl, who was blameless in all this. I decided to leave home and live by myself somewhere else, even if I had to claim that this was on the advice of my psychiatrist.

While walking half-drunk through the downtown streets after midnight, I remembered my old loneliness, my innocent loneliness. It may be the point at which this story began—a young boy alone in a big apartment, his mother always out, speaking to imaginary brothers, inventing disagreements and reconciliations with them. The strange thing is that for a moment that isolation had a pleasant taste again, but this time it would not be the isolation of an adolescent in his family's apartment. No, I would set off into the world like a stray bullet. I might separate with Shireen and she might find herself a real man. Even the company could be wound up and closed down, because in fact it was just a respectable pastime for the son of a famous actress, so that people didn't see him as a lay-about living on his mother's wealth.

While I was making my plans and imagining how I would put them into effect step by step, I heard a clear voice calling me. It was Omar Nour in the middle of a late-night drinking spree. He welcomed me, gave me a hug, and introduced me to some of his friends and colleagues. They said they were celebrating the fact he was leaving for Kuwait in two days to work on a newspaper there. Everyone was happy and singing, so I thought I would take refuge with them from my personal hell. I soon ended up with them in a large apartment in Bab al-Luq, where a German woman lived with her Egyptian boy-friend. I abandoned myself to the noise and the drinking, and danced like crazy.

I remember that at a certain moment I was sitting on the floor crying, with a foreign woman speaking Arabic nearby. She patted my shoulder and massaged my head as I told her about Abdel Aziz, until I collapsed on the spot, dead to the world. I woke up midmorning and found myself lying on the carpet among strange bodies, cans of beer, empty wine bot-tles, and bowls overflowing with cigarette butts. I washed my face and sneaked out. After drinking a coffee in a nearby cof-fee shop and racking my brain, I remembered where I had parked my car the night before.

Before I could carry out any of the steps in my plan to escape and keep my distance, Mother had a serious heart attack and I came around from my adolescent fantasies. All my brave plans fell apart as if they had never existed, and the only thing that mattered to me was the sudden danger that I might lose my mother. For ages I hadn't considered this possibility at all. I had thought of her as immortal, maybe from the time Aunt Husniya had died. But now we were car-rying her out on a gurney, and prying eyes behind windows took pleasure in seeing a once-powerful woman lying on her back, tied down with straps. I just couldn't imagine her ceasing to exist. I said she would recover, that it was just a temporary setback to her health. I spontaneously looked up to heaven in tears and pleaded with God, reproaching myself for having moved away from Him all these years. I asked for His mercy and forgiveness, not for my sake but for hers. Then I thought again and admitted to myself that I needed her to live more than she did. As if God were right in front of me, I begged Him to spare my mother for me, if only for a few more years, until I was strong enough and ready to part with her, if ever I could.

After she left intensive care, I would sit by her side reading the Quran in a whisper or steal snatches of sleep in the visitors' room, which was piled high with bunches of flowers sent by famous people. That's all that most of her acquaintances did, and only a handful took the trouble to visit her—an actress from her generation or one from the next generation who cultivated her image as a woman of compassion. Then Adel al-Murr, her former secret husband, turned up looking like a very old man. His hands were trembling all the time, and he was leaning on both his stick and the arm of a handsome grandson of his. At first I was upset to have him visiting my mother but I soon laughed at myself and felt grateful for his visit, which finally made her smile as she went over pleasant memories with him. It was he who spoke, while she laughed with difficulty.

"Do you remember Ismail Arar, the lighting guy whose body produced electricity?" he asked. "I remember once we set him on Madiha Gouda because she didn't want to work. He touched her elbow and shoulder, giving her electric shocks, and she was screaming and saying, 'Okay, damn it, I will go and act, but get him off me!'"

With Mother he only brought up things that weren't embarrassing—things to do with their work together and pleasant memories, stories they weren't embarrassed to tell in front of his grandson and me. We stayed in the background in silence, exchanging friendly looks from time to time. He planted a kiss on her hand before going, and tears glistened in her ashen eyes. I watched him walk off down the corridor in a silk suit as white as the little hair he had left.

As soon as Mother had recovered a little and could get up, go to the bathroom, and perform her prayers while seated, she insisted on coming back home, indifferent to the doctors' advice that she needed care and observation during her recuperation. She overruled us all and was content to have just one nurse visit her at home every day. I thanked God for answering my prayers, and I had every intention of being grateful for those divine blessings to which I had been blinded by my foolish obsession with the knight of my dreams.

It was like a celebration, with all of us gathered around Mother, meeting her slightest desires for some days, until the afternoon of that inauspicious Friday in September, less than two weeks after she had come out of hospital. She was sitting on her favorite sofa with fruit and the remote control on the table in front of her, holding the latest issue of the magazine *Radio and Television*, tracking the lines with her magnifying glass held up close to the page. Without lifting her eyes off the magazine, she mumbled, "Hey kids, they're going to show the serial *Saqiyat al-ayyam* from the first of the month. We have to record it this time."

"We'll record it every day, Mother. That's one of your finest roles," Shireen replied immediately.

Silence reigned in the living room for some minutes, till Mother lowered the magnifying glass, put it on her lap, and lifted her nose a little as if sniffing the air. "What's that nice smell, Shireen?" she asked. "Did you light some incense?"

Shireen looked at me and said she hadn't lit any incense, but if Mother wanted, she could fumigate the room with incense. Mother wagged her finger to say no, but insisted she could smell something very pleasant. "It's like a rose garden floating in the air, kids," she said.

We smiled, unsure what to say. She smiled back at us and then, as we watched, her head abruptly slumped forward onto her chest.

29

I TOOK PART IN THE various acts of the funeral drama without shedding a single tear. I played my role perfectly when I prayed for my mother in the Kawakbi mosque in Agouza. Then the coffin left for the Basatin cemetery. I was surprised that the unknown director had managed to muster all these actors and crowds at such short notice, then put them in place so skillfully and have them identify with their roles so successfully.

I knew she was now hidden in that box, covered with a drape embroidered with Quranic verses in gold thread, making fun of us all. With them I laid Mother's body on her white linen shroud, and took it down into the women's enclosure in the family vault. I was convinced I was dreaming. Everything would come to an end in a few minutes. I would wake up lazily and leave my bedroom to find Mother in her favorite place on the sofa. That's why I was so fearless. I was playing a role with Mother and all the time I was having an imaginary conversation with her, and together we were making fun of everything happening around us. We were shooting her last movie, and she had insisted that I take part in it. "My son has promising talent," she told them. "Give him a chance." But would the director fire me if I still couldn't cry?

I stood there receiving condolences, Mother, as if you really had died. Everyone wore black and some of them played their roles well. They even cried and hung their heads on their chests as they sobbed. Then they stood in front of the cameras to say a word or two about the late actress. Toward the end of the condolences session, I sat down for a moment to relax, smoke a cigarette, and ask myself when Mother would turn up, stick her tongue out at them, and make fun of them all. I shut my eyes and listened to the famous Quran reader repeating verses from the Maryam chapter, ringing all the possible changes. My mind wandered for a while. In my reverie I saw Mother's face as she had been thirty years earlier, smiling at me as she tried on a new dress I remembered well—a Chinese-style dress with a row of buttons running at an angle down the front, made of satin and printed with large bright flowers. As she spun around on her high heels, she asked me, "Ha, so what do you think, Mr. Hani?"

Before little Hani could answer her, I felt a hand touching my shoulder. I opened my eyes to see Abdel Aziz standing next to me, looking at me with honest sympathy. He offered me his condolences and told me that he had arrived back from Germany only a few hours ago and that otherwise he would have been by my side from the first moment. He could have been anyone else who had come to offer his condolences. Mother's last movie had undermined all his magic and allure. My little dream about my mother had turned my head and I was almost euphoric, confident she hadn't really died. All the time I was wondering when all these people would leave. When could I be alone with Mother again, to tell her what I thought of her beautiful Chinese dress?

I slept alone in her bedroom for days, taking in the smell of her clothes, teetering on the brink of madness. Sometimes I felt that the time had come to cry, if only a few tears. Only then could I admit that Mother had died and that I was crying for her. Only then could I release all the anger and fear inside me. I gathered up the old photo albums, the family videos and CDs of her performances, her letters and postcards. I packed up these treasures and decided to cut myself off from the world in the office until I could cry. I gave the staff indefinite paid leave and made sure I had an adequate stock of whisky. Then I camped there, switching between the old video player and the computer screen.

I started with the oldest documents, from the time when the sisters, Badriya and Husniya, were budding performers with ivory complexions and honey-colored eyes. I went inside the photographs and spoke to them, and we laughed. I heard their laughter echo around me. They confided many things to me as we drank glass after glass together, about the days when they dipped bread in oil because they didn't have any other food, about waiting for their dresses to dry, about the single kohl pencil and the single tube of lipstick they had, about their joy at their first speaking role in a movie, about the groping they had to put up with from actors and studio workers.

Over the next few days I switched from photograph to movie to serial without a tear ever wetting my eyes despite the whisky, the solitude, and the confinement. I often saw her among the specters of my drunkenness: she was vivid, alive, and more tangible than everything around me. She laughed, came up to me, and wrapped her fur with pistachio-green feathers around my neck. There was nothing in the whole world but me and her.

Make me weep, O Lord, so I can escape this delirium and accept that Mother is dead and have a rest. How I had wept in the past, for the most trivial of reasons, and now I couldn't. I went from room to room in the company offices with my glass in my hand, half-clothed, without a ray of light seeping in from the outside, talking to myself. If I couldn't cry, I'd rather die. She had been there at home all those last years, while I was loose on the streets, madly following my desires and seeking my pleasure, and now where was she? Then I addressed Mother: show yourself, appear, Badriya, Badridar, Badara, enough of playing coy. Where are you hiding? Have you really gone to the Lord as well? Then I addressed God: "Take me, now that You've taken her. How can You leave me alone like this, when You knew that I didn't have anyone else and that I am the weakest person in the world without her? Why her? She was devoted to worshipping You night and day, and she was charitable to the poor and the wretched, so why have You taken her from me?"

After I don't know how many days Shireen couldn't take any more anxiety, especially as I had turned off my cell phone and disconnected the landlines at the office. She had to check on me through the doorman, who told her how I was, based on brief encounters whenever I asked him to go and buy things for me. When she dared to come and visit me, I almost threw her out. She noticed I was drunk and mentally disturbed and that the office was in chaos, so she panicked and started to appeal to others for help. She spoke to Asma and told her she was terrified that I had been in such a state for so long and that I might do something to myself. Asma suggested that Abdel Aziz come to see me in the office and try to talk me out of this reclusive and overindulgent form of mourning.

At noon one day I woke up to the sound of the door-bell ringing persistently. I got up from the sofa, irritated and ready to explode at the doorman or whoever it was. I opened the door and found Abdel Aziz standing in front of me with a solemn expression on his face, like someone on an official mission. I was taken aback and thought of several things at the same moment: my unshaved face, my puffy and bloodshot eyes, my anger toward him, as if he were the hidden reason why my mother had died, and about how I wanted to cry right now if I could. Several moments passed before I invited him in. I closed the door and turned to him. He took me in his arms all at once and started to rub my back with compassion.

I stood immobile for some moments, unwilling to hug him back. But I breathed in a familiar smell from his body and it surged through my bloodstream, like the smell of my father. Only then did the miracle happen. Small pools of tears gathered in the corners of my eyes and I almost gasped for joy when I felt that I was finally close to crying. I then embraced him too, clung to him, and let the tears flow gently, without any sobbing. It was just lines of salty water running down my face. But within seconds the pace picked up, and I started heaving and whimpering on his chest. "My mother died when I was eight years old," I heard him whisper in a trembling voice, his hot breath on my bare neck.

He joined in the crying as we hugged each other. We stayed like that for maybe ten minutes. It seemed like a whole lifetime of mourning, and neither of us was weeping just for the loss of a mother, whether a few days ago or decades ago. We were also weeping at the loneliness we had lived through and that was still with us, but this time we did so together.

30

I T   W A S   T H E   F I R S T   T I M E in my life I had seen it raining in May.
This was after they moved us to Tora Agricultural Prison. We
had appeared before the prosecutors, who decided to extend
our detention pending further investigations.

On arrival they made us stand in the yard in two lines, and
it was then that it suddenly rained for a few minutes, despite the
May heat. I still haven't seen any explanation. I remember that
Karim Saadoun looked up furtively to catch some of the big
warm raindrops. Some of them slid down the lines in his weary
face. The hint of a pained smile had hardly flickered on his lips
when a massive slap landed on the back of his neck, accompanied by a large dose of insults. It was the end of the day and,
although they didn't spare us the obligatory ministrations with
their tongues, fists, and boots, they didn't seem to have the time
or the energy to give us a proper reception, so they postponed
that till daybreak. They soon stuffed us all, more than fifty
men, into a room that hardly had space for twenty. There was
no light and nothing to cover a floor that was splattered with
dried shit. I fell asleep anyway from exhaustion and woke up
to something crawling on my neck. I sprang to attention and
grabbed the large spider in my hands. I wanted to talk to it, to
ask it why it and all its kin had been singling me out for pursuit
rather than everyone else, ever since I was a child. A single spider seemed to have been weaving the thread of my life since I
was born, and would leave me only when I died.

In the morning the guards took us out and ordered us to strip down to our underwear. They stopped in front of one man who looked unusually effeminate and ordered him to take off all his clothes, possibly to make sure they didn't have a real female as a guest in their cells. When he covered his shriveled little penis with his hands, they hit him and told him to take his hands away. When they saw it they had a good laugh at it. Then they handed us over to the prison barber, who looked rather like the handsome actor Abdel Salam Mohamed, famous for playing the jester in a play by Yousef Idris. Abdel Salam had visited my mother at the Shamm al-Nisim spring festival a few months before he died and had eaten the traditional salted mullet, kippers, and onions. Pleasant and affable, he never stopped laughing and joking. But our barber was nothing like that. He had a hideous, venomous, jaundiced face and kept insulting us and hitting us on the head with his clippers. "I'll have to burn all my gear," he said every now and then. "No doubt you all have AIDS and you'll infect all the innocent prisoners."

Then the orgy of beatings began, at the hands of other prisoners who had been ordered to attack us. I don't know how long it lasted but when it was over and I was quite sure I no longer had to protect my head with my hands and curl up in a ball on the ground, almost completely naked, I felt like the happiest person in existence simply because it had stopped. The pain felt normal and tolerable now that the assault was over.

We had to be sorted out somehow, in case we resumed our debauchery on government premises. They divided us into two cells, one for the married men and one for the others, on the premise that this was the only reliable way to separate the passive homosexuals from the active. They were uncertain how to deal with an unmarried man who had the physique of a champion bodybuilder and was called either Wissam or Bassam, I no longer remember. His appearance didn't suggest any sexual deviance, so the officer simply decided to put him in a room by himself, isolated from all the others, until his status could be determined. For the next three days this young man was held alone in a tiny room for twenty-four hours a day, until he almost went crazy and screamed at them to put him with the others, either with the bachelors or the married men. I acted quickly and tried to persuade a sergeant in whom I detected a trace of kindness to put the muscleman with the married men and put me with the bachelors. After a short discussion he agreed. All I wanted was to be in the same cell as Karim. As soon as Karim saw me coming into the cell, he stood up and greeted me at the door like someone greeting a long-lost brother. I rested my head on his shoulder and cried, and he patted my back with affection. We ignored the silly comments from here and there in the room about us and the film *Love in the Prison Cell*.

We spent a whole month trapped in that cell and if it hadn't been for the lavish amounts of money that Prince dispersed, I would have starved to death before I died of shame, claustrophobia, or dark thoughts. They opened the cell door only once or twice a day, to give us our rations and the food that some of us had been sent. The guards had dug their fingers into the bowls of rice, the inside of the loaves of bread, the packets of cheese, and all the other dishes we received, to check for drugs, sharp instruments, or SIM cards for cell phones. But despite the searches some pills did slip through— whether with the guards' connivance or behind their backs I don't know—and some of the warders would secretly pass on to me a few five- or ten-pound notes to help me out with necessities, thanks to Prince, of course.

There was water in the bathroom for only one hour a day, between five and six o'clock in the afternoon, so every day arguments would break out at that time over who could go in to wash his clothes and his bowl and cutlery. A senior prisoner would settle any arguments that arose, usually based on his personal preferences. Karim, Mohamed Sukkar, and I learned to give way, doing the impossible not to provoke anyone. We filled our bottles one way or another during that one-hour period, however much we were abused or harassed, but for the rest of the day we were not immune from attempts to seize our bottles. Later, when the other prisoners realized that I was ill and that someone in authority had given orders that no one should stand in my way, they started treating me with more circumspection, maybe even pampering me a little and trying to please me.

They gave out one blanket per person and when we went to sleep we used our shoes as pillows. We covered ourselves with half of the blanket and laid the other half on the floor to ward off the dampness of the concrete, which we could feel in our bones at night. There were no visits, no letters, no contact of any kind with the outside world, and for several weeks, I don't know how long, the only air we were allowed to breathe was the putrid air in the cell. After that, for just two hours a day, one hour in the morning and one hour at the end of the day, they let us out, not into the open air of the courtyard but only into the corridors between the cells. I remember how happy I was with every minute of those breaks, as I took in breath after breath of pure air, leaning against the wall and hardly moving my body.

The various cells at Tora Prison contained some bright stars in the worlds of crime, terrorism, and opposition to the regime. President Sadat's assassins were serving their life sentences there and there were plenty of people from the Muslim Brotherhood, including their leader at that time, as well as extremists, Egyptians, and foreigners, who belonged to various organizations, such as al-Qaeda and other jihadi groups I had only heard about on television. I saw many of them after they allowed us out every day. I saw men with long beards coming together to exercise, and I also saw how discussion groups were formed between their various schools of thought and between them and the liberals and the leftists, who were fewer in number. Besides all those, there were Christians who had converted to Islam, and Muslims who had converted to Christianity, and others who had been detained for countless other reasons. We were all colors of the rainbow, an extraordinary mix brought together by just one thing—the fact that our masters were angry with us, whether that anger was justified and had legitimate motives, or simply because they didn't like the look of us.

In the midst of all this, Karim was the only window that God gave me through which I could look out at something different, something that offset and subverted all the ugliness. Looking furtively at Karim's face became one of my habits in prison. His voice was like a radio station in my head that consoled and reassured me. I no longer cared whether his extraordinary stories were events that had really happened to him or were as fantastical as the vision of the blond Kurdish lad who would defeat all religions in order to advance the cause of Lot's people in the end times.

Karim started telling these stories only when I asked him, one dark night that I remember well. It was after an argument that I unintentionally provoked in the cell. The initial disagreement arose when two men who traded in prescription drugs competed over who would sell me what I needed. It was clear to everyone that I depended on the pills to breathe easily and go to sleep. After I and the guard on duty agreed that he would supply me with them, another man approached my mattress with a large bottle of water he wanted to sell me as a decoy, while secretly slipping me two Apetryl pills as a gift to win my business. I don't know how word of this reached the guard, but a fight broke out in the cramped space, with followers of the two men scrapping with each other for some time before calming down to patch up their injuries and get their breath back. That night Said the Skull had taken a massive quantity of pills and in the middle of the fighting and the chaos, he just stood up, and went to a plastic bag hanging on a nail above my bed, which contained some loaves of white bread, cheese, olives, tins of tuna, and a few vegetables—my food that one of the guards brought from time to time and that I shared with Karim and Mohamed Sukkar, because none of their friends or relatives had yet asked after them.

Said took the bag despite Mohamed Sukkar shouting at him and our disapproving looks. Then Karim stood up and tried to stop Said, whereupon Said gave Karim's beautiful face a slap that echoed across the cell. "Didn't we tell you to turn the television down a little, you bastards? I can't sleep because of you," Said told him.

Of course there wasn't a television in the cell and Said was imagining himself at home with his younger brothers, or that's what some people guessed from what he said before and after the argument. Karim stared at him with tearful, stunned eyes, then came back cowed to his bed by my side. As the whole cell laughed in derision, the guard on duty sent someone over to hit Said the Skull on the head repeatedly with his fist in the hope of bringing him to his senses. He took the bag of food from him and gave it back to us. Said did come to his senses for some moments but he quickly relapsed. "You come and hit me in my own home as well?" he said.

Everyone laughed again, and they laughed even more a little later when Said called out to his sister Huda and told her to prepare a bite for him and his guests to eat. Even Karim laughed, wiped a couple of tears away, and asked me for permission to make Said a sandwich. Yes, I saw Karim Saadoun splitting a baguette open with his fingers, putting cheese and pieces of tomato inside, then standing up, walking over to Said's mattress, and giving him the sandwich. Said, off in his own little world and moved by his little sister's kindness, said, "Very kind of you, Huda. I'll find you a husband, God willing."

The roars of laughter and wisecracks filled the cell from floor to ceiling for quite a while. That same night I was so tired

190

that the pills I had started taking to excess had no effect. When Karim hadn't said anything for ages, I asked him to talk, to tell me about his life or anything else so that I could escape my dark thoughts and go to sleep. From that night on his whispered stories continued, until we emerged from the depths of that grave about seven months later.

That night, lying on his back, his gaze fixed on the ceiling as if he could see something there that no one else could see, Karim said, "Once upon a time there was a boy called Karim, who lived in a small town south of Tanta called Khorset. It's an old Pharaonic name, meaning the place where Set, the god of evil, was worshipped. Imagine people worshipping the god of evil. Would they act like him too?"

He smiled at his musing and his dimples showed.

31

KARIM NEVER SAW HIS FATHER, except in an old photo that his mother kept among the paltry treasures she hid in the storage compartment under the seat of the sofa. But she spoke to Karim about him, without affection in her voice, but with amazement and reverence as if she were talking about a pious holy man rather than just a petty criminal.

I don't know if it was Karim's mother who stuffed his head with nonsense, or whether he was born with a natural disposition for such things. In his childhood, she told him about his father in brief moments of respite while catching her breath and having a rest from hardship, on the eve of a religious holiday for example, after bathing him in the small washtub, dressing him up in clean clothes, and taking him in her arms in their tiny room in her parents' house. His head was full of myth-like stories about Saadoun al-Halabi, the tough guy and hashish dealer whose forefathers were said to have come from Syria to Egypt long ago, married local women, and had children. The family name Halabi—"the Aleppan"—was a clear indication that he did indeed have distant roots. I no longer remember much of what he told me over the weeks and months in prison. But I remember, for example, that this Saadoun supposedly acquired his extraordinary strength when he drank the water of the river when it was steady—that is, when the Nile was completely still, undisturbed by a single ripple, which is something that happens only once in a thousand years. Whoever drinks from the river at that moment gains a strength that no other creature can overcome.

It is certain that Karim's mother gave birth to him when she was close to forty. She was a woman who was slightly mentally disturbed, with a brazen rustic beauty. She had no children with her first husband, so he divorced her, and for years she roamed the lanes of Khorset selling vegetables, crying her wares in a rich voice: "Fresh rocket! Radishes sweeter than bananas! Finest lemons! Lettuce sweeter than honey!"

At least that's what Karim liked to whisper to us in our corner of the cell, imitating her call in a singsong voice. She lived under the protection of her brothers—a beautiful divorcee pursued by malicious gossip as she came and went. Then Saadoun saw her one morning as he was starting his day in a coffee shop, and he was stunned by the sight of her whiteness amid her black rags. "Do you have a lemon, pretty girl?" he shouted.

"The only pretty thing is your tongue," she replied with an idiotic smile.

Like everyone else, she was afraid of him. He picked up a lemon and with his big teeth bit into it whole with the peel on, his eyes pinned on the naïve peddler, who was clenching her teeth in a sullen attempt to resist vomiting, though she did manage to maintain her smile.

After that first encounter, the tough guy asked where she was from and who her family was, and because he was a man who feared God and cared about his fate in the afterlife he sent a messenger to her brothers on the evening of the same day. Within a week Shafya, Karim's mother, had joined the long line of women that Saadoun had married. He rented a room for her on the roof of a building not far from her family's house, the same room in which she would give birth to this beautiful boy and where he would live until he decamped to the capital.

I couldn't even imagine how a young man could live with his mother in one room, with a mud ceiling and wooden beams that always needed repair. When it rained there, water would drip down on them and his mother would arrange empty pots and pans under all the spots where the roof was leaking. Karim told his tales without turning them into sob stories, but always with irony and with a smile that came and went. I imagined the scene with the pots and pans collecting the rainwater as it dripped, with my mother suddenly appearing in this scene of poverty on the screen of the black-and-white television in the same room, whispering to her lover on the telephone that the coast was clear at her place and he should come to her at once. Karim smiled under his cover, identifying with the beautiful actress, not with the handsome lover. And then the pots and pans filled up and he stood, sighing irritably, to empty them in the only bathroom, which was on the ground floor, making his way carefully so that his feet didn't slip on the mud on the roof and on the stairway.

Shafya had been married to Saadoun for about a year when her only offspring begin to stir in her belly. The tough guy was not destined to hold this baby in his arms because the government arrested him in a well-executed ambush. As expected, the police were able to find him only after one of his closest associates betrayed him, much as happened to Adham al-Sharkawi, a Robin Hood character who was active in the Nile Delta. The government didn't just arrest him and his young accomplices; it also humiliated them in front of their families, dressing them up in women's headscarves, mounting them back-to-front on donkeys, and parading them through the streets in disgrace as a lesson to others. Karim hadn't been weaned yet when they heard that Saadoun al-Halabi had died in prison. Some said it was from grief, others that they had murdered him, and others that he had dug a tunnel and escaped but the government had covered it up to save face, so maybe he was still alive somewhere and would reappear one day to reunite his children, now dispersed in Cairo and Gharbiya Province, so that they could live like princes in his restored kingdom.

Even in those dark hours in prison, when I was gasping for air and snorting crushed pills through a rolled-up banknote, it was obvious to me that, in weaving the legend of his father, Karim had borrowed from many films, such as *The Harafish*, *Mulberries and the Cudgel*, and *Saad the Orphan*.

"So later they threw me out of the institute," Karim added suddenly, skipping ahead a number of years.

After preparatory school, he had joined an Azhar institute that taught religious instructors for primary schoolchildren. He left the institute for many reasons, including his eccentric behavior, such as daydreaming and saying strange things about how God sometimes talked to him. That exposed him to ridicule from the other children and threats from the pious among them, especially when they caught him in the bathroom with one of the janitors, which confirmed their suspicions about his sexual orientation. They disciplined the janitor and took Karim to the principal. "I don't want to see you here again except for exams. You can come like a dog, sit the exams, and then go. Otherwise, on my mother's honor, I'll hand you over to the police and have you arrested."

Karim wasn't upset. On the contrary, he was relieved that he was spared the long trek to the institute and back every day. He looked for work to help his mother, who went out at the crack of dawn to sell vegetables and continued to hope that one day he would go back to the institute that had expelled him, to obtain a qualification he knew would do nothing to help him achieve his grandiose ambitions. He was a chronic daydreamer who rarely stopped dreaming. Although he loved moulids and Sufi musicians and dervishes, he was also obsessed with fashion. He would sit for hours imagining himself in fine clothes, and he drew sketches of models in strange garments, although he wasn't a very good draftsman. He hoped one day to meet a famous fashion designer, whose name he told me. When he asked me if the man was like us, I said, "God alone knows." He imagined the conversation they would have and how he would convince the designer that he had talent and a feeling for fashion, elegance, and carefully choosing and matching colors.

When I heard about this passion of his, I ended up telling him about my father and grandfather, in sentences that faltered at random, disjointedly and breathlessly. I told him about the old workshop in Adli Street, about the ladies and the film stars, and how I played between their feet as a child. In a slip of the tongue I told him that Mother was the actress Badriya Amin. He gasped loudly and put his hand over his mouth. Some of the people near our beds noticed and one of them asked him mockingly, "What's up, nancy boy? Just lost your virginity, have you?"

He pursued me with questions about my mother for days after that, and sometimes I saw her sitting with us in the cell, listening to us with a sad smile.

32

ALEXANDRIA IN EARLY APRIL IS like another beautiful lie. I pushed the balcony door open and the end-of-day sun blitzed us—Abdel Aziz, Essam, and me—with red light. We had reached Agami two hours earlier, and the old villa seemed to be yawning and rubbing its eyes. The watchman and his children had done what they could to clean it up before we came, but erasing the hidden wrinkles was an impossible task. We sat on the cane balcony chairs, relaxing after a fish dinner with the women, who were staying in a more modern apartment in a building not far off. Mother and I used to sit here alone whenever we were lucky and she wasn't busy with work, if only for a week or ten days. It was growing old but I only saw it as it used to be, since every nook and cranny brought back clear memories of my mother.

After she died, I had to force my body through the motions of living—having a shower, eating, drinking, going to work, and doing errands. I was merely improvising, contriving a life without savor for the sake of my mother's memory, and then for Shireen and little Badriya. I received special treatment from those around me, as if I were a precious glass ornament that they held with trembling hands for fear it might break. Mother never stopped visiting me in my daydreams and when I slept. I would suddenly see her quite clearly, as she had been ten years earlier, when she was at the height of her glamour and glory. She would be laughing or singing, and I would drift off with her, indifferent to those around me and what they thought of me, because madness, like death, brings relief.

Then I started pretending that I was back to normal, just so that others would stop worrying about me and asking me how I was—especially Shireen. As soon as she felt I had withdrawn inside myself again, she would hurriedly try to draw me out of my shell. Even Abdel Aziz maintained his support with irritating devotion. During this period he seemed to be pursuing me and I didn't know what his motive was. He wasn't good at making jokes, which sometimes made me feel sorry for him. For their sake I forced myself to talk and laugh and went back to taking an interest in myself, in what I ate, and in taking my tranquilizers. I went out, went to the office, and even appeared on television programs to talk about the talented actress who had died. But I hid from everyone the fact that she visited me all the time and that our conversations at her bedside sometimes lasted for hours, until I fell asleep. Only Dr. Sameeh knew this, and he was reassured only when I told him I knew they were just fantasies that comforted me and eased the pain of her death.

The only point of the trip to Alexandria must have been to help me recover. I no longer remember who was behind the proposal but it came up suddenly while we were having dinner at the home of Shireen's uncle. Everyone was soon enthusiastic about the idea, as if they had already agreed to it behind my back. Even Abdel Aziz, who was always busy, seemed willing. But Uncle Sallam wouldn't let Asma go with us unless her younger brother, Essam, came too. He was a law student who was as light and agile as a monkey and who always gave me a strange feeling that I was now old, by the way he dressed and spoke, the music he listened to, and of course the way he soon grew bored of everything.

While Essam was having a shower, I sat on the balcony with Abdel Aziz. We began the evening in silence, each of us apparently waiting for the other to speak. This may have been the first moment we had been alone with each other since he hugged me at the office after I locked myself up there a few days after my mother died. No, his tearful embrace hadn't had the same effect on me as the prince's magic kiss had on Sleeping Beauty, because I hadn't yet recovered from my grief for my mother and it hadn't led to us rolling around on the floor and stripping naked in a frenzy. Our embrace that time was something small and fleeting but it was more eloquent than anything I had dreamed might happen between us; something that wavered between brotherliness and sympathy, between denial and acknowledgment. Here we were together, alone again. I got up, fetched my laptop, and played an Umm Kulthoum song. I could hardly listen to anything else, simply because my mother loved her so much. When Essam came out of the bathroom, I went and showered and changed my clothes. I had chosen to sleep alone in a small room with one big bed, so that Abdel Aziz could share the other two-bed room with his young brother-in-law. I wasn't ready to sleep in the same room as anyone else, especially Abdel Aziz. The room wasn't the only thing that Abdel Aziz and Essam shared; there was also hashish. They had started the ritual by the time I came out of the bathroom a few minutes later, as Umm Kulthoum toyed with the question she was singing—"Does love triumph over all?"—giving it a different coloring each of the many times she reprised it. My mind drifted with her voice, and the sweet aroma of hashish smoke took me back to when I was a child pretending to be asleep on the maroon armchair in my father's workshop, sneaking a peek out of the little window from time to time at the penises of urinating men. Then a cell phone started ringing with a dancing ring-tone. It was Essam's and he jumped out of his seat. "That must be the guys and they've reached Alexandria," he said.

We could hear his voice from inside cussing his friends playfully and agreeing to join them downtown immediately. Abdel Aziz asked me gravely, "So tell me, Hani, can you remember the first song you heard when you were young that stuck in your head?"

I was taken aback by his strange question. Without racking my brain for very long, I told him it was a song by Aida al-Shaer that I often used to hear on the radio as soon as Grandma Sakina turned it on at seven in the morning. I started singing it to him, pretending to be cheerful:

Open the window for me, my dear.
I love the air, my dear.

Essam came back all ready to go out and started imploring us to lend him one of the cars. His driving license had been suspended and his father had banned him from driving because of his recklessness and the repeated accidents he caused. I firmly refused, so he worked on Abdel Aziz until he relented, to my surprise. Abdel Aziz just gave him the car keys, saying, "If you get into trouble, I'll say you stole the keys."

Essam told us not to wait up for him because he would be spending the night with his young friends at the home of one of them in Raml Station. He then disappeared from the face of the earth and we sat in embarrassed silence pretending to listen to Umm Kulthoum. I fetched two cans of beer from the fridge and then I remembered the question Abdel Aziz had recently asked. "And what about you?" I asked.

"Me what?"

"The first song you remember from when you were very young."

He smiled as if remembering something we had spoken about years ago, not just a few minutes. He started telling me a long story, as if his whole self had reverted to that distant moment in his childhood in Minya. It was when he was very young, maybe before he went to school or maybe when he was in the first year of primary school or maybe it was the first time he went out alone at night to buy ice cream from a store that was far from home. The shopkeeper didn't see him at first from behind the high counter, but he kept banging his coin on the glass front of the cabinet where the biscuits and chewing gum were on display until the shopkeeper noticed him. Anyway, the radio was on, playing a song that Warda was singing at a concert. She was repeating one particular verse:

What do we care for our critics?
We've been through enough already.
We toiled and we suffered
Until we met one another.

In his rich voice and with a laugh, he said, "The audience at the concert was going wild. I took the ice cream and headed home, and all along the way I was singing those words: 'What do we care for our critics? We've been through enough already.' And even now I don't know what the song's called. Every few years I hear it by chance in a café or on the radio, exactly the same verse, as if it's chasing me, and every time I hear it I tell myself I must look it up and find it; that I must for once listen to it from start to finish and then forget about it completely until I hear it again. Imagine, it's been about thirty years." He started laughing with a certain bitterness.

Smiling enthusiastically, I said, "I remember that song, but I don't know what it's called either."

Then the silence returned and neither of us was able to break through it until the Umm Kulthoum song was over. I didn't bother to play another one. The balcony was charged with tension and the slightest breeze could have whipped up a storm. He had his right hand on his left shoulder and started to groan and massage it languidly. "Didn't you tell me once that you know how to give a massage?" he asked me frankly, stubbing out the joint he was smoking.

I nodded, my heart racing, overawed by the moment I had long awaited and imagined.

"Because my shoulder's been stiff all day. Could you . . . ?"

I interrupted him, knowing that I mustn't let slip the opportunity he had offered me. "It wouldn't work properly here, in the open air. Come into the room," I said.

In my bedroom, with two rapid moves Abdel Aziz took off his traveling clothes and then his undershirt. All he had on were his white briefs, tight around his bulging genitals. The little room glowed with the pure bronze of his skin. He lay down on his stomach and relaxed, turning his face toward the wall. Like a professional masseur, I took my time. His broad back stretched in front of me like a desert wet with dew. I focused the pressure of my fingers on the shoulder he said was stiff and he started to groan, making subdued sighs that sounded sweeter to my ear than all of Umm Kulthoum's songs. Then he turned over to lie on his back and the shape of his penis was clearly visible under his briefs. He gave a serene smile that pained me.

"It's good like that," he whispered. "You're doing well."

I was hesitant for a moment and didn't know what I should do. I looked at him and he was silent and smiling too, as if he was enjoying the moments of suspense before the icy barrier collapsed. Finally he pulled me toward him and whispered, "Come and lie next to me."

I didn't want anything more than that. I tasted his lips slowly and we held each other's hands. Then my face burrowed at length in the thicket of hairs on his chest and stomach and I licked his navel. Suddenly we were naked and our arms and legs were locked together, flesh to flesh. My friend penetrated me and it was like the first time in my life. I didn't want that moment ever to end. I wanted us to die like that, him and me, or the planets to stop turning and time to stand still. When he hugged me after coming, he could feel I was crying. He touched my eyes with his lips and licked the tears away with his tongue. It wasn't pure joy because a sadness was present among us too.

The first time wasn't as I had imagined it in my dreams, where there was no sweat, no breathlessness, and no fumbling over the insertion. In my imagination fireworks in psychedelic colors had exploded and flashed across the sky of the universe. But the real version, although it was rough, had a feel to it, and a taste, a sound, and a smell. His inclination toward men was an obvious fact and not just a whim or a matter of curiosity. He had come prepared with packs of condoms and I realized that he had decided in advance that we would come here.

My excitement was edgy, looking around for the punishment that would surely be imminent. I was so excited I almost forgot I was still afraid of what was hidden for me in this brown body with its toned muscles, and inside his head, which was sculpted like a pharaonic statue.

I wanted to scratch his skin and flesh off to reach whatever was beneath, and I wanted to get into his head, to open all its dark rooms and fill them with light and air, just to be sure, so that my fears could dissipate and my joy be undiluted.

After a second round that was long and less frenetic, sleep stole him from me. I kept looking at him, listening to his snoring, which was like the bubbling of a water pipe, and smelling the rough animal aromas of his body, mixed with his cologne. I smiled contentedly, only because in recent times I hadn't woven fantasies in my imagination. In the taste of his sweat, I sensed a victor who didn't know what to do with his victory.

33

AT NOON THE NEXT DAY we were all on the beach. I sat alone, watching them from behind my sunglasses. I was watching his body, as vibrant as the sea, the sun, the sand, and the wind. It was a warm April day and the weather was pleasant. The light was astonishingly pure, despite a trace of dust from time to time that irritated Asma, who had a sensitive nose and often complained for the most trivial reasons. High in the sky, fragile wisps of cloud like cotton candy dispersed almost as soon as they appeared. I started to think about my tremulous happiness, examining it with the curiosity of an expert appraiser. It wasn't that old superficial happiness that was the product of the moment, the kind that made me jump and shout and sing. It was its elder sister, sensible and staid, the one that smiles at a cup of tea and a cigarette after the afternoon siesta or that purrs with affection when she hears little Badriya laughing as she splashes Shireen and Asma with water. Just to have Abdel Aziz in front of me in the sunlight, covering his firm body as little as possible, was another form of happiness, secret and buried like a bean that the soil cradles, a seed that sleeps and dreams of the journey that awaits it, the long journey that will one day be its life aboveground.

After lunch I told them I'd like to take a walk alone for a short while. I walked until I found an Internet café, where I searched everywhere for the mysterious Warda song. Eventually I found it, downloaded it, and burned it onto a CD.

I took Abdel Aziz by surprise with it that night as we were sitting on the balcony. He couldn't believe it, and he hugged me while Essam the little monkey wasn't looking. He looked contented as he listened to the opening section of the song from his childhood for the first time:

On the nights when the tears in my eyes have stayed awake singing,
For loved ones whose only pleasure is to do me wrong.

When Essam had the impression that his sister's fiancé had run out of hashish, he stood up to go to bed. We sat up with Warda, a bottle of wine, and an assortment of nuts and cheeses. We chatted about everything under the sun. I told him the story of my first relationship, with Ra'fat, when I was a naïve adolescent, and how he had abandoned me and eventually offered me to one of his colleagues. I wasn't embarrassed and I didn't hide anything from him. I wanted to encourage him to be honest with me about himself, without overtly pushing him to do so. Then we reminisced and laughed about the days after we first met, and I told him how I was mad about him as soon as I saw him at his engagement party and about my strange dream about him and the uncertain memory of the kiss. Even in this heart-to-heart, with the April breeze sometimes harsh and sometimes gentle, he didn't satisfy my quest for the truth about that kiss. He ignored my reference to it as if it were unworthy of attention, and I didn't press him.

He took a small piece of hashish out of his pocket and proceeded to crumble it into a joint. "I hope Essam doesn't get a whiff of this and wake up," he said.

He lit the joint and handed it to me. I took one short puff and coughed so violently that my eyes watered. He reached out and wiped my tears away, while sneaking a look into the living room. After a while he admitted sweetly that in my company he had found something he hadn't been used to, maybe something that was simple but that now seemed necessary. He said he had never experienced the pleasure of "playing," and he had never been brave enough to break free from considerations of rules and conventions, right and wrong. Now he had suddenly discovered what it meant to be like a child again, a child other than the old one who trembled in fear of his big brother, and naturally of his father, the army man who was absent most of the time. They were a clan of males who watched each other constantly, in a big cold house that hadn't been graced by the spirit of a woman since their mother had died. They ate, drank, watched television, and did everything at fixed times and under a strict regime. Dissent or rebellion was banned, even in their imaginations. Any disagreement could easily end in a heated battle, and then the leather belt from their father's army uniform would come out to resolve everything, leaving its mark on the boys' young backs. Compared with my childhood, Abdel Aziz's was one long nightmare. I had once thought it was too much coddling that had sapped me of my masculinity, but long ago I had stopped bothering about the reasons, because I had come across so many diverse cases among gay men, some of them almost contradictory when it came to the backgrounds in which they had grown up. We went back to listening to Warda in the calm of the night:

The joy of our love was our hopes.
The hours when we meet pass in seconds.
All our lives, from our joy, the world sings to us.
All the flowers, even the birds, rejoiced and became like us.
They sang to us, to us, and we together,
And I learned the meaning of love.

He was about ten years old when one of his brothers caught him with another local boy in the bathroom at the youth center. His eldest brother tied him down and beat the soles of his feet twenty times with a thick piece of wood. His brother added another punishment—blindfolding him with a coarse black rag and making him stay home for two days under constant observation. If he tried to lift the blindfold off, even for a second, the two-day period would restart. Abdel Aziz was willing to take any punishment as long as his father knew nothing of what had happened. He spent two days stumbling from room to room, banging into pieces of furniture and falling over every few paces, while his brothers laughed at him and insulted him in the vilest language. Even so, his eldest brother told their father everything as soon as he came home. Abdel Aziz couldn't tell me how his father punished him. He was completely silent and tears welled in his eyes. When he tried to talk again his voice trembled. I wanted to spare him the memory, so I asked him jokingly, "And what were you doing with the boy in the bathroom, bad boy?"

He smiled and slapped me gently on the shoulder. "Nothing," he replied. "We were seeing what he had and what I had. Not even kissing or playing."

Toward the end of the pleasantly cool night I found myself wondering if I was happy now. I didn't know the answer. I thought that maybe happiness was the carrot that they put in front of us so that we keep walking forward whatever happens, and maybe it's not even a real carrot, but just a picture of one and nothing more.

What do we care for our critics?
We've been through enough already.
We toiled and we suffered
Until we met one another.
Until we met one another.
Whatever they say about us, let them say.
What they say isn't on our minds.

When Abdel Aziz heard this part of the song, he suddenly livened up. He rose to his feet and started to sing along, swinging his firm body right and left like a second-rate showman. "There's only the ice cream left now," he said ecstatically.

He gave me a mischievous conspiratorial look, and a few minutes later we were out looking for ice cream in the streets of Agami, which were quiet at two o'clock in the morning. Eventually we found a grocery that was still open. We licked our ice creams as we walked along laughing. Not far off, customers were going in and out of a fancy nightclub, the men in full suits, some of them swaying slightly, accompanied by women in furs and jewels. We watched them from a distance like schoolboys playing hooky.

"We and the gang should come and spend the evening here some time," he suggested.

"Or without the gang."

"That would be better," he replied.

On our way back a pack of dogs behind the wall of a small villa barked at us when we went too close, and we started barking back at them. When lights came on in the villa, we ran off to our dilapidated beach house, which was hidden among smart new buildings.

Before I fell asleep I heard my bedroom door opening slowly and felt his warm body slipping under the cover by my side. "I can't sleep for Essam's snoring," he whispered.

"Really?" I said.

He went back to his own bed before dawn. In the meantime we had shared each other's bodies without making the slightest sound, as frightened and cautious as thieves.

34

EVEN BEFORE ESSAM SAW US together and blew our cover, the pleasures of the body were not completely undiluted. Every now and then a sense of guilt tormented me when I admitted to myself that I was betraying everyone with Abdel Aziz. We were clearly taking advantage of their inadvertence. I mentioned my unease to him but he didn't seem at all interested in the idea, and I felt from what he said that he saw what we were doing as just innocent play, like something that any two men might do together, such as play backgammon or cards, smoke a joint, or talk crudely about women. I went along with him but without conviction. Then I was surprised to notice that he openly ignored or belittled Asma, his fiancée. They weren't doing any of the things that an engaged couple is meant to do, and it didn't matter whether her brother Essam was present or not. He didn't spend time alone with her or go for walks along the beach with her, for example. Most of their conversation was with us as a group, and it didn't focus on their future, but rather on best-selling books and writing and publishing in Egypt. Asma would often get emotional and accuse him of promoting bad books based on personal considerations and relationships. She would put aside her feminine persona and turn for some reason into something else, something resentful and indignant, maybe because she was no great beauty or because she felt she was inferior to him in every way. After lunch in the apartment one day, she told him, "You're very clever at knowing how to make everyone happy, but your own attitude is mysterious—if you even have an attitude in the first place."

He smiled and didn't answer. Then he left us and disappeared for the rest of the day, coming back quietly to the beach house in the evening, as if he had forgotten what had happened. Maybe he saw her as a stubborn child that he would gradually have to tame, and if he didn't succeed he would leave her where she was and move on as if nothing had happened. Shireen and I patched things up between them the very next day but the seeds of the problem had been sown and it complicated what should have been simple daily pleasures. Our clandestine trysts became more tempestuous, with a certain violence and roughness on his part. Repressed anger seemed to have accumulated over his lifetime and now he was finally letting it out, disguised in the form of sex with a man who submitted to him voluntarily.

I told him I knew that no sex could be real without an element of violence in it, however hard one tried to make it gentle, but we could steer it in the other direction, toward tenderness, if we wanted. I carefully avoided using the word *love* or any similar words, but Abdel Aziz seemed to switch from one state of mind to another at a moment's notice, and he wasn't in control of what he was doing. After he had come, he came back to the real world around him like someone in a Sufi trance who no longer knows where he is. He avoided looking me in the eye and seemed embarrassed about what he had done.

I no longer sat on the beach with them with my chest and shoulders bare. To hide the dark marks he left on my skin I started wearing something light, on the pretext that the wind was cold. I didn't give up hope of clipping the monster's claws, as if I were living out some myth. But, unknown to us at the time, the sandcastle came crashing down two or three days before our vacation was due to end, when Essam saw us embracing. He had left us at nine o'clock to visit his friends, and as usual we took advantage of his absence to have sex. We finished and calmed down and then we went back to sitting on the balcony. I was trying to coax out of Abdel Aziz whether he'd had any previous experiences with men. He was evasive but I pressed him, and eventually he gave in and started to tell me about what he claimed was his only experience.

It was in his first year at university, when he started to break loose from the family network and discover himself alone. He was moving from one furnished apartment to another, and at one stage he had to move out of one and wait three days before moving into the next. He didn't know where to go. He thought of going to a small hotel but a colleague suggested that he stay with him. The colleague tempted him by promising that they would binge on alcohol and hashish during Abdel Aziz's stay. Abdel Aziz agreed and went with him, leaving the cardboard boxes with his books and other stuff with the doorman at his new apartment. His colleague carried out his promise, but the alcohol and hashish were only one part of the plan. He had wanted Abdel Aziz for some time and didn't how to get him, or if he was available in the first place. That's what he admitted to Abdel Aziz after the incident. Maybe, like me, the man had detected secret signals that Abdel Aziz transmitted.

They spent three days out of their heads, trying out every possible pleasure, without of course deviating from their designated roles as master and slave, as man and catamite. With every hour that passed, Abdel Aziz had to resist his feelings of contempt and disgust toward his friend. But the feelings rose silently inside him like an incoming tide. Even the alcohol and the drugs could no longer mask his revulsion and enable him to get an erection. He told himself that as soon as he moved into the new apartment he would end all contact with this colleague. That's what he did, without looking back even once or giving him a word of thanks or saying goodbye to him. He threw him away like a used condom that we hold between our fingertips in disgust and drop into the nearest trash can. In a remorseful tone that I felt was insincere, he said, "Even when I saw him on campus, I steered clear of him."

Suddenly he noticed I was looking at him disapprovingly. He raised his index finger and looked at me warningly. "You're another matter, and anyway, I've changed," he said.

He reached out toward me, inviting me to approach, like someone encouraging a young child to crawl toward him. I rose from my chair and sat on his lap, resting my head on his chest. The darkness on the balcony concealed us from view from outside, but then we found Essam standing behind us. He stood still in embarrassment for a moment and I saved myself with a quick lie, claiming that I had remembered my late mother and had started crying, and Abdel Aziz had tried to comfort me. Then I started wiping away nonexistent tears.

Essam didn't seem convinced. He said nothing and looked suspicious, and at that point we noticed a large bandage on his head. He had been in a fight. We latched onto this injury as a lifesaver. Cleverly, Abdel Aziz started bombarding him with questions about what had happened, while Essam was rude and evasive about answering. I left them and went off to my bedroom to be alone. I could hardly settle in one place and my whole body was shaking. I reproached myself for not being careful enough and for exploiting the memory of Mother to escape. I wanted to cry to myself, so I went outside. I walked toward the beach and only noticed I was barefoot when I felt the cold sand and found it difficult to walk in. My fears were creeping around me in the dark like silent dogs. When I'd had my fill of crying, I saw Mother again and she scolded me, saying, "I hope you had a good time."

"Essam saw us and it's not impossible he'll tell them," I said.

"The chickens always come home to roost," she said.

When I told Dr. Sameeh what happened in Agami between me and Abdel Aziz he asked me about Shireen, my feelings toward her, and whether I felt any guilt or remorse. I didn't know what to say, except that I slept with her from time to time. He smiled strangely, as if he knew I understood his question well but was being evasive. Since my mother's death I had become reliant on Xanax and antidepressants, and maybe that was another reason why sex with Abdel Aziz seemed a little lackluster once he had finally yielded. I knew that these drugs affected one's appetite for food and sex and everything, and now I could rarely get an erection without ridiculous effort. Our last two days in Alexandria were absolute hell, and as soon as we were back in Cairo I felt really relieved. I went back to my old routine as if nothing had happened. I spent hours asleep, like someone with jetlag, and I learned as much about my dream world as I knew about the real world. I started looking at the world through a hazy screen, smiling to myself for no good reason. I regained my ability to dream of things that soon came true in reality. I even dreamed that Shireen told me the news that Abdel Aziz and Asma had broken off their engagement, about twenty-four hours before she actually told me. I was sitting on the carpet sorting out dozens of photos of Mother that were scattered around me when I heard the news. Shireen had just finished a long conversation with her cousin. She came and said just one sentence: "Asma's engagement has been broken off."

She twisted her lips as if she couldn't stand the taste of the sentence in her mouth. I pretended not to be interested. "I sensed it," I said sagely.

We made some trite remarks about luck and fate, and then some scathing words about Asma being stubborn and highly strung and Abdel Aziz being arrogant for no reason. Eventually I managed to slip out of the circle of photos of Mother spread around me. In the bathroom mirror I looked at my pale, plump face and at the new lines endlessly being etched in it by an invisible pen in a hand that had neither compassion nor understanding.

35

WHEN I LISTENED TO KARIM's stories in our corner of the cell in Tora Prison, I couldn't possibly tell where the facts ended and the fantasies began. Sometimes I envied him his ability to live in another world. I tried to learn this skill from him so that I could escape at times from the nightmare around me, if only for a few stolen minutes every day.

Karim said he had talked to God since he was young, sometimes to himself and sometimes aloud. God was his best friend, even if it was a one-sided conversation, but he soon discovered there were many ways God could whisper secrets to him—through a phrase a passerby used in the street, in which he detected a secret message meant for him, or in the first thing he heard when he turned the television on. The chirping of a sparrow might sound like the answer to a question he had asked himself. He liked to listen to God's voice in all such things, although he knew he was cursed because he committed the sin of the people of Lot. But then he consoled himself by saying it was God who created him as he was, and maybe God had some purpose he would never understand however hard he tried, and maybe He would help him repent someday.

He had tried to pray regularly, to fast on Mondays and Thursdays, and to remember parts of the Quran he had forgotten. His uncle, who knew of his sexual activities, once asked him, "Have you made friends with some fundamentalist?" Then Karim decided to move to Cairo in search of a private life away from his uncle, who smoked marijuana all the time, and from his mother, who lived on alms although Karim, as a man, should have provided for her. Maybe he struck out in search of the man in his life, the dream that never left him however many books on Sufism he collected and however many hours he spent engrossed in them, though he didn't understand much of what was in the books and they only made him more puzzled and confused. Sometimes he would interrupt his own storytelling, look at me, and ask me questions such as, "Do you think God is inside us or outside?"

When I reacted by pursing my lips and shrugging to mean I didn't know, he would volunteer his own answer: "Both, and anyway it doesn't make any difference."

He made sure he took those books on his move to Cairo, where he slept on the floor in the home of "Captain" Salah, one of his mother's cousins, who agreed to put Karim up with his own children until Karim found somewhere else to live. Within a day of arriving in Cairo, Karim was working with Salah in a small nightclub called the Arizona in the Tawfikiya district downtown. On his first night, while changing the ashtray at one table, he knocked over a bottle of whisky worth a small fortune, and half of it spilled on the floor. The manager insisted on firing him but the customer who had bought the bottle saved him, forgiving him and giving him a twenty-pound tip. He then gave him a tape of the Lebanese singer George Wassouf to play until the band turned up and the live music began. That customer was Fathi al-Touni, a dealer in car spare parts who liked nothing better than toying with people and who saw young Karim as just another opportunity for fun and amusement.

Karim learned a great deal at the Arizona. With every night that passed there, he discovered there was a massive gap between what he saw on television and what took place around him. In the downtown environment he mastered the language of eyes and discovered that he was really handsome and that he didn't need to make much effort to seek out men and attract and seduce them. He just needed to act naturally. Even his Nile Delta accent gave his voice a distinctive timbre. He memorized the words of George Wassouf's songs so that he could sing them to Fathi al-Touni as he stood next to him in the early hours. The other staff in the nightclub worked out what he was up to but he didn't care. They called Karim "his cousin" because of his distant relationship with "Captain" Salah. When he plucked up courage and objected to this name, they started calling him unpleasant names such as "the pansy," "the fairy," and "the queen," so he decided he would leave the place, especially as he had already moved out of Salah's house and rented a room in an apartment in Omraniya, which he shared with other newcomers to Cairo.

One fresh morning, when he left the Arizona after mopping the floor for the last time, he had Fathi al-Touni's business card in his shirt pocket close to his heart, checking every few minutes that it was still there, as if it were his lifeline. Before looking for another job, he decided to visit Fathi in the spare-parts emporium that he owned, close to the Rivoli Cinema. When he went into Fathi's glass-walled office, the owner, puffy-faced and contracting into a scowl his bushy eyebrows, dyed glossy black, gave him a quizzical look as if he didn't recognize him. After a silence that lasted longer than the few seconds one might expect, he shouted at Karim in a harsh, hostile voice: "And what can I do for you, boy?"

It was like a bucket of cold water poured over Karim, who didn't understand and didn't know what to say. Was it conceivable that Fathi had completely forgotten him, when only a few days earlier he had been making eyes at Karim and saying nice things to him whenever he came close to his table, such as, "Aren't I lucky? You're prettier than this fruit here"? And now this look of surprise. "I'm . . . I'm Karim, from the Arizona. 'Love is king, love is king,'" the pretty boy stammered in a muffled voice.

"Are you an idiot or what, boy?" Fathi said, in the same rude tone.

Karim realized that for some reason Fathi was pretending not to know him, so he decided to leave. "I'm sorry I disturbed you," he mumbled.

He turned away and was reaching for the handle of the glass door, with a lump in his throat and tears in his eyes, when he heard the laugh, the malicious laugh he knew well, the laugh that the devil laughs when he enjoys playing with his victims. His hand froze on the door handle and he heard Fathi's voice revert to nightclub mode. "Come here, boy. Come here, Karim. I'm only joking with you," it said.

Fathi laughed and laughed at his prank. He took Karim's hand, and they left the store to go for a walk downtown.

"My god, if you'd seen your face in the mirror at the time!" Fathi joked.

They had lunch at a kebab restaurant nearby, and then settled in a bar called the Cyprus, where Fathi peppered him with questions about everything in his life, especially about his previous sexual experiences, which he seemed to enjoy hearing more than anything else. Karim told himself that maybe he had found what he had long been seeking, and he overlooked his irritation at the way Fathi behaved, spoke, and ate. I still remember the glint in Karim's eyes and his serene smile when he mentioned the beautiful clothes that his boorish patron bought him, describing in detail the colors, materials, and brands. His world suddenly expanded. He tasted kinds of food he hadn't even known the names of and visited places where everything was permissible.

He spent a few weeks in Fathi's heaven and Fathi didn't make any physical advances, except for some kisses, embraces, and light flirtation at drunken, dissolute parties with a number of Fathi's acquaintances, which puzzled Karim and made him wonder. Although he was frightened of the moment he expected would come, he was also impatient for it, because afterward either the dream would continue or it would come to an end and he would go back to being alone and hanging out on the pavement with Mohamed Sukkar.

Then Fathi called him one night and abruptly summoned him to a hotel. Karim had often fantasized about this encounter in advance. He imagined special preparations, rituals, candles, and wine. He imagined that every kiss would be like something out of *A Thousand and One Nights*. But the reality fell far short of his dreams. The hotel was just a cheap boarding house in Clot Bey Street, quite inappropriate for Fathi's status.

In a horrible room, Fathi thrust his short thick penis into the boy's ass nonstop for a full two hours until Karim was worried the pain would overwhelm him and he would scream and cause a scandal. He couldn't work out what exactly Fathi's problem was, but he noticed that Fathi's scrotum was almost flush with his groin and didn't hang down at all, unlike with other men. He also saw that his testicles were obviously withered, so maybe he had some defect that meant he couldn't ejaculate.

Anyway, Karim was bleeding from his anus, crying, and begging Fathi to have mercy and set him free. The man started hitting him like a maniac, with his hands and his feet, and Karim didn't try to defend himself. Karim began picking up his clothes, covering himself as best he could and saving his skin. In the minibus home he was crying and people were looking at him, and he could still feel warm blood wetting his clothes from below.

Karim didn't cry after telling his story. He smiled out of the side of his mouth, as if remembering a silly joke. Then he turned his face away and took out his little Quran.

36

I STILL TURN TO KARIM and his stories for help in erasing my memories of prison. Sometimes the ordeal seems like a long soap opera that I followed lazily, episode by episode, distancing myself from all the cares of the world. Possibly under the influence of Karim also, I sometimes imagined that I had started to rediscover God while in prison. I had previously thought we had no right to be pious because piety was clearly incompatible with our desires, which nagged at us day and night, so much so that we couldn't resist submitting to them. Karim had a different opinion. He saw it as a personal test, different from other people's tests, and everyone had his very own exam to sit. Even in our circles, he believed, everyone faced his own test or trial that no one else could take on his behalf. I say "imagined" because I now know that I was insincere about turning to God. There was something deceitful about submitting to God's will. Somehow it was like trying to bribe fate to save me from the trouble I was in. Or maybe I converted my submission to the government, the law, and its henchmen into a spiritual state of mind that was ridiculous and fragile. Nonetheless, I would often cry when Karim read from the Quran in his fine voice. The remorse was delicious; it could evoke the same guilty pleasure, as if with a magic wand.

A victim can easily turn into a saint, at least in his own eyes. That was another trap I almost fell into. In the eyes of those around us we were just dirt that had to be disposed of somehow. The state found itself in an embarrassing position, caught between international pressures on the one hand and on the other hand the local media, which blew the case out of all proportion and never stopped sniping at us, while the state posed as the protector of society's immutable values against deviant beliefs, immorality, and perversion. Even the wretched guards seemed to enjoy hurting, humiliating, and making fun of us. Whenever we went into the yard at the courthouse they insulted and abused us endlessly. "Hi faggots, hi devil worshippers, hi perverts, you sons of whores," they would say, and often they would beat us with sticks and fists to accompany their chants of welcome, as long as we were somewhere away from prying eyes or cameras.

During the sessions of the trial, the security presence was absurd, as if we were indeed terrorists and as if someone were going to try to set us free. A permanent wall of policemen separated us from everyone else—the lawyers, the journalists, and the families. Even the relatives were subjected to the vilest forms of abuse. When some poor-looking women asked the police about their sons, the police said, "Are you the mothers of the faggots?"

All this was a godsend for the media. Dozens of journalists and camera crews turned up. The cameras lapped us up like celebrities strutting along the red carpet at some international film festival. Right from the first session we covered our faces with anything that came to hand—plastic bags, handkerchiefs, small pieces of clothing, with holes cut out for the eyes.

When I see some of the pictures of the trial that were published in newspapers or on the Internet, with us hiding our faces, I tell myself I wish we hadn't done that. I wish we had shown our faces to the people there and to the cameras. We looked like strange faceless creatures, not people like other people. This may have reinforced the sense that we must be guilty. Besides, what was the point of hiding our faces when some government newspapers had already published our names, professions, and ages in full detail. Even before the verdicts, most newspapers and magazines behaved as if the verdicts had already been issued and treated us as Satanists, followers of "Lot's tribe," or advocates of a new religion that promoted debauchery, homosexuality, and same-sex marriage.

Eventually one journalist picked out my name from the list of names and discovered I was the son of the late actress Badriya Amin. He then started writing one article after another in a trashy weekly newspaper. On the surface he was writing about the case, but in fact he was writing only about me and how the way my mother brought me up might have affected me, philosophizing about the "mother's boy" theory, the absence of a father, and the origins of "perversion." These were ideas that I myself might once have found convincing, until I met dozens of men whose backgrounds and upbringings were completely different from my own, though they too were born with a sexual orientation toward men. The zealous journalist went even further: rummaging around in the rubbish of the past, he discovered that my aunt was the singer Husniya, that her life had ended with a drug overdose, and that she had spent her last years in rehabilitation clinics. When he ran out of treasures from the past, he invented another scoop: that I had married a woman of ill repute who worked with me. At this point, naturally, Shireen gave in to her family's demands and asked for a divorce.

After signing the divorce papers that morning, I came back from the superintendent's office, sat in my corner, and started to cry because I missed my daughter Badriya and didn't know when I would be able to see her again. Karim woke up to the sound of me crying and started rubbing my hands between his warm hands and comforting me until I calmed down a little and took a pill I'd been saving for the evening. I found Karim smiling and telling me he'd been dreaming about Salah Jahin, the poet and cartoonist, and that Jahin was singing his song

"Pianola" to him. Karim then rose to his feet and started singing, swaying slightly to the rhythm:

> I'm worn out and the soles of my shoes are worn out too, from searching for loved ones so long. My goodness, if I come across someone I love, I'll be so excited I'll dance, like this, like this, like this.

He swayed to the left and right, and some of our cellmates who were awake early clapped for him. I wiped my tears away and, in a voice like a torn rag, I whispered with him: "Like this, like this, like this."

I finally lost the ability to speak after many months without medicine or medical care, to be precise in the session of the trial before the one where they gave the verdict—the first verdict. While we were in the holding cell at the courthouse, waiting to be moved again, I wanted to ask someone for matches and was surprised to find that my tongue felt like a stone and my throat was making a strange noise, like an animal that has been hit with a tranquilizer dart. Before muteness descended on me, like a vampire bat sucking out my ability to speak, I pointed at Karim, who was crouched next to me in the corner of the cage in the courtroom. The last thing I said was: "See that guy in the black suit over there? That's Abdel Aziz."

I said it breathlessly and in fragments, but at least I spoke. Karim looked up slowly, and from behind the white T-shirt with eyeholes that covered his face he looked at Abdel Aziz and whispered, "What a beauty!"

I cried all the way back in the truck because I didn't know what had happened to me. In the cell I signaled to Karim that I couldn't speak. "Impossible. Try," he said.

He repeated that simple but impossible word *try* every two or three minutes and looked at me encouragingly and sympathetically. But all I could produce was an incomprehensible wail that made some of the men around us laugh, in the belief that I had taken so many pills that my tongue was tied.

That's when my relationship with writing things out began; writing became a substitute for my tongue. I was suffering from a form of transformational hysteria, as I later understood from Dr. Sameeh. When I could no longer take any more pressures and conflicts, my mind transformed them into a physical symptom to reduce their impact.

When I saw Abdel Aziz in the courtroom, before I became completely mute, I didn't feel anything special. No tremor ran through my body and tears didn't well up in my eyes. To me he was just like all the others in the room, another free man. And the most important thing was that they were clean, and their names were clean too. Even if I were to forget everything that happened to me during those dark months, I would never forget the day when he and I were arrested. Nor, of course, would I forget when they read the verdict, which was an international farce—a moulid without a saint, or a street carnival. Everyone had come to play their roles—the people who sold cold drinks outside the courthouse, the mothers looking for someone to take pity on them and help them into the courtroom, the foreigners from human rights organizations and Western satellite channels. Some of them came into the courtroom and started to record the events with video and audio, before the session began. One of the prisoners spoke to them from where he was in the cage. Everyone was talking at the same time and I kept to myself in the corner next to Karim. Many of them were criticizing what had happened and denouncing the government to the whole world for the torture they had undergone, trying to prove themselves innocent one way or another. I could hear them shouting over each other in the clamor of the courtroom before the judges came in.

"We want everyone to be treated fairly," they said. "The press has slandered us and ruined us, and after the verdict they should write the truth. Many people have been released.

They let them go. People with connections, or foreigners, or Arabs. Lots of Arabs."

The noise didn't help diminish our fears in anticipation of the verdicts that would soon be announced. Yet some of those with us in the cage had the courage and presence of mind to talk to the Western media in English, asserting for the thousandth time that we didn't know each other, that we had been arrested in different places, that this alleged network that held religion in contempt and promoted perversions existed only in the case documents, and that we still didn't know why we had been detained all these months. I admired those people for their courage, especially when they spoke about the physical and psychological torture they had undergone. I wished I had been born as brave as them and I realized that my recent muteness was merely a natural extension of my past passivity. For a few fleeting moments I thought of emulating their bravery and uncovering my face for a few seconds, at least enough to let Prince and Abdel Aziz see that I was so close to them, but my hand froze and within a minute the whole courtroom came to order with the arrival of the judges.

The noise outside the courtroom was unbearable. Many relatives of the defendants couldn't get in so they started banging loudly on the door and shouting, while the court usher began calling out the names of the defendants one by one. When my name was called, Karim took the initiative of answering "Present, sir" in my stead. Then the judge started reading the verdicts and sentences, with a calm, firm confidence. We couldn't hear a word he said. The judge stopped a moment and looked around the room, then resumed reading the list of verdicts and sentences as if nothing had happened. Some of us dared to shout out: "We can't hear anything! We can't hear, pasha!"

People started shouting out loud when we heard snatches such as "three years' imprisonment" and then "so many years' imprisonment for defendants number so-and-so to number such and such."

"No justice! No justice in the whole of Egypt!" people cried.

I burst into tears, and people in the cage kept shouting. The banging and screaming on the other side of the door grew louder, but the judge, his face placid and composed, took no notice of any of this. The noise was like one loud buzzing in my ears and I could no longer bear it. I no longer wanted to hear what the verdict on me was, whether I would be sent to prison or acquitted. I just wanted them to let me go, to disappear, to let me go back to my corner of the cell as soon as possible.

Some people fainted or had convulsions. I squeezed Karim's wrist, panting and sobbing so much that I couldn't breathe. Then I passed out, and came round only in the police truck when someone poured some water onto my face from a bottle. In the truck, it wasn't much different from when we were in the courtroom—crying, screaming, and wailing, and more than fifty men in a state of collapse. None of us knew anything about what our fate would be, although the verdicts and sentences had been announced. The whole world knew our fate, but not us. Around me people were asking each other frantically, "What did he say? Did you hear? Did you hear the verdict? He said the acquittals were from number what to number what?" But it was pointless. Neither the guards nor the other policemen had heard or even cared to know anything. I leaned back against the side of the truck and ended up banging my head against it again and again with all the energy I had left. The defendant who was handcuffed to me, a stranger to me, looked at me in shock and didn't know what to do. I suddenly stopped crying when I saw the blood gushing from the side of my forehead. Within moments, Karim had managed to cut a path through the mass of bodies and pressed his hands on my shoulders, although he was still handcuffed to someone else. In a violent voice, as if threatening devils that only he could see, he began to recite:

"Ya Sin / By the wise Quran / You are one of the messengers / On a straight path. / This is the revelation of the Almighty, the Compassionate, / To warn a people whose fathers were not warned and so they are unaware. / The Word has proven true for most of them, and they do not believe. / We have put chains on their necks up to their chins, so that their heads are forced up. / We have placed a barrier in front of them and a barrier behind them, and we have covered them so that they cannot see."

37

IN THE WRITING GAME OVER the past weeks I have wavered between remembering and forgetting. Whenever I wrote anything down in these notebooks, I somehow erased it from inside me. I had to ignore everyone else around me—Shireen, little Badriya, Prince, and Abdel Aziz—so that I could first of all find the real Hani Mahfouz that lay behind the visible forms he took, his disguises, and the roles he played. I managed to forget the months of imprisonment, if only for a few hours a day, and I even forgot those who were like brothers to me in prison—Mohamed Sukkar and Karim, of course, who gave me many gifts, possibly without knowing how valuable they were.

I left them behind me, in the same way I abandoned the other Hani, the asthmatic prisoner who wanted to die but didn't die. Death remained a fragile hope, maybe an insincere one. My attempt to kill myself in the police truck was just a reaction to the shock, and I didn't really need the magic spell that Karim cast on me when he recited the Ya Sin chapter of the Quran for me. I just needed the few stitches that the prison doctor gave me, without any anesthetic, while he smoked and made fun of me.

We didn't hear the verdicts until we were back at the prison. The principal defendant in the case, Samir Barakat, was sentenced to five years' imprisonment, with three years' imprisonment for the second defendant, Barakat's dearest and closest friend, and two years for twenty other defendants, to be followed by years on parole. Most of them were people who had the misfortune to be associated with Barakat, for example because they had had their photos taken with him at parties. One defendant was sentenced to a year in prison and twenty-nine were acquitted, most of whom had been picked up from the streets or from outside the Queen Boat. They had no connection with Barakat and there was no proof that they regularly engaged in gay sex.

There was both sadness and joy, weeping, shouting, wailing, cries of celebration, excitement and dancing, kisses and hugs. Those who had been acquitted pretended to be sad for the sake of the others and tried to encourage them with kind words about the verdict being only the first stage in the legal process. They said there were still plenty of opportunities for appeals and legal challenges, that the world was in uproar over the scandal of the case, and that they were all certain to be pardoned sooner or later. Those convicted pretended to be happy for those who had been acquitted. They wiped away their tears and took part in the dancing and singing. Some of them claimed they didn't want to leave prison and face the scandal and the shame. They preferred to stay in prison until people had forgotten them. At that stage I suddenly realized that, because the relief of acquittal had been so overwhelming, I had been ignoring an ordeal I had yet to face. How would it be to leave prison? What would I do? Who would I see? How would I survive after everything that had happened? The noose that would strangle me wasn't just my inability to speak; it was fear of everything.

For weeks I imagined that someone was following me or that a hellish hand would descend on me at any moment. In the first weeks after my release, I took showers obsessively, many times a day. I succumbed to sleep most of the day, and despair almost drove me to end my own life several times, until I made friends with the spider and found my way to these notebooks, which started to proliferate in the drawers of the dressing table, like silent witnesses in a case where no one knows who the final verdict will favor. As line followed line and page followed page, I felt I was shedding an old skin. The skin just fell away, with a pleasant kind of pain, and at the same time I didn't know what new kind of skin had started to form. I wasn't sure I would find my own reflection in the mirror in front of me if I stopped writing for a moment and looked up from the paper. I was a ghost who slowly faded away with every line I wrote.

Sometimes writing was harder for me than speaking. My fingers would freeze on the page, sometimes for quite a while, as if my inability to speak had paralyzed my hands, my mind, and everything about me. At other times I would write very slowly, as if I had to cut each word out of my flesh with a knife made of wood or stone. I would implore some mysterious entity inside me—the custodian of a secret fortress where words, images, and stories were stored—to let me in for just a few minutes or to let the words sneak out. When I was lucky this custodian would disappear, all the fortress gates would swing open, the towers would be razed to the ground, and the inhabitants could mix with the troops in the garrison. I would see words slipping between my fingers in such abundance that I couldn't catch them or organize them into meaningful sentences. At such moments I forgot practically everything. I turned into some unknown other person who was watching Hani Mahfouz from afar, or maybe imagining him and creating him out of nothing through words. The more progress I made in telling my story the lighter I felt, like a slave buying his freedom by the sweat of his brow at every sunrise, and losing another link in his chains at every sunset.

I might have identified with Karim the storyteller during this period, which has almost come to an end. Sometimes I heard his voice in my ear, repeating the words I was writing one after another. I tried to imagine how he might tell this or that story and then I would follow his lead. I tried to be like him, a man who is about halfway through his life and whose experience of life doesn't amount to a hill of beans, but I wish I had some of his talent for fantasizing, laughing, forgetting pains quickly, making fun of the world, and soliciting God's love, even if the inhabitants of this world and the next deny it to us.

Karim's wounds soon healed. Whereas for years I remembered with rancor what Ra'fat did to me and threw myself into every possible trash can for any man who was willing, Karim had not given Fathi al-Touni, for example, any chance to dominate his thinking for long. He seemed to have forgotten about him completely within days. He moved on, busy with his fantasies in spite of hunger and the risk of poverty. He thought of going back to the Arizona, but he didn't do so. He borrowed money from his relative, "Captain" Salah, several times until the man hinted that he couldn't lend him any more. At about the same time, I might have been hurting and railing at heaven and earth because my beloved Abdel Aziz had abandoned me.

Karim found work in a clothes shop near Roxy Square and, although it was a long way from his home in Omraniya, he was happy to be among all the expensive clothes, even if he didn't own them. He revived his old dream of fashion design and with his first salary he bought beautiful sketchbooks, pencils, paints, and old fashion magazines. He started sketching in his spare time and every now and then nostalgia drew him to the cloth bag that contained his religious books and his Sufi texts, and he would leaf through them before falling asleep.

At night and on his days off, he would wander the streets and maybe satisfy his sexual urges with brief adventures here or there, without precautions or practicing safe sex as Prince had taught me to do when I started out, and without feeling anything but the lust and the pain of the moment. Despite himself, and without knowing it overtly, he was waiting for his knight on a white charger. From the way he looked at me

I often felt he was wondering if I was the one, even after I told him in brief one night about my relationship with Abdel Aziz. Besides, he should have been able to see for himself, with his own always startled eyes, that what was left of me was no longer of any use to anyone.

He went wandering the streets with Mohamed Sukkar, who on that distant day had persuaded him to go for a night out in the Queen Boat, with their surplus cash, which was hardly enough to last them till the end of the month. They knew that gay men gathered there every Thursday evening and stayed almost till dawn—and who knew, they might meet someone, and maybe the unknown prince would not be another version of Fathi al-Touni this time, but a wealthy young man who was looking for the right partner to dance with and hold tight at the end of the night. The only time they went there, they were arrested. On the boat no one was interested in them, Karim said.

"They felt we were strangers to them. From the way we dressed, the single bottle of beer that we kept holding all evening, from our shocked reaction to the place, from the way we danced, they knew we were outsiders. We're not their people, and not like them. We couldn't possibly be friends, them and us."

I pointed to him and to myself, and then I brought my right and left index fingers together, and separated them and put them together again several times, to say that he and I had become friends, almost brothers. He understood, but said, "Here it's one thing but outside it's something else. Maybe if you'd seen me outside, you wouldn't have been at all interested in me. Who knows?"

I wasn't tempted to make any easy promise that we would stay friends after we were out, if we did see the light one day. I knew he needed me as much as I needed him, as the nurse and the patient need each other, and as a story is coupled with its audience.

Sometimes I imagined I was telling Abdel Aziz everything that had happened to me in prison, including the stories of Karim, Sukkar, and the others, but in my own style and in my own way, forgetting that I had promised myself I wouldn't go back to him whatever he did, and forgetting that I didn't know whether I would recover my ability to speak. The seed of these pages took shape unconsciously in those days—the seed of the story that started knocking persistently on the door from the inside until it broke free and came into being and lived a life that may turn out to be longer than the lives of its author and of those who read it. While Karim was the voice I heard inside me, repeating every word I wrote, Abdel Aziz was the ear at which I aimed my story, from start to finish.

Then I discovered I was playing the role I had longed to play with my friend Abdel Aziz before they shredded the fabric of our fledgling relationship one night last May. I wanted to be Scheherazade and tell him everything that had happened to me and to other gay men. I wanted to pull him by the hand into our world and make him see and know and understand. I would speak to him without any order or system, blurting out things I hadn't even said to myself before, or to Dr. Sameeh. Only now do I admit that I have been imagining only us reading these pages, yet at the same time I imagine Karim's voice guiding me through the corridors of that secret fortress inside me, the fortress of words that is constructed by a smile of acceptance and demolished by a disdainful look.

In my old bag of memories I started coming across the strangest possible things, although I did not write them all down. It was like diving into the hull of a ship that had sunk four hundred years ago, not just forty: our neighbor the bicycle-repair man in Abdin, spitting toward me when he noticed how I was looking at him day after day and biting my lower lip; my teacher in secondary school slapping me when I reached out to touch his thigh during a private lesson; my colleague at university who took me aside in the bathroom, emptied his lust into me, and then started cursing, insulting, and kicking me. Then I wanted to tell my friend about the diseases and physical hardships of the path that we follow, with our regular nightly excursions and hunting codes. I told him about the curse of pubic lice, the affliction of crotch itch which clings to the body like a tick, the pain of piles and anal fissures from time to time. A gay man might decide to renounce the short-term pleasures that bring him all this pain, but as soon as the fissure starts to heal and little calluses form around the anal opening the longing revives, like a green shoot on a plant.

I wanted to talk about the bodies on display on the sidewalks in the squares and other well-known places as soon as night falls and even after midnight; about the eyes hungrily looking around for a message, for reassurance, for another chance, if only for one night. I wanted to talk about crowded buses and the valuable opportunities they offer; about deprived young men who find what they seek in gay men and treat them as an outlet for the semen that seethes in their bodies and drives them crazy. With time these gay men see themselves as merely cum dumps, and it becomes normal that they are beaten till their faces are swollen and their bodies are bruised. It is expected that everything they have on them will be stolen at any moment if they let down their guard and trust people unwisely. As the days pass we become strange creatures, warped to be cunning and wary. Their code is mutual deceit, and their weapons are their tongues, their words, and conversations that can take you to the sea and then bring you back thirsty.

I wanted to talk about a bearded young man with beautiful eyes who one of our friends picked up some years ago in Ramses Square. He told our friend how the sheikhs in one of the religious extremist organizations would take him at night and then lead people in prayers at dawn. About a senior official in the Ministry of Education who jumped off the balcony of his apartment after his enemies set a trap for him and caught him in an office sucking the penis of a security guard who had volunteered to take part in the sting. And about many others, more than necessary. I wanted to tell my friend that all these men were Hani Mahfouz, but I truly understood this fact only under the impact of the nightmare that was prison, when I was struggling for words and out of breath. I understood this only after meeting Karim Saadoun and listening to him, because then I realized that some people have an inner light that cannot be snuffed out, even if they are imprisoned seven levels underground.

38

I WAS WOKEN UP BY the phone ringing and then by Prince's
voice on the phone.

"Wakey, wakey, lazybones," he said. "Come down and
have coffee with me once you're awake."

He hung up without waiting for me to answer, of course,
although I'd had a feeling that I was about to speak to him.
When I put down the phone and tried to speak, nothing came
out but a horrible wail. It was a false alarm, as they say. I
looked at my latest notebook on the nightstand. Without taking any tranquilizers or sleeping pills, I had fallen asleep while
writing.

I sat down next to Prince on a sofa in the hotel reception.
He was talking nonstop and every now and then I reached
out for my pen and notebook to jot something down for him.
He didn't speak openly about the need for me to go back
to living and working and being with people, but there was
a hint of that behind every sentence he spoke. He told me
scraps of news about other people he knew who had been
imprisoned with me in the same case and had been released,
about the arrangements they had made to emigrate, and how
some others had completely vanished. He told me that Abdel
Aziz had called him every day to check up on me, and he said
that Abdel Aziz had completely changed: he had shaken off
his fear and moved out from under the shadow of his family,
as shown by the fact that he had found it intolerable to be

working in the Emirates when I was on remand awaiting trial, so he had broken his contract after less than a month and had come back to be in Egypt and follow the trial with Prince and the lawyers.

Prince made me dizzy with his news and his stories, while all I wanted was to be alone. I didn't want to go back to my old life. I still wasn't ready to meet Abdel Aziz, even if he really was a transformed character. All I wanted from the world was to be left as I was, in my room with my nightmares for company, along with my little spider that was weaving a little home close to me in the corner of the nightstand, now that I had freed it from imprisonment in the drawer.

I wanted to tell Prince that I had a long journey ahead of me and I had to make it alone, without help from anyone else, otherwise I would never recover, however much I traveled and spoke and sang and danced. It would be a journey back into the past and then forward to the present. I might find out where I was, who I was, and what I wanted. But I didn't write any of this down. I just nodded until he had finished, and quickly went back to the spider's room, like someone who misses a secret lover.

Two days later Prince set a trap for me and I fell into it unprepared. He invited me to his small private suite in the hotel, to talk about something important, he claimed. As soon as he opened the door for me, I saw Abdel Aziz. For a moment I thought of turning round and simply going back to my room, or leaving the hotel completely and roaming the streets, since it was almost evening. But something held me back, maybe the sudden realization when I saw him that we would meet sooner or later and that delaying such a confrontation was not a solution. I also took it lightly because I couldn't speak, so I wouldn't have to open my mouth and say anything in response to him unless I wanted to, in which case I would use paper and pen. All these explanations and justifications came later; at the time I was interested only in hearing his voice.

I let Abdel Aziz embrace me warmly but I didn't reciprocate. My arms hung by my sides, as if I were declaring from
the start that I had no desire for him. That was insincere, but
at the same time I was terrified that I might in fact be acting
sincerely. I could smell his old perfume and his body. Prince
left us within minutes. There were some snacks on the table in
front of us, together with a bottle of Dewar's whisky that was
almost full. I poured myself a glass and started to look around
the little suite, ready to listen. For a moment I wanted to rush
off to my room and fetch the notebooks that were my therapy,
to offer him a summary of my life, to show them to him and
point to particular pages and passages for him to read, and
then we could laugh or weep together.

He didn't seem to be in a hurry. He took his joint-
rolling gear out of his pocket and sat opposite me calmly, rolling patiently and intently as I was accustomed to see him. I
stole glances at him, wondering who this man might be. Nothing about him had changed, yet a pall seemed to hang over
him, a transparent pall that enveloped him on all sides, cutting
him off from me and from all the ways I remembered him. As
he took the first puffs on his joint, after the expected remarks
on loss and loneliness, he started telling me a story, and I realized how much I missed his voice, with that delightful way he
pronounced his r's. He offered me the joint and I took one
drag, as if I were throwing myself in the sea.

He told me about an old colleague of his from university days. He was a strange young man, poor and arrogant,
who didn't like anything—not the professors, not the government, not the regime, and not religion. He might have
been a communist but he was crazier and more extreme
than all the other leftist students. Even they saw him as an
isolated case. He brazenly proclaimed his atheism to all and
sundry, whether or not it was relevant. Maybe he enjoyed
shocking people with his strong opinions and his contempt
for their beliefs. The problem wasn't with the way this young

man lived, but with his death, which came as suddenly as a slap on the back of the neck from an unseen hand. He died in a fire on the train to Upper Egypt, along with dozens of others, ending up as a charred indistinguishable corpse among nameless and featureless fellow human beings. Abdel Aziz went south to attend the burial and funeral of his atheist friend, in a village near Esna, a beautiful little village tainted by the drabness of poverty. All the time in the village Abdel Aziz was thinking only about his dead friend and his contempt for all these rites and rituals. He imagined him cracking up with laughter at how they were praying for him at the funeral when he didn't believe in God or any religion. This idea weighed on Abdel Aziz's mind, but he suffered in silence as he sat on a yellow mat outside the mud house where his friend's family lived and listened to a Quran recitation from an old tape player. All the while he was almost certain he could hear his friend's roars of laughter from somewhere, maybe from inside himself. He didn't understand, and he found the whole business disagreeable.

I pulled the pen and paper toward me. "And the lesson to be drawn?" I wrote provocatively.

He took the notebook, read my question, and smiled. He didn't answer in spoken words, but took the pen from me and wrote: "There isn't a lesson to be drawn."

He gave a little laugh and rolled another joint. In a while he was blowing the smoke in my direction, as he went on talking.

He said he had remembered that old story the day they arrested us in Tahrir Square and took us to Abdin police station, specifically after his family's lawyer managed to get him out and he went home safe and sound. He had imagined himself as that dead friend of his. Maybe he had grasped a painful truth at that moment: that we do not belong to ourselves. Throughout our lives we can fill the world with noise, bravado, sarcasm, atheism, craziness, and aimless wanderings, but at the end of the journey, even if it's after a hundred years, we are just an embarrassing object that has to be hidden away quickly, just something that had gone missing and has now been restored to its original owners, for them to do with it as they see fit. In other parts of the world, you can say in your will that you don't want any funeral rites when you die, or that you want to be cremated and have your ashes scattered somewhere you love. You can change your religion, your sex, your sexual orientations if you want, simply because you are free, but where we are we don't have the right to do anything like that. We're just things, as far as we, our families, the government, and everyone else are concerned. We're not free to do what we want with these bodies. In the end we're their property, even if we're not burned to death on the train to Upper Egypt.

This truth weighed on Abdel Aziz's mind during the month he spent in his new job in Dubai. Every day he tried to ignore it and forget about his relationship with me. He had tried to emulate the insensitive attitudes of the men in his family, but he had already been cursed, he said, and the genie was out of the bottle. "It was you who broke the bottle, Hani." That's roughly what he said and I wanted to cry, but I held myself back. He contrived some problem in the institution where he was working in the Emirates and broke the contract. They were lenient with him, out of deference to the people who had recommended him. He came back to Egypt in a rage, ready to flare up at the slightest affront or friction. He blew up in the face of his elder brother, admitted his sexual orientations, turned his back on the tribe of strict males in the ranks of his distinguished family, and started again from scratch. All the time the guilt he felt about me weighed on him and he didn't know what he should do to get rid of it, other than aid our cause in the ways he knew through his work, with help from Prince and some human rights activists, although this alienated him from his family and most of his former friends and meant that his reputation as a journalist was almost completely destroyed. He said he didn't want anything from me now and that he had come only to thank me because I had set him free, whether or not I had intended to do so.

I didn't feel sorry for him and I didn't feel flattered. On the contrary, I envied him and was angry with him as I listened to him talking so objectively and logically. He was talking about the outrageous injustice inflicted on me and on dozens of others, in the same style as the statements issued by human rights organizations. Apparently for him it was only concern for the public interest that finally helped him to take a more robust attitude and then to change his life and face his family and then the whole of society. Should I applaud him for it? Should I bring down the final curtain now that our hero had repented of his errors? He gave the impression he had never played a part in the saga, had never been involved in an argument or an embrace, had never hugged the friend they had locked up and tried and whose body they had abused when he was naked and defenseless before them.

I don't know what I expected from him. I felt that he was telling the truth, and that he really had changed, but at what price? I had lost my voice, and earlier I had lost things I didn't even know one could lose. With a hand that now felt heavy, I wrote: "I don't want anything from you. I just want Hani Mahfouz."

I gave him the piece of paper torn out of the notebook, turned my back on him, and left. Then I left the hotel, without knowing where I was going. Signs of preparations for New Year's celebrations were evident everywhere. I could see the lights and decorations through my dark glasses and I felt lighter and braver as his lovely voice echoed in my head.

After an hour or two wandering around, I was alone with my notebook in a small bar I had recently discovered. I had made friends with the waiter, Milad, who was tall and agile, with bronze skin. He was used to my muteness, my sitting alone, my obsession with writing, and my generous tips. He suddenly suggested we go to a wild New Year's Eve party in a few days in an upmarket nightclub at the top of a hotel not far off. I was unreservedly enthusiastic about his suggestion, although I had already promised Prince I would spend that evening with him in the roof garden, as I did every year. Maybe I knew that nothing could go back to the way it was before, however much we pretended and however much we hid the marks of pain and degradation under our clothes. Or maybe it was because Milad did not know me and had not heard the story that stretched out behind me like a trail of blood.

On New Year's Eve, I slipped out of the hotel without Prince noticing, like a teenager leaving home at dawn before the rest of the family woke up. When I arrived at the bar, I found the party was in full swing. The customers were wearing red party hats or Santa Claus masks and were joking and singing together. I drank unhurriedly, watching the clowning and the drunken rowdiness. After a brief dispute between Milad and a fat and resentful colleague of his, who didn't want to be left alone on such a night, we set off together at about midnight. I ended up with Milad in the elevator, both of us smelling of beer and as impatient as little kids. At this distance, with the light so close, I could see the color of his amber eyes. A spot of blood floated like a little island on the white of his left eye.

Through a colleague who worked in the nightclub, Milad had booked us a small table close to the dance floor. I promised myself that I wouldn't reveal my sexual preferences to him, however hard that was, so that our innocent friendship could last as long as possible. I was spending the last night of what had been a horrible year in a state of ecstatic abandon. I was escaping from everything—Prince, my notebooks, and Abdel Aziz. It was like my last night alive. I hadn't taken any

tranquilizers that day so that I would be ready to get conspic-
uously drunk, emboldened by a false identity and the illusion
of a new beginning. That old imp inside me had reawakened,
after months subdued by sedation.

As soon as I entered the place, I caught the attention of
the staff and some of the customers because of my appearance, my expensive coat, and my red scarf. Milad walked
behind me like a page who plays his part well and knows his
place, and at that point I knew what role I wanted to play
there for the rest of the night—the mute rich man seeking
pleasure, especially women. A decent bottle of whisky, ice, a
large bowl piled high with a selection of fruits, and another
one full of nuts, cheeses, and cold cuts. Close to our table
stood a woman around forty years old who looked like she'd
stepped out of a film from the 1970s.

My new friend and I swilled down glass after glass of
whisky, and soon the woman, whose name was Afaf, was
filling our glasses whenever they were empty. Our eyes were
pinned on the little stage, where the dancers came and went
about every half an hour, interspersed with pieces of music
requested by the customers. Every now and then I stole a
glance at happy Milad, and noticed the alluring spot of blood,
his thin lips, and the small regular teeth behind his permanently broad smile, but I reminded myself of the pledge I had
taken in the elevator, and downed more whisky.

I no longer remember much of what happened that night.
I handed out loads of banknotes to the women and the band.
Flashes of scenes come back for a moment but soon disappear into a chaos of noise and idle talk. I remember that at
one point, between two dancers, I asked the band to play any
song by Farid al-Atrash. The singer was useless, with a grating
voice, but I enjoyed his singing as if he were a musical legend.
I stood up and danced with him. I danced and pulled Milad
along with me. I showered him with small banknotes after
Afaf gave me change for a large amount of money.

May I never be deprived of you, my love,
Or of the pleasure of seeing your eyes,
Those sweet eyes of yours, those sweet eyes of yours.

For a moment I thought I had caught sight of my father sitting at the tables, blowing out hashish smoke and laughing as he watched me dance. Then I sat down, panting, with sweat dripping from every pore. The gathering broke up all at once and we heard the call to dawn prayers. I insisted on going on drinking and Milad tried to persuade me that we had to go. Some of the junior staff were cleaning the place up, lifting up chairs and throwing downcast glances at us. I explained to Milad with signs that I wanted us to take a room in the hotel to go to sleep, and he went along with the idea. In the hotel room I threw up at length in the bathroom, and when I came out I saw Milad lying on the bed in his underclothes. The sight of his brown underpants tight against his strong thighs turned me on, so I sat down on the edge of the bed, reached out my hand to his body and started to fondle him. Within a minute he woke up, startled and on his guard, and pushed me away. Then he stood up, dressed in haste without looking at me, and left without a word.

My body was on fire and dripping with sweat, although the air was cold. I grabbed the remote control for the air-conditioning and lowered the temperature setting to the minimum until the room felt like a fridge. I suddenly fell asleep and then just as suddenly woke up with a headache like bells ringing between my temples, or maybe the trumpet blasts on the Day of Judgment. One of the hotel staff was banging on the door and asking me whether I was checking out or would stay another night. The room was almost rigid with cold and I was completely naked and yet my skin was still hot. I sneezed a big sneeze and realized I had caught a vicious cold. Straight off, without thinking, I answered the unseen woman's question in a drunken voice. "I'll get up and leave right away," I said.

At first, I didn't notice the miracle that had taken place. Then I repeated to myself what I had told her in a low voice, incredulously. I wanted to get up to clap and dance, but I collapsed on the bed again and the walls of the room spun around me with demonic speed. With some difficulty, I managed to get dressed and hurried out of the hotel. I couldn't find my dark glasses in my pockets so I didn't bother to hide my face. In the taxi I heard Layla Murad singing and I sang along with her, indifferent to the driver's smile:

How can people say it's a world of sorrows,
When it has all this magic, in all its shapes and forms?

When I collapsed on the bed in my room in the Andrea Hotel, I left this world behind me for I don't know how many days.

39

I SAW MY MOTHER SITTING among many women, who were sitting around her on the living room floor in our old apartment in Abdin. I was hiding in the corner, spying on them. I was following a ritual they were performing, apparently some form of celebration. When I heard the pounding of a pestle in a mortar and saw them scattering salt and seeds around, it soon become clear that it was a subua, the ceremony marking the seventh day after the birth of a baby boy. In the middle of the room, in a large flour sieve, there was a bundle of white swaddling clothes that must have contained the baby. I went up to where they were sitting without them noticing me, and when I was within their field of vision, I realized that I was invisible. That didn't bother me; on the contrary, it reassured me somehow. All I wanted to do was sneak a peek at the baby, maybe to confirm my suspicion that this in fact was my own subua. I couldn't see anything protruding from the folds of cloth, no signs of a little body or a face like that of a kitten with its eyes closed. Floating in the air above them, ignoring their cries and their advice to the baby that he obey his mother and father, I reached out and touched the swaddling clothes. The white cloth was very light, like the gauze used to bandage wounds or like a very small shroud. This filled me with terror, and I started searching frantically inside the cloth. But whenever I undid one layer of wrapping, a smaller bundle of cloth appeared underneath, as if the layers were replicating as

I took them off. It became clear that there was nothing inside, and I never did get to that hidden little core that they were protecting with all these wrappings. I wanted to scream at the women at the ceremony, to proclaim the truth: that there was nothing in the sieve but bits of cloth, and that I was there among them, an adult, a man of more than forty, and that this wasn't my subua, and that my mother had never had another child. But my voice let me down again.

Prince said he couldn't believe his ears when I started ranting during my fever. I wasn't interested in asking them about it later. In a period of consciousness, I saw Abdel Aziz sitting beside my bed, putting compresses of icy water on my forehead and stomach. He hadn't waited for permission from me before turning up. So I wasn't completely alone. When he saw that my condition wasn't improving, he carried me to the elevator in his arms and put me in his car wrapped in a blanket. With the wisdom of the sick, on which I was now an expert, I told myself that maybe the secret was this—that the savage is tamed and becomes human, that we manage to pull out our claws or at least trim them, so that we can touch others without injuring or frightening them. I looked at him driving his car, silent and serious, while I was a lifeless lump on the back seat. It occurred to me then that inside each of us there lurked a monster that might ooze the milk of human kindness at the right moment. I took my hand out from under the blanket and massaged Abdel Aziz's head from behind. He smiled at me in the rearview mirror and his eyes sparkled.

He took me to a small private hospital. I had many tests done, just to be sure, and stayed there for more than a week, fed intravenously. Whenever I was alert, I couldn't stop talking with anyone who happened to be in front of me. Apparently I still couldn't believe I had recovered the ability to speak. Once I woke up to see Karim smiling, his dimples dancing. He took my hand, oblivious of the nurse standing nearby, and kissed the palm.

"Thank God you've recovered, Hannoun," he said. "Didn't I tell you that you were going to speak again?"

I immediately remembered my recent dream about him, when I saw him in front of me just as he was now. In my dream he was crying and telling me he was ill and that he wouldn't get better unless he walked along the river all his life. I opened my arms and he leaned toward me and embraced me. He was cheerful and optimistic, and he told me that a human rights organization was helping him, Mohamed Sukkar, and others, along with some doctors and specialists who were giving them psychological rehabilitation and taking an interest in their health and their lives. He said he felt he could now start everything from scratch. I wasn't sure he was telling the truth. Maybe his optimism was real, or maybe it was just a ruse to make my illness and breakdown easier to bear. He visited me again with Mohamed Sukkar and was silent and uneasy, maybe because Prince was scowling in their presence. When they had gone, Prince advised me to cut off ties with all such people I had met in prison, so that I could turn that page and focus on myself and my life. I didn't argue with him. I recognized that, despite the invaluable support he had given to me and others, he was still the same old Prince. I realized that he hadn't been inside with us, he hadn't fallen asleep to Karim's stories, and he hadn't seen Said the Skull speaking to his sister Huda, who was present only in his drug-crazed mind. Alongside Prince's kindness and generosity and all his good intentions, there was always a trace of arrogance about him, and he loved to be in control. He enjoyed what he had been doing for years—mentoring young gay men and prescribing the course of their lives, as sole compensation for the status he had not achieved in the world of music, as he had dreamed of doing since his youth. For all those reasons I agreed to stay with Abdel Aziz in his furnished apartment when I came out of hospital, since I could not bear Prince's insistent compassion, which made me feel like a child he was helping to take its first paces.

On my last night in the Andrea Hotel, it was the usual Thursday night party, so I packed one big suitcase, stacked my notebooks by themselves in a smaller bag, and then went upstairs to the roof garden, where I witnessed a minor drama between Prince and one of his lovers, a young actor who had received much help from Prince until he started to get serious roles. In the heat of the party, after a few drinks, Prince had made fun of his lover and his modest talent, whereupon the young man exploded, insulting him, reminding him that he smelled bad, and describing him as a living mummy. Then he stormed off, as an embarrassed silence descended on the place.

I quickly sent one of the staff to fetch the oud for Prince, who pretended to be composed and indifferent to the argument. Absentmindedly, he tried to put the incident behind him by concentrating on his whisky. I passed him the oud and insisted he play his old song, which his late brother had set to music for him. He was reluctant at first but finally agreed, saying he was singing only to honor me and celebrate the fact that I was over my breakdown and returning to the world. When he started to strum, it sounded like colored tongues of fire. He stopped several times to get the tuning right, and then he sang:

> Light, light the air.
> I am hurt and you're the cure.
> However long I haven't laughed,
> I laugh again when we're together.

His voice was shaky and scratchy. The last vestiges of its melancholy beauty were gone and he forgot the words of the song once or twice, so he just hummed the tune sheepishly. I don't know why, but I felt I was hearing this song from him for the last time; that I was hearing it for the last time from anyone. As soon as he finished he hugged his oud and asked leave to go. He stood up with difficulty, walked a few paces, and then remembered he had forgotten his stick and his hat. So he went back, put his hat on his head, and held his stick in his right hand, then bowed to us theatrically before making his way a little unsteadily to the elevator, his shoulders slumped and the hem of his jacket on both sides flapping in the wind on the roof, rather like a bird in danger of extinction.

Before I was fully awake the next morning, and after I had everything ready to move with Abdel Aziz, Mohamed Sukkar knocked on the door of my room, clearly in a state of agitation. He kept saying something incoherent about Karim disappearing after finding out the truth about a disease he had. I asked him to calm down and tell me everything from the start. I gathered that the organization that was looking after them and others had offered to do some medical tests on them, if they wanted, to make sure they weren't HIV positive. They agreed, and the results were bad news for our young friend.

A little spider in my heart bit me when I heard Mohamed say, "We found out from the tests that Karim is HIV positive."

I rubbed my forehead, trying to concentrate and catch my breath. There are poisonous varieties of spider too. Then I saw that Mohamed had started sobbing. He said they had been told that although Karim was HIV positive he could live a completely normal life if he took the medication and looked after his health. They had told Karim that the medication was available and free. He went along with what they said and pretended to agree. But then he suddenly left, turned off his phone, went back to Tanta, took his clothes and other things from his mother's place, and said goodbye to her, saying he was going to work in some other province. When Mohamed Sukkar and one of the staff from the organization went looking, they couldn't find a trace of him. Karim's uncle told them he had heard that Karim had gone crazy and was walking along the irrigation canals day and night, talking to himself.

I went up to Mohamed and patted him on the shoulder to calm his sobbing, but he completely collapsed in tears. "Karim really loved you," he sobbed. "His health might get worse if he doesn't take his medication. He has to come back and take care of himself so that . . . so that he'll live."

I agreed to meet Mohamed Sukkar in Ramses Square the next morning so that we could go to Tanta together. I called Abdel Aziz and told him everything. I told him I'd decided I had to go and find Karim and bring him back with me, even against his will. We agreed to meet in an hour. He insisted we meet in the same place in Tahrir Square where the nightmare began the day we were arrested. I dragged my suitcase of clothes with me, the bag full of notebooks slung over my shoulder. I went with my face uncovered in broad daylight, without dark glasses, and pretended to be brave as I walked. As we headed to the car together, he reached out and held my fingers in his large hand. And at that moment, everything seemed possible.

Thanks and Acknowledgments

IF THESE PAGES CONTAIN ANYTHING worth reading, the credit is not due to me alone, but also to the many people who agreed to meet me and tell me their stories and other people who provided useful documents relevant to the Queen Boat case. Of course I would also like to thank my dear colleagues who read the first draft and offered valuable advice, and I would especially like to mention Yasser Abdel Latif, Sherif Bakr, and Hassan Yaghi, without denying the contributions of others who encouraged me over the years to continue with the work. I must emphasize my gratitude to two friends: Hussam Mustafa Ibrahim and Ahmad Ayed.

One last observation: Although the events of this novel are based on real events, in their final form they are based on those events only in the sense that dreams are based on the elements of waking life. I gave my imagination free rein to play and roam, without any direct reference to real people, because imitating reality is an objective that is neither possible nor desirable.

SELECTED HOOPOE TITLES

The Televangelist
by Ibrahim Essa, translated by Jonathan Wright

Embrace on Brooklyn Bridge
By Ezzedin C. Fishere, translated by John Peate

All the Battles
By Maan Abu Taleb, translated by Robin Moger

hoopoe is an imprint for engaged, open-minded readers hungry for outstanding fiction that challenges headlines, re-imagines histories, and celebrates original storytelling. Through elegant paperback and digital editions, **hoopoe** champions bold, contemporary writers from across the Middle East alongside some of the finest, groundbreaking authors of earlier generations.

At hoopoefiction.com, curious and adventurous readers from around the world will find new writing, interviews, and criticism from our authors, translators, and editors.